For Butterfly

2018 Rabbooks Publishing First Edition

ISBN-13: 9780998247427

ISBN-10: 1542441536

Illustrations by Alex James

Mary & I

The Real Story of

Miss Mary Mack

Book One

MACKNOWLEDGMENTS

Special thanks to all the people who helped in one way or another, either by inspiration or perspiration, to place this book in your hands.

A special thanks to Melissa Ehman, Luke Neher, Azusa James and Mikaela James for their tireless editing and support.

Contents

Photo taken in 1915 of the person believed to be Mary Elizabeth of the House of White.

Part One
MISS MARY MACK

Wednesday, August 10, 1892.

Chatsworth, Illinois. A young girl of five is sitting between her parents on the front seat of a squeaky, wooden, horse-drawn wagon. The crackling of dirt under wheels is the only sound they hear as they return towards their small, one-room cabin on a small plot of land they have yet to own. The father is a beaten-looking man who has always worked earlier than the sun has ever made an appearance, until long after it has gone. The mother is equal in shabbiness, working as a garment worker at a local factory, making dresses she will never be able to afford. They are poor farmers, as were their parents and their parents before them.

Today they are returning from an unsuccessful trip to get the bank to give them more time to pay off their loans. Unless there is a financial miracle, they will lose the small plot of land they call home and will have to move. To say the least, this is a somber moment. The little girl was completely unaware of the family woes and is just happy to be in the front of the wagon instead of the back, where the crops or animals usually ride. The evening air is warm and still and the crickets are silent. The carriage was making perhaps one of its last journeys before it will have to be sold to the bank. The little girl looked off in the distance and noticed an eerie orange glow. She nudged her mother's shoulder to draw her attention to it, but she was already aware of it.

"What is that? A fire?" the mother asked.

"Don't know…" answered the father. "…Reckon we better have a look-see."

On the next crossroad, he steered the horse right and they traveled on to the glow. The closer they got to the light, the more they saw it was not an out-of-control fire but the controlled burning of hundreds of lanterns illuminating the air of a very large field full of striped tents. A large sign announced their arrival into the area currently occupied by the Berkeley Brothers' Circus. The little girl was ecstatic, as if magic was happening her own town. "Mama! Mama! It's a circus!"

Hundreds of people, many of them strangers, crowded in and out of the entrance, some walking, others riding on horse carts.

"I know, sugar...Noah? I didn't know a circus was coming to town, did you?"

"I knew, I just didn't say anything."

"Why not?"

"Can't afford it."

"Well..." She realized he was right.

"Can we go, Mama? Can we?" The girl asked, clasping her hands in prayer.

The wife glanced at her husband.

"Can't afford it," he repeated more sternly.

"Can we look?" the girl asked.

Again, the wife looked to her husband, her eyes were even sadder than her daughter's. He thought for a second. "Okay, we can look...don't cost nothing to look." He guided the cart to an area full of parked carts and carriages. They pulled up next to a large, all black, double-horsed carriage with a driver patiently waiting for the passengers to return.

"Look who else is here," the father complained.

The carnival around the big circus tents was alive with activity. Hundreds of men, women and children dressed in their Sunday clothes sauntered around, marveling at the sights: Fortune tellers beckoned from tents, freaks entertained the eyes, and a small brass band played jaunty music for the ears. The little girl was in the most over-stimulating heaven one could be in. Every direction she turned, she saw something she has never seen before: a monkey in a cage, a woman dressed as a cowboy, shooting plates out of someone's hands, a wild-looking, dark-skinned man from a faraway land shaking a spear. At the end of the alleyway was the entrance to the big top tent. A carnival barker yelled through a large cone: "Come one, come all to the Berkeley Brothers Circus! We got acrobats, elephants, tigers and eagles! A feast for the eyes and ears! Keep you young for years! Come one, come all, Summer, Winter and Fall!"

"Time to go," Noah muttered.

"Can we go in, Papa?"

"No!"

"Please?"

"No! We can't afford it."

The wife read the admission sign. "Noah? Adults are $1, but children are only 50¢. I have 50 cents. We could just let her go in?"

"Can I really, Mama? I've never seen an elephant before, can I have 50 cents?"

Noah sighed: "That doesn't make sense, Mabel. Let's just head on…" A family caught his eyes—a husband, wife and their eight-year-old daughter, on a much higher financial level. Noah recognized the well-dressed family. The father's suit was even better than the banker's who had turned him down, the wife looked like she was going to a picnic and the little girl could put her frilly white dress directly onto a life-sized doll.

"Noah?" yelled the well-dressed gentleman as he led his family to the tent entrance, "How are things?" he asked, smiling, oblivious to the family's woes.

Noah shuffled his feet. "Fine…fine."

"I talked to Jeremiah at the bank, he said you were having trouble with your loan. Everything okay at the farm?"

"Everything is fine."

"Sure you don't want me to talk to him for you…"

"I SAID EVERYTHING IS FINE!" There was an awkward pause. "…It's fine."

The well-dressed gentleman's daughter walked over to the little girl. Her hair was in golden ringlets and bounced whenever she tossed her head around. She was carrying a white parasol, which the girl thought was a strange thing to have at night.

"You're poor!" were her first words to the little girl.

The little girl didn't know how to respond. She didn't even know she was poor, because she had always felt she had everything on this earth to be happy. As long as her family was together and they had a roof over their heads and food in their bellies, that was enough, but the way the rich girl had hissed 'poor' was not stating a fact, it was a verbal backhand to her life. She wanted to slap the rich girl, but because her mother was standing next to her, she settled for saying: "No we're not!"

"Then why didn't you go in?" the rich girl volleyed.

"C-cause we don't want to."

"I've seen your house. You're poor."

"Stop!" the rich girl's mother yelled. "Watch your manners! I'm sorry, Noah."

"No worries, no worries."

"You want us to pay your way, Noah?" the well-dressed gentleman asked.

"Don't need your charity! Let's go!" He grabbed his daughter's hand and started to head off.

"See!" yelled the rich girl. "I told you, you're poor!"

"That's enough!" the well-dressed gentleman yelled. "Any more out of you and we're going straight home!"

Noah paused and looked around. Then he turned and stomped back to the tent's entrance. "Where's that 50 cents?" he asked his wife.

She dug into her purse and pulled out the coins. He snatched them away and placed them in his daughter's hand. "Here! You go on inside! We'll wait for you out here!"

The well-dressed gentleman looked in his pocket for some change. "Noah, let me pay for y—"

"I DON'T NEED YOUR DAMN CHARITY!" He gently pushed his daughter toward the entrance. "Now git!"

The girl slowly walked inside, pausing one last time to look back at her dad. He seemed like he was either going to yell in anger or cry. She gave a gentleman the coins and entered the tent.

"There she is!" exclaimed the well-dressed gentleman. He directed his family to where the girl was sitting. Although many people were filling the wooden bleachers, there were plenty of seats available for the family somewhere other than next to her.

She wondered briefly if her father had put the man up to sitting next to her, a way to watch after her and keep her company. Knowing her father's pride, she realized this was unlikely. The daughter sat next to her, creating an instant discomfort. No words passed between the two, their awkward silence filled by the band playing 'March of the Gladiators', over and over.

The interior of the tent was a wonderland of colorful fabric, lanterns, and paintings of wild animals and savage-looking, black-faced Africans with white lips. A short wooden fence kept the audience from getting too close to the tent's center. A parade of exotic animals she had thought were myths were carried in garish cages past the audience: Monkeys, alligators, and even ostriches came within arm's reach of the onlookers. The rich girl maintained her lack of enthusiasm for everything she saw. When she was not silent, she would comment with sarcasm. After the exotic animals, came a group of Nigerian men and boys in loincloths, ushered in like freshly captured, unchained slaves. Tribal scars formed intricate patterns across their faces. Many in the audience gasped, and some sensitive women fanned themselves to prevent fainting. A young West African boy, around the same age as the two girls, looked over at them. The little girl smiled at him, but her cousin's face formed into a scrawl.

"We used to have slaves, but my daddy freed them," her cousin commented. "Now we have to pay them—so stupid. Why pay someone who was working for free?"

The little girl ignored this. She began imagining what her life would be like if she could journey around the world hunting exotic animals and meeting people whose skin was not the same color as hers and who spoke in different languages and accents.

The crack of a whip and a fired rifle caused everyone to sit up straight, as cowboys on horses galloped into the tent. They did various horse tricks: Standing on the galloping horses' backs, leaping on and off, jumping over ropes, and shooting at china plates thrown in the air by a Native American wearing a chief's feathery headdress. The Africans then retook center stage and performed various feats of strength: lifting huge barbells, forming human pyramids, tumbling and flipping acrobatically, and hurling spears at a bullseye painted on a tree trunk. The little boy who had stared at them played a large drum. The little girl wished she could at least touch the animal skin drum. That would be just enough exotic adventure.

The ringmaster, a short fellow with a top hat and a large curly mustache announced three African elephants: Hannibal, Samson and Cleopatra. Everyone clapped, but nothing came in. The ringmaster looked back and then repeated the names of the three elephants. Again, everyone clapped but nothing happened. The little girl had butterflies in her stomach, anticipating the excitement of being close to something she'd only seen in storybooks. Right when the ringmaster started to stomp to the back entrance, a large African elephant bustled into the tent, knocking over a wooden bucket and nearly running over the ring master. The man rolled out of the way and picked up his fallen hat; his face was not a happy one. On the elephant's back rode a man not dressed as any type of performer. He wore no exotic costume and could pass as a farmhand taking a ride. The elephant trotted around the center circle, its large tusks came dangerously close to several members of the audience. Some laughed it off as an exciting thrill. The little girl found this exhilarating, but realized she would not be too happy being impaled by the large ivory tusk.

There was a crashing noise from the outside, followed by much yelling. Two more elephants entered the tent. Although not as large as the first, the second one was instantly recognized as more dangerous. Impaled on one of its tusks, like a marionette on a stick, a man's lifeless body was flopping in whatever direction the elephant turned its head. People's screams filled the air. The third elephant ran off course, jumping over the wooden fence. Audience members in its path scrambled, except an old couple who ended up trampled.

Everyone fled. The entrance was too narrow and formed an hourglass of death. The second elephant whipped its head around, flinging the dead body into the bleachers. The well-dressed gentleman grabbed his daughter, his wife grabbed the little girl, and they tried to push through the crazed, panicked crowd. The little girl was in shock. She should be scared and running faster, but it all seemed like a weird dream. A flash of orange caught her eyes. She looked back and realized one of the elephants had knocked over a lantern, setting the tent ablaze. Impossibly, this created even more chaos and panic. A wooden brace fell from the ceiling and landed on several people.

"How did that happen?" the little girl asked herself. She looked up and saw a huge hole torn through the tent's roof. Then she heard frantic screams and looked back down. The lead elephant was knocking circus workers out of its way, throwing some as high as 20 feet into the air. The man riding it, instead of trying to gain control, laughed with no hint of remorse. This scared the little girl more than the rampaging elephants.

The crowd was pushing harder on each other to fit through the exit. Someone got the idea to duck under the tent's bottom edge and escape and others began to scatter like ants whose hill was being stomped. Grown men and women got on their hands and knees to crawl under the tent. Many struggled, because it had been tightly pegged down. The lead elephant, like an anteater gathering up ants, snatched at the people trying to escape, dragging them back and flinging them over its shoulder. The little girl, transfixed, watched a body hit the ground like a sack of wet flour. She could only see two of the elephants. 'Was the third outside causing trouble?' she wondered.

A powerful wind knocked her backwards and threw hay and dust into her face. After she had cleared her eyes, she saw another hole in the tent's roof and wooden planks and debris falling down onto one of the cowboy performers. Now she could only find one elephant.

"There she is!" It was her own father. He and her mother had crawled under the tent and were pushing against people and reaching out their hands for her.

"My parasol!" yelled the rich girl.

"What?" her father asked.

"I forgot my parasol!" She released herself from her father's hand and, ignoring the fire and calamity, worked her way against the crowd back toward her seat.

"NO!" her father yelled.

She was out of his reach and quickly made it back to her seat. She picked up the parasol and was about to rejoin the escapees when something grabbed her and lifted her into the air with its trunk. She screamed almost as loudly as her mother. The man on the elephant's back said something to the elephant. Instead of flinging her away into the air, it curled its trunk around her and held on as if she were a prize.

"Oh, God, no!" her mother screamed.

"I'll get her!" yelled Noah. Leaving his daughter in the care of his wife, he stepped over a fallen beam, picked up a torch and rushed at the elephant. The elephant reared up for a moment, lifted up its trunk and flung the rich girl onto its back. The man riding it caught her and clutched his new hostage. She wiggled and screamed, but the man, now laughing harder, just held her tighter.

The captive's mother fainted. With its trunk free, the elephant swung it fast and knocked Noah into a tent support. His wife ran over to help him, completely oblivious to the elephant. With one strong swoop, it sent her flying into the air, through the tent roof and screaming out of sight.

The little girl let out a high pitched scream, louder than any she'd ever made. She slowly walked over to her fallen dad.

"No! Don't!" yelled the rich man, tending to his wife.

"Release me!" the rich girl squealed.

The little girl was almost close enough to see whether her father was still alive when she felt a hot breath on her neck. She turned to face the murderous beast. Its eyes had turned blood red, even to the whites and pupils. It had become a demon. The elephant lifted up a front leg and started to bring it down at her chest. Her father somehow picked himself off the ground and placed his body between the foot and his daughter. The two fell back onto the ground as the elephant pushed thirteen thousand pounds onto them. The dad screamed in pain and tried to protect his daughter, spreading his arms and legs over her in a push-up position. The weight of the beast won and he collapsed onto his daughter. There was a horrible crunching sound. The little girl saw a flash of bright red, and her body went numb.

Then the foot lifted, the elephant drew back. The girl's vision was becoming blurry. The elephant shook itself like a bird in a bath and then, with a grand gesture reminiscent of an eagle, shot giant grey wings out from its side. It reared up and gave a loud cry and a groan. The wings flapped three times and with a powerful force of air, the elephant exited through the tent's roof. Fire and screams were still everywhere. The girl could not physically move. She didn't want to. If elephants could fly, then other miracles were possible. She lay on the ground for a long, long time and waited for one to happen.

Her vision faded to black...

Part Two
ALL DRESSED IN BLACK

April 30, 1915.

They had expected at least five women to show up but instead, twenty-two made an appearance. Some bought signs which read:

SHOW YOUR FAITH IN THE WOMEN OF NEW YORK! VOTE YES ON THE AMENDMENT ENABLING WOMEN TO VOTE!

She carried a drum, to equate them with soldiers in the American revolution. The women, all in white dresses and hats, marched toward the city hall. Some onlookers jeered at them. When she saw a sign in the window of a bar that read: 'NO IRISH ALOWED!', she thought: 'Even if I become treated as a political equal, my red hair still gives people reason to discriminate.' She could see, in most of the women's eyes watching the parade pass, a yearning to join them. She wished so much they would walk away from the loutish husbands clutching heavily onto their arms and join the parade for freedom.

Unlike the larger protests which took to main streets and were more like parades, their group hit the smaller streets and neighborhoods, places where the message would get to the more common masses. The audience in these neighborhoods, with their narrower streets, produced a more active counter-protest, louder jeering and a thrown beer bottle, which narrowly missed one of the older females in the group.

"Should we stop?" asked one of the women.

"No! Not until we circle back to city hall," the drum-carrier answered with a slight British accent. They carried on, nervous, but marching with signs and heads held high. A figure was running up from behind her and she braced for an altercation. She put herself into a fighting frame of mind and gripped her drumsticks, prepared to hit whoever it was. The thought of shoving a stick up their nose entered her mind. It was Thomas. As if he had entered her house, he took off his straw boater hat before greeting her. He was a tall, slim man with attractive, almost feminine facial features. Even though his clothes were supposed to help him blend in with the civilians, the grey, dapper suit he wore was a lot fancier than anyone would wear in the bad neighborhoods and bars where he investigated crimes.

"Miss White?" he yelled nervously, trying to speak over her banging drum.

"Well, hello, Detective Vanderbilt, beautiful day, is it not?" she yelled back.

"Miss White, what are you doing?" He walked beside her, uncomfortably looking around and trying to keep up to her pace.

"It's obvious, we're standing up for a woman's right to vote."

He leaned in closer and spoke in a hushed tone: "It's...it's not like I don't agree with your position, but Chief O'Riley doesn't want any more protesting."

"I'm not worried about that grouser, and there won't be any more protesting right after President Wilson gives us the right to vote...and rights for Colored people—but we'll work on that later."

"Miss White..."

"I told you, Thomas, you may call me Mary."

Thomas blushed a little. "Miss Wh...Mary. It's not right for a woman of your standing to be stirring up trouble like this."

"If not me, Thomas, than who? Is it not the job of all citizens to stand up for those who cannot stand on their own?"

"Like I said, it's not that I don't agree with what you're doing, but I don't think it will help your cause if you're dragged to the hoosegow."

"On the contrary, it may draw more attention to the plight of all women if it gets attention."

"Of all the people who need any attention, you already get plenty of that in spades."

Mary laughed. "That is true. I do stir the pot from time to time, don't I?" she laughed again. Thomas loved her laugh, it was like listening to a song bird.

"Go home, ya floozies!" a man yelled from a window. He threw an apple at Mary's head. She stopped playing the drum just long enough to put the sticks in her left hand and caught the apple with her right hand. "Thanks for lunch!" she yelled.

Thomas briefly put his hand on the derringer he kept hidden in his coat pocket, next to his watch. "You see?"

"Ignore that ding-bat. Even the message to breathe would be lost on him." She tossed the apple to Thomas, he put it in his coat pocket. Mary went back to drumming.

The procession made a turn back towards the main road. Thomas relaxed a little but kept a vigilant eye out for danger.

A young, uniformed officer ran up to him. "Detective Vanderbilt!" he yelled.

"What is it, Peters?"

"They're going to do a raid in Chinatown."

"What, at the opium den? Finally."

"Yes, apparently there have been rumors of gambling and illegal fights."

"Well...that's new."

"Chief O'Riley wants you there."

"Wants me? Why?"

"Don't know. Because you speak Chinese?"

"Not very well. Besides, I speak Mandarin, and I think they mostly speak Cantonese." Thomas sighed and turned his attention back towards Mary. "I guess I should go. Until I return, please do me a favor and don't do anything silly."

"Oh Thomas, I'll be fine. Go, do your raid on the opium den... and say hello to Mr. Lee for me."

Thomas did a double take, not sure if she was making a joke or not. He trotted off, following the uniformed officer.

Across town, in a dark basement, two shirtless, muscular Chinese men faced each other. They were both in different battle poses: one with his arms spread out like a crane, and the other with his two hands in a claw like motion to resemble a tiger. Surrounding them, various voices yelled and cheered them on. Cigar smoke polluted the air, mixed with the smell of sweat and coal dust.

Almost faster than the eyes can follow, punches were thrown and simultaneously blocked. The gentleman using crane style bent and extended his wrists into blocks and threw punches, while the other raked at him and did grabbing motions like a tiger. Every blow which met its target, sounded like a sledgehammer hitting a side of beef. After much back and forth, the Crane Master landed a successful blow to the Tiger's throat. The Tiger doubled over, allowing his opponent a follow-up kick to the side of the head. Faster than it started, the fight ended, with the Tiger hitting the concrete floor, unconscious and near death.

Raucous cheers erupted in the room. Many handed money over to the lucky winners of their wagers. The loser opponent was dragged away to an unknown fate as the winner was patted on the shoulders and given back his shirt. A bald, mustached Chinese man strolled to the center of the room and raised his hands to quiet the loud conversations around him. Although he is speaking in Cantonese, and half of the patrons do not understand a word of that language, everyone knows what he is saying: He was introducing the next gladiators that will take the arena. A ponytailed fighter even larger than the previous ones, strutted into the room, exuding such confidence one has to assume he is the recipient of many victories. He flexed his arms and manipulated his pectoral muscles independently. The crowd responded with thunderous cheers. When the opponent was announced, the room became silent with anticipation to see who in their right mind would even think of taking on such a brute. A young Asian child walked into the room. He was wearing a newsboy cap and clothes which were a little too big for him. Everyone looked to see who the child was escorting. After a moment, news spread throughout the room; no one else was coming. Murmurs turned into complaints and finally protests for what was obviously either a joke or an uneven contest of extreme child abuse. The bald, mustached Chinese man did his best to reassure the patrons, these really were the next contestants. The betting only took a short time, they all put their money on the adult pulverizing the child. No one else protested the set up and the fight was signaled to begin.

The large man looked around and shrugged his shoulders, his way of saying: 'this is ridiculous, but what can I do?' Some in the crowd laughed when he lumbered over to the child to quickly end the fight. He chose to use a quick backhand, which would be enough to incapacitate the child. He smirked at the child and then quickly swung his big arm at him. The arm came in contact with... air. The child took advantage of the height difference and had lowered his body into a spread legged split onto the ground. By the time the large man realized where the child was, the child had managed to land five punches to his groin. He doubled over in pain. The child rapidly spun back onto his feet and then jumped into the air, continuing their spin, into what is know as a flying tornado kick to the side of the man's head. This rendered him instantly unconscious and flung his motionless body onto the floor.

The prediction of a fast fight everyone thought was correct with one exception, the victor. There was silence in the room. The child walked over to a slightly chubby Chinese gentleman wearing a fedora. He laughed and bowed to different people while he collected various amounts of cash from them. He, and he alone was the only one to bet on the child winning. Complaints and resentment filled the air with words like: 'cheater' and 'fixed.' This did nothing to keep the Asian in the fedora from smiling, bowing and grabbing the hand of the child and trying to leave.

The two never made it to the stairs which will lead them to escape. A loud banging and crash announced a police raid. The doors at the top of the stairs flew off their hinges and a loud whistle was blown.

"Jǐngchá!" Thomas yelled. "Nín zhèngzài fánnǎo (Policemen! You are under trouble!)"

Like bugs underneath a lifted rock, the patrons scrambled in different directions. Groups of black uniformed policemen, armed with batons, descended on them. There was little restraint shown as the policemen randomly started clubbing anyone that didn't look like them in dress or in race. Thomas found the scene a little barbaric. The whistle continued to be blown as a few managed to rush pass the wall of policemen. Thomas took note of the guy in the fedora dragging the child through a door. 'Was that a child?' he thought before giving chase. He shoved past gambling participants and policemen alike to get to the exit. Kicking the door open revealed the exit into an alleyway. To the right the alley was blocked off by a brick wall. He raced left as fast as he could, thinking: 'A child is being kidnapped!'

Not far ahead, the child was pulling on the man's arm and digging their heels into the ground. The child yelled: "Wǒ bùxiǎng hé nǐ yīqǐ qù! (I don't want to go with you!)" in Mandarin. He was slapped across the face for protesting. "Bì zuǐ! Nǐ shì shǔyú wǒ de! (Shut up! You belong to me!)" the man yelled. After the stinging slap, the child offered less resistance to the pulling arm.

When they had almost reached the alley's exit, Thomas yelled: "Bú yao `jruh `yiaun! (Don't do it!)"

They stopped and Thomas walked over to grab the child from the man. Suddenly, at lightning speed, the man delivered a kick to Thomas' chest that sent him flying backwards into a pile of wooden crates. It hurt a lot. He held his chest while the man again argued with the child. Thomas used this opportunity to regain his composure and get back on his feet. The man seemed shocked Thomas was even alive after the blow. He stepped forward to make sure his next strike would render him unconscious, if not dead.

Thomas pulled out his derringer and repeated: "Bú...yao... `jruh `yiaun`!"

The man stopped in his tracks. He looked at the child and then at Thomas. He stepped behind the child as if he were going to use him as a shield. This was the plan. He pulled out a large knife and held it up to the child's throat. "Suànle ba! (Drop it!)" he yelled.

Thomas, unwilling to let any harm come to the child, raised his hands, slowly crouched down and placed the gun on the ground. The man smiled a sly and sinister grin. He removed the knife away from the child's throat. Then, with a quick flick of his wrist he was now holding the blade end. Thomas knew what this meant, It was going to be thrown it at him. 'Do I have time to grab the gun off the ground and shoot him?' He thought. He knew the best he could do was crouch down and even then, the knife would get him in the top of his head or shoulder. "Oh, nuts," was going to be his final words.

Faster than either one of the men could move, the child had taken action. The Asian man found a foot imbedded his face. Thomas was almost as shocked as the Asian man. The flexibility and speed it took for the child to stretch themselves into the letter 'I' and kick back with such force was quite impressive. The Asian man's eyes rolled back in his head and he fell backwards, unconscious. The child slowly lowered their right leg and looked down at the victim.

"Thank you...Xièxie" Thomas apprised, walking forward. "...I guess you saved my..." the child got into a fighting stance; legs apart and fist in a pose conveying the message: 'You can be next!'

"Oh my, No, no, no!" Thomas raised his hands. "I'm a friend... Friend? Darn, what's the word for friend...Péngyǒu?" This didn't seem to satiate the child's skepticism. "Oh...uh, let me see...do you speak English? Nǐ shuō yīngyǔ ma?" The child said nothing. "Hmm, don't know if that's a yes or no, or you only speak Cantonese...but that man spoke Mandarin. Maybe you're deaf; can you hear me? Sorry, I don't know that one in Chinese. I'm actually quite surprised about how much I remember. I was in your country...in Peking during the rebellion. What's your name? My name is Thomas...Nǐ jiào shénme míngzi? Wǒ de míngzì shì Tuōmǎsī. I hope I'm saying this right. Far as I'm concerned I could be insulting you." Thomas giggled at a memory. "...Ha, there was this one time in this club in Peking...no wait, that story is not appropriate for children...So, is that man your father?" The child gazed at the unconscious man and then back at Thomas. Their face looked displeased. "Not sure if you understood me or not. Either way, we have to figure out what to do with you. Do you want to come with me to the station?" He held out his hand. The child backed up and looked over their shoulder at the end of the alley, leading to freedom. "No wait! Don't go...er ah, Bùyào...qù!" The child started to back away to the exit. There was a rumbling gurgling sound coming from somewhere. It took Thomas a moment to realize it was coming from the child. "Is that you? Is that your stomach? Are you hungry? Chī fàn le ma?" Thomas remembered the apple, Mary had given him. He reached into his pocket. The child raised their fists. "No, no, no! It's okay...Look." He slowly took out the apple and offered it. The child looked at it and Thomas with extreme skepticism. "It's okay, it's good. Freshly thrown at my head this morning." Thomas smiled. The child's stomach growled again. He quickly grabbed the apple and devoured it as if he had never eaten an apple before. "My, you are famished." The child ate the whole fruit: core, seeds and all. "Poor lad. Let's go get you a nice bowl of soup and some bread." Thomas reached out his arm and tried to place his hand on the child's shoulder but they flinched out of the way. "Okay. Here's an idea; follow me and I'll take you to a café near the police station. First let me go tell my men we have an extra passenger for the hoosegow who may or may not be your father." Thomas took the lead and walked around the child. He slowly followed Thomas, always staying out of arm's reach.

"Mary, we're tired," whined one of the women in the women's voting rights march.

"We're almost at city hall," Mary informed. "One more block and then we can rest." The party vigilantly pushed on, lead by Mary and her drumming. On the last block of their journey, Mary could hear someone yelling at them. It wasn't unusual considering some have shouted rude comments or made nasty faces. She lowered the volume on her drumming in order to make out what the person was saying. It was the word "Hey!" She stopped drumming completely in case the person was yelling for an important reason.

"Hey!" yelled a large man. He was wearing a poor-boy cap, the kind usually seen on young boys, a white tank top and suspenders. "Hey!" he yelled again.

Mary recognized him. He was the person who had thrown the apple at her from a window. "Well," she exclaimed smiling. "Look who it is. Are you coming to give me more apples? It is getting close to lunch time."

"I'm coming to give you a piece of my mind!" he yelled, walking beside her.

"Are you sure you have some to spare?"

It took a second for the insult to register with his brain. "You think you're sooo funny? Cork-headed women like you are what's ruining this country! Why don't you go back in the kitchen and shut yer yap?"

"I can tell that convincing you of the virtues of equal rights for women would be like discussing Nietzsche with…well, actually discussing Nietzsche with you."

He looked confused, then angry. "I should rap you in the mouth!"

"Well, as luck would have it, we have arrived at our destination and our journey is ended." Mary gestured to the city hall building. "So no rapping is needed. You may go about your merry way."

"What's the matter? You dames ain't got a man at home go to? Real man wouldn't let his wife run around on the streets. If I were your man, I'd put you over my knee and spank you!"

"I said, good day to you, sir," Mary sternly repeated, hoping he would get the cue to leave. The words seem to finally sink in and he turned around and started to walk away. Mary turned her back on him to give instructions to her women's group about what course of action they should take next.

The man stopped walking away, turned around and walked back to Mary. He then proceeded to slap her right butt cheek and said: "See! That's what you need!" He turned around and laughed to himself. This was a bad idea, because it created a target that wouldn't dodge the drum Mary had taken off her shoulder and thrown at the back of his head. He hit the sidewalk like a seal flopping onto a rock. He slowly picked himself up, fuming with anger and rubbing his head. "Why you! I'm gonna black your eye! You Bit…" Mary didn't move as he lurched towards her with murderous intent. He got within three feet of her which was just close enough for her to deliver a perfect right punch to his left eye. He staggered, fell backwards over the drum and landed with his back on the ground. He looked up and saw the women's group surround him in a circle; they had angry expressions. The women looked at him and then each other, nodded in agreement and began to stomp on him while using their signs for bludgeoning. Off in the distance, a police whistle was blown.

The Bowery neighborhood, which was lined mostly with flophouses, clothing stores and shops selling cheap goods, was a little shady, but it also had the Blossom restaurant which served a decent dish of lamb and oxtail stew. Thomas knew it was decent because the child was now on their second bowl. The lamb and oxtail stew, costing 15¢ was supposed to be for himself. He had actually ordered the soup with bread for 5¢ for the child but the boy grabbed it from him. Remembering the child could knock out a grown man with just one kick, he waived and ate his sour soup with hard, crusty bread.

"Now, what am I going to do with you? I guess the orphanage is the best option…if they'll accept you. That, or send you back to China–how did you even get here? I'm quite sure only grown men are allowed to come to this country." Thomas looked across the street at the police station as a long, black, Ford Model T. paddy wagon pulled up to the front. Numerous Chinese men were taken out of the back and escorted inside the station. "I should have stuck around longer to help investigate," Thomas lamented, "but… I guess I haven't been that excited about detective work lately. I thought I could be the next Sherlock Holmes. Truth be told, today has been the most exciting day I've had in months. Otherwise it's the same thing, over and over." Thomas felt embarrassed: "…But, why am I telling you this? You're a child that doesn't even speak English. So…" Another paddy wagon pulled up.

Thomas looked to see if more Chinese men were being booked. To his surprise, he saw Mary White and her women's group gently escorted from the back and lead inside. "Nuts!" he yelled standing up.

Inside the station, Sarah, the youngest member of Mary's group, held tightly onto Mary's arm while they were escorted to their cell. On the journey, they passed by multiple cages with voracious criminals all yelling, either for justice or for the women to be put into their cells where they can do various inappropriate harms to them. The cell of the jailer's choosing was one filled with other women. None of them wore white or expressed the virtues of any woman who would wear white. Like the men, they were just as glad to receive the new group, like lions, waiting on a deer carcass to be thrown into their den. The rusty cell door was slammed shut and locked, those who had been sitting stood up. They grouped together on one side of the cell, while Mary and her group cowered on the opposing. Unlike the others, Mary stood steadfast, unafraid of their situation. A large older woman took the lead of the thieves, beggars and prostitutes and approached Mary. Mary held her ground. Sarah dug her frightened claws into Mary's arm and physically shivered. The woman, larger and taller than Mary came within one foot of her face. The woman's pockmarked skin and missing teeth told of a life of hardship and bitterness. The tension was so high, everyone in the other cells went quiet to hear what kind of exchange was about to happen. Mary moved her face closer to the woman's. The woman's eyes widened in surprise as did everyone else. Mary looked at the woman's face, it appeared she were examining it,

"Wha' you want? Fish!" The woman growled.

"You're eyes…"

"Wha' 'bout 'em?"

"They're simply…gorgeous!"

Like a deflated balloon, the woman shyly grinned, turned her head and smiled while fixing her hair.

In the police lobby, more Asian men were ushered in. The mixture of Cantonese and English being yelled, created a bit of chaos in the room. Thomas held the hand of the Chinese child and pushed past the crowd being escorted to the jail cells, to get to the police chief's desk, located behind a decorative waist-high wooden barricade. The chief was a heavyset man, causing his black uniform's gold buttons to buckle a little. His head sported big bushy side burns Thomas couldn't resist staring at. The chief was writing some things down in a book, deep in concentration, evident when he looked angry at being interrupted by Thomas.

"Chief O'Riley!" Thomas yelled.

"Yes, Detective…" he inquired in a rich Irish accent. "…What are yeh doing with that Oriental lad?"

"He was part of the raid, sir. I was thinking of dropping him off at the orphanage. Was Miss White just taken into custody?"

"Ahh, yes."

"What for?"

"Seems she got into a bit of a brouhaha down near city hall."

"Really? With who?"

"With me!" yelled a voice from behind Thomas. It was the man who had fought with the woman's group. He was holding a steak on his swollen eye. "Bunch of floozies tried to rip my head off."

"Wait. I recognize you. You threw an apple at us," Thomas complained.

"Oh really?" said the police Chief. "Ya left that part off about yeh starting the kerfuffle."

"Well…I"

"Well yeh can rot in jail while you think about throwing food at police officers. Take him away."

"What?" the man protested before being lead to a cell.

"What about Miss White?" Thomas asked the chief.

"She broke the law, Vanderbilt. Yeh can't be going around beating up people that break the law—that's our job."

"But sir…"As though a reverse explosion had taken place and sucked all the noise out of the room, everyone went silent. A tall, dark skinned African man in a black suit and tie entered the room, carrying a green, crocodile skinned brief case. On his face were intricate tribal scar tattoos of little raised dots. He slowly approached the police chief's desk. Expressions on some faces in the room revealed they had not only never seen an African before, but not even anyone darker than themselves, on this side of town.

The chief sighed. "And what might yeh be wanting, Abel?"

The African man spoke in a rich British accent. "Good afternoon, Chief O'Riley…" He looked at Thomas. "Detective Vanderbilt…" He bent down and looked at the child. "…And hello to you." The child stepped behind Thomas in fright. Thomas found this interesting and humorous for someone of their fighting skills. "…I am here to procure the release of Miss Mary White."

"And how did yeh know she was here?"

"I was instructed by Miss White, in the event she was not home in time for lunch, I should come here. Was she correct?"

"Ahh, yes. She's here all right. She broke the law and will have to spend some time in the slammer."

"She has given me permission to negotiate her release and post bail for her."

"Okay, then. $10!"

Thomas gasped at the high cost the chief had quoted.

Abel opened the briefcase, reached in, took out $10 in cash and handed it to the chief.

The chief counted the money. "Sorry, I meant to say, $20!" Abel reached in and pulled out $20 and handed it to the chief. Caught by surprise, he counted the cash. "Well…I mean it's—"

"Chief O'Riley…" Abel interrupted, handing the chief $100. "Miss White has also instructed me, in case of her tardiness, to release the other members of her women's group…" He handed him $200 more. "…And to donate $200 to your police charity fund."

His eyes widened. "What police…"

"…To be spent by YOU on any charity you deem worthy."

"Ah,…yes, me charity. Well now, that's very generous of Miss White." The chief yelled to an officer across the room: "Donovan! Release Miss White and her gang."

In the cell, things were of an almost festive mood. The tough woman who Mary had discovered was named Big Alice, sat on the floor with her back resting on Mary's knees while Mary styled her unruly hair into nice presentable fashion befitting of a proper lady. Meanwhile, the other women in her group were leading the rest of the detained females in a spirited, women's rights version of the Glory Hallelujah song. Mary finished Alice's hair just when the guard came to tell them her group was free to go. "There you go Alice…" Mary concluded. "…When you girls get out, I'll see to it you all get jobs at the soup kitchen."

Mary and her group came into the police lobby. Mary thanked Abel, said goodbye to her women's group and then noticed Thomas and the Asian child. She squatted down to the child's level. "And who do we have here?"

"I don't know his name," Thomas answered. "Doesn't speak a word of English. He was part of that raid in China Town. I was going to take him to the orphanage."

"What do you mean?"

"Well, it's either that or ship him back to China."

"No, I mean why do you keep saying HE."

"Pardon? What do YOU mean?"

Mary rolled her eyes, reached over and pulled off the child's hat. Long, ponytailed black hair slipped out from under the hat and extended to the middle of the child's back. "See? HE'S a SHE."

"But…but, I've seen boys with long pony tails while I was in China."

"But why would one hide it?"

"Good point, but that doesn't mean he's a girl."

"Really?" Mary pointed her two index fingers at the child's chest. "Didn't you notice the tiny bubs?" She poked the girl twice in the chest. Thomas knew this wouldn't go over too well. The child's eyes widened in rage and she drew her fist to punch Mary's face. When the punch was delivered, it instead hit Abel's arm which quickly blocked it. The child looked at Abel and was about to do another strike, this time at him.

"Tíngzhǐ!" Thomas yelled. The child stopped their attack and looked at Thomas. "Oh, so you DO speak Mandarin."

Abel rubbed his arm and mouthed the word "Ow…"

"My…" Mary marveled, standing. "…she is a live wire. What are you going to do with her?"

"I told you, the orphanage."

"You can't do that."

"Why not?"

"A Chinese girl in an American orphanage? They'll make her life quite miserable."

"There's not even supposed to be any Chinese women in this country. The man with her, who I assume is her father, must have smuggled her in. I guess the only choice is to ship them both back home…when he gets out of jail."

"And where will she stay in the meantime?"

"No idea. You're right about the orphanage. Maybe she can stay at my sister's place."

"What? At that little flat, with those five ragamuffin kids? Even the roaches can't turn around in there. I think the only solution is for her to come stay with me."

"WHAT? Are you hopped up? With someone who almost punched you in the face?"

"Strangely enough, not the first time today. It'll be fine." Mary squatted back down and looked at the girl. "…I'm sure by the time she leaves, we'll be the best of friends."

"Hold on!" yelled Chief O'Riley. "Is that an Oriental girl? That's against the Exclusion Act!"

"Abel…" Mary inquired, "…did you donate some money to Chief O'Riley's favorite charity."

"Yes, Miss White."

"Donate $200 more to the Policeman's Ball." Abel reached into the case, took out the money and handed it to the chief.

"Okay. Fine…carry on." Chief O'Riley said.

Lighthouses are not uncommon in New York State. In New York City? not so much. Away from the shore and in the middle of a neighborhood, surrounded by large mansions, very improbable. The Asian child might not have been familiar with American architecture, but even she could tell the lighthouse, standing on the grassy parcel of land on Fifth Avenue was out of place. She looked at it and then Mary, who was also riding in the back of the Rolls-Royce Silver Ghost, an elongated silver version of a model T. convertible.

"Yes, I know. Wait until you see the inside!" Mary winked.

The fancy, silver automobile parked in front of the white lighthouse. The beacon, reserved for ships was painted with a few red stripes on the bottom, matching the red front door. Thomas followed close behind the luxury car in his very modest, little red Model T. breezer. It barely had enough room for two people and no roof, but it served its purpose. He got off of his car, and joined the others walking up to the lighthouse. "Hěn qíguài (Very strange)," he muttered to the girl, while pointing to the lighthouse. She seemed to understand and nodded.

"Isn't it lovely?" Mary bragged to the little girl, oblivious to the fact she might not speak English. "It used to be in Long Island, but they were going to demolish it so I bought it and had it moved here. I used to run the lantern, but my neighbors weren't too keen on the light shining in their bedroom windows."

Abel unlocked the front door and allowed everyone to enter the tower. The inside was painted white. In the middle, 72 black, cast iron stairs spiraled up to the lantern room. Lining the wall from the bottom step all the way to the top were wooden, curved bookshelves. Hundreds of volumes of literature adorned the shelves, illuminated by porthole-style windows and electric lights. Mounted on the wall near the bottom shelf was a metal devil head, mounted on the wall.

The girl started walking up the stairs while touching some of the books.

"This is one of the libraries..." Mary informed. "...I keep all the ones about religion here. The ones towards the bottom are about demons. That way, the higher you climb, the more references there are about gods. Come along, they'll be plenty of time to browse later." She gestured for the girl to come down the stairs.

"Lái-lái (come-come)," Thomas ordered. She traveled down the stairs.

"Please, stand to the side," Abel instructed everyone.

"I know what you're thinking…" Mary foretold. "…How can Abel, Helga—Helga is my maid and I live In such a tiny space?"

Abel reached inside his shirt and pulled a hidden necklace from around his neck. On the end of the necklace was a large metal key, barely smaller than his palm with a hollow end, resembling ones used to wind up music boxes. He placed the key inside the metallic devil's mouth and turned it. The eyes on the sculpture glowed red and there was a metallic clunk followed by the sound of metal gears turning. The center of the round, iron floor they were standing on, dropped, spiraled and unraveled downward, revealing a continuation of the spiral stair case, this time, leading even further down to a subterranean level.

Mary took the lead and walked down the stairs to an area resembling a large, windowless drawing room. A crystal chandelier illuminated the room used for receiving guest but this wan't enough to explain the presence of natural lighting filling the room, just as bright as the outside. All around the room were plush red couches and chairs all in a neoclassical and revival style. It was richly adorned with statuary and objects gathered in foreign land. In place of windows, paintings from the Renaissance of Greek mythological themes. The Asian girl's mouth was agape, as her brain was trying to take in how a large, elaborately decorated well lit room could exist under the lighthouse. Mary didn't give her mind time to rest as she lead a quick tour of the complex. They walked down another spiral staircase to another elaborately decorated room, this time with Victorian era furniture and decor. The ornate, plushy chairs and curtains were yellow. In different parts of the room, a grand piano, harp, violin and African drums were placed.

"This is the music room. Feel free to play any instrument," Mary offered.

Down another spiral staircase led to the parlor room, decorated in pink, Rococo style. It had desks, chairs and a large fireplace. Another level: The elegant Edwardian style dining room, sporting a green theme. Its large table could seat 16 people. The levels seemed endless: The white kitchen, befitting of a restaurant; the bedroom level with 12 chambers all with huge canopied beds, large armoires and writing desks, all illuminated by the mysterious natural light, the marble tiled Roman bathroom with cherub statutes all spitting or peeing water into a large, mosaic tiled tub which could hold 10 people; a gymnasium; a bowling alley; two more libraries; an underground greenhouse and on the final level, a room containing no furniture or decorations, only a large, metal vault door with a silver engraving of a winged elephant.

"You may go anywhere in the house. But, you cannot go into that room...well...neither can I, because I don't have the key."

"I've always wondered, why do you have a room without a key?" Thomas asked.

"You'll have to ask my father. He's the one who designed this house." Mary looked at the little girl. "Now, if you ever get tired of walking up and down the staircase, there's an elevator behind the red curtain on each level."

"What!" Thomas yelled. "You have an elevator? You never told me that! All this time I've visited, I've had to go up and down those stairs."

"Did you really think they carried a grand piano and a credenza down a spiral staircase? Of course there's an elevator." Mary bent down to the girls level. "Now, then, what may I call you?"

"She doesn't speak English."

"Then translate."

"I've asked her many questions, she hasn't said a word."

"Maybe it's because you ask questions like a flatfoot. Let me try." Mary lay her hands on her own chest. "Mary...Mary...Mare-rreeee?" She gestured to the girl. They stared at each other in a moment of awkward silence. Mary did it again. There was no result. Mary did it again but this time, touched the girls chest to give her a hint to reveal her own name. The girls eyes widened and became angry. Mary remembered what happened the last time she touched the girls chest. "Oh nuts," Mary groaned before being head-butted and knocked unconscious.

Thursday, August 25, 1892.

She looked at the ceiling. Was she at home? No, this ceiling was too clean. If she were at home, the ceiling would be made of wood that leaked whenever it rained. Her house usually smelled of cheap cuts of pork. This one smelled like iodine. She wanted to look around but she couldn't move her head. There was a wheezing sound; she realized it was her own labored breathing.

A woman wearing a white nun's habit, appeared over her. 'An angel?' No, she had a red cross on her hat. 'A nurse?' The nurse adjusted the blankets on the girl's chest, The look in the woman's eyes were sad in such a way as though she were staring at a dead body. Another nurse made an appearance. She put her hand on the girl's head. "Is she awake?" she asked the first one.

"I can't tell. She comes in and out of it," the first one said.

"Poor little lamb."

"Indeed. No one deserves this."

"I hear she lost both of her parents," the second nurse said.

"It's true…" she sighed. "…Many people were killed. Heard it was rampaging elephants."

"Oh, dear, she's lucky to be alive!"

"God has spared her."

"He has. Does she have anyone to take care of her.…when she gets out?"

The first nurse whispered to the other one, but the girl could still hear what they were saying. "She's not getting out. The doctor thinks she won't last more than a day longer. It's a miracle that she made it this far with her injuries."

"Oh, dear."

The two women looked toward one side of the room, where a door must have been. "May I come in?" a man's voice asked.

"Yes, are you a relative?"

"Uhh, yes." The man's voice sounded unconvincing.

The only relatives the girl could think of were her aunt and uncle, and they have yet to make an appearance.

"Visiting hours are over in 10 minutes…We're so sorry for your loss."

"Thank you. May I be alone with her? I'll be quick."

"But of course, take your time."

She heard footsteps leaving the room. The man leaned over her, she could now see his face. He was unfamiliar: tall and slim, in his 30s, wearing a grey suit and on his head, a black derby hat. His ginger beard and mustache were sharply trimmed and pointed at the ends. On his nose, a thin pair of gold wire-framed sun glasses. He looked her over and his face became saddened.

"I'm so sorry," he whispered. "This is all my fault." He looked back towards the door to see if someone was coming in. He grabbed her left arm. She couldn't move it on her own but she could feel his grip. His fingers had many cold rings on them "…So sorry. I'm going to fix this…I'm going to fix all of this." He stopped whatever he was doing, looked back at the door and wiped a tear from his face. He reached into his suit pocket and pulled out a huge hypodermic needle. She had no idea what he was going to do or if he was even a doctor. She wished at that moment she could scream or pull away, but the lung power and motor ability weren't there. She was at his mercy. He took out a bottle of silver liquid, inserted the needle and drew the liquid up into the valve. She knew what was coming next. Before he did it, he said: "sorry" one more time. She felt the needle inserted into her arm and red-hot liquid being injected into her. The pain was like pure fire in her veins. "I know…it hurts. But it'll be over soon," he soothed. He put the needle and vial back into his coat pocket, held his hands over her stomach and closed his eyes. *"Gwessla orga-na,"* he chanted silently. *"Gwessla orga-na,"* he repeated. In an instant, the red hot liquid had turned cold. The chilled liquid spread from her arm up to her shoulders into her heart and then her lungs.

She felt her consciousness slipping away from her. 'Why is he trying to kill me?' she thought.

"Visiting hours are over," a nurse's voice reported.

"Thank you. I'm done here," the girl heard the man say before the darkness came.

Helga was a silver-haired British woman in her late 40s. She had a pleasant, chubby, motherly face that usually bought pleasure to Mary whenever she saw it. But the sight of Helga's face, when Mary opened her eyes, was more confusing than pleasurable.

"There-there, love…" Helga comforted with a cockney accent. "Just 'old this on yuh 'ead."

Mary felt an ice-filled cloth on her swollen forehead. She reached up and held the icepack in place. "What happened?"

"That little bugger done knocked you out, she did."

"How long was I out?"

"Not long."

Mary sat upright on the plush fainting couch. She felt along her back. "Where's Abel?"

"Don't worry Miss, I took care of that, already."

"Thank you, Helga. Where is the girl?"

"Detective Vanderbilt is taking 'er to the orphanage."

"No!" Mary hopped off of the couch, ran over to the wall and drew open the curtain. Behind the curtain, was the elevator shaft, separated from her by a golden gated, ornately decorated door. She pressed a black button summoning the elevator.

"Where yeh off to, Miss?"

"I have to stop him."

"From taking that 'ooligan?"

"She's not a hooligan, Helga, she's just scared." The elevator quickly lowered into place. Mary opened the gated door and stepped inside.

As luck would have it, Thomas was having trouble starting his car. He fiddled around under the hood. The young girl sat on the passenger seat, looking bored.

"Thomas!" Mary waved her hand and fast-walked over.

"Miss White?"

"Mary—Thomas, where are you taking her?"

"To the orphanage. If I hurry, I can get her there before lights out."

"But she's staying here."

"Miss Wh—Mary, she knocked you unconscious!"

"I know that, Thomas, I was there. But I'm sure the little dear is just scared."

"Her? Scared? That's a riot. You should be more afraid of her! You know that raid in Chinatown? I'm starting to think that she wasn't brought in as someone's future bride. I think she was one of the fighters!"

"Even so, Thomas, she's staying with me."

"I don't feel comfortable with leaving her here. What if she tries to kill you?"

Mary pointed to the girl's chest. "I'm sure as long as I don't touch her bubs without consent, things will be fine."

Thomas sighed and put his arms akimbo. "As you wish. It's getting late and I know better than to argue with you. I'll be on my way...as soon as I get my car started." He returned to looking under the hood of the model T.

Mary peeked at the engine, "Have you checked the ignition timer or the manifold retaining stirrups?"

Thomas slowly looked up at her.

Part Three
WITH SILVER BUTTONS

May 1, 1915

The young Asian girl awoke in a large white canopy bed. Carved, two-headed snakes decorated the wooden bed posts. The surrounding walls displayed paintings of children by artist, Mary Cassatt: 'Child in a Straw Hat,' 'Children on the Beach' and 'Jules Being Dried by His Mother.' It took her a second to remember where she was. It was hard to believe, because sunlight penetrated the wall and gave the appearance of the morning, streaming into her room. She knew this was impossible, the bedrooms were all on the negative fifth floor, underground. There was a knock on the door. Helga entered the room without waiting for a response to come in, carrying many dresses over her arm. "Good morning, luv. Did yeh sleep well?" Helga knew better than to expect an answer from the girl and continued talking. "Lovely day outside...You can tell, even from down 'ere. I never did understand 'ow the professor was able to bring the sunlight from the outside, all the way down 'ere. 'E tried to explain it to me, something to do wiff mirrors, magnifying glasses or magic—never mind that. I brought you some pretty dresses to wear." Helga laid out the assorted dresses onto the bed, each one of a different color and varying degrees of frilliness. "Miss Mary went out and bought these the second them stores opened up. Pick out whichever one ye like, luv. Breakfast is in the dining room...You understand...?" Helga made eating motions with her arms, pantomiming shoveling a spoon into her mouth. "Brrreak-ffast?" She shrugged her shoulders and left the room. The girl looked over the dresses. One of them looked like it could be a pink wedding dress for a child. She sneered and then threw it onto the floor.

Even though Helga had not explained breakfast was being served in the dining room, the girl found it easily by traveling up the stairs. Mary, Helga and Abel sat eating at the large table, enjoying the bacon, eggs, oatmeal, orange juice, tea, toast, deviled kidneys, chops, and kedgeree. The girl went straight for the kedgeree and, ignoring the knife and fork, started shoving in the rice, eggs and white fish, just like Helga had demonstrated.

"Good morning young lady..." Mary greeted. "...whose name I simply MUST know....and who ignored the dresses and is still wearing the same exact clothes from yesterday," Mary laughed with vim. When the little girl came up for air, she looked at Abel and Helga.

Able registered her confusion and he put down his newspaper. "You may be wondering why the servants are sitting at the table, eating with the misses. Miss Mary doesn't treat us like servants, we're more like...like her friends. We only put on airs when we have to go outside, or have company. Otherwise, it would get awkward for me to be too familiar with my White, female employer."

"But one day, things will be different, I'm sure of it," Mary added. She rested her elbows on the table, put her chin on her hands, faced the girl and smiled with her eyes wide open. "Would you like to spend the day with me? I have a full schedule of activities."

Mary's schedule started with...

8:30 a.m. : Exercise

Mary emerged in the gymnasium dressed in a black-and-white striped body suit, and spent most of her time doing stretches and lifting a large medicine ball and small dumbbells. She had excellent coordination and balance. Helga lifted some heavy dumbbells, some of which even a male would have trouble lifting. Abel shadow-boxed and worked a punching bag mounted on the ceiling.

The girl walked around the room and lifted various objects, looking for something to do. When she approached Abel, he gestured to the punching bag as a clue for her to give it a try. She regarded it for a moment and then proceeded to jump up and kick the punching bag off its mount, sending it flying across the room against the wall. Mary smiled. "We must get her to teach us that!"

9:00 a.m. : Running

Mary jogged down the avenue of her neighborhood, wearing a long-sleeved white shirt and black, bloomer-like pants. Abel rode behind her, the heavy iron bike, more than enough exercise for him. The little girl ran close behind Abel, completing the strange interracial parade. Some of Mary's upper-class neighbors stared, but others were so used to her shenanigans that they ignored her. Whenever she spotted them looking out their windows, she would wave hello and address each one by name: "Good morning, Mrs. Astor," she yelled. "Hello Mr. Morgan!" A large automobile, similar to Mary's, but black, pulled up next to them. Abel readied himself like a bodyguard, in case the passengers meant ill will. A young woman wearing a fur coat, in spite of the coming of warmer weather, leaned out of the window and waved with her white gloved hand.

"Good morning, Mary."

"Oh, Mayoress, good morning..." She saw the mayor riding next to her. He was an attractive young man of 34 wearing a light grey suit. "Good morning, Mayor Purroy," Mary acknowledged. The mayor pretended not to hear her. "Mayor Purroy...John?"

"Don't mind him, Mary..." the mayoress consorted, "...He's just mad because he heard you had tea with that socialist, Hillquit."

"Don't be mad, John. I like to hear everyone's opinions, including yours. Tell you what, tea next Saturday?" He didn't say anything. "...They'll be cake." He nodded and smiled.

"No one can resist Helga's deserts, Mary," the Mayoress giggled. "Speaking of get-togethers, next month I'm co-hosting a soiree at the Astor's mansion. They're welcoming a group of expatriate socialites from Europe, escaping from the big mess. I was wondering if you're going to be free?"

"And, by chance, are any of these expatriates, single men?"

"A couple of them."

"Jane, are you trying to play matchmaker, again?"

The mayoress smiled and rolled her eyes. "You've found me out. You know you're not getting any younger, Mary. How many proposals have you turned down, seven?"

"Eight, and I told you, I won't get married unless I can keep my own name, and no man has ever agreed to it."

"Such a stubborn girl."

"Jane. I'm the very last branch on my family tree. The rest have all passed."

Wednesday, September 14, 1892

The rain trickled down the window of the hospital room like hesitant tears. She looked out at the black, horse-drawn ambulance cart. Two gentlemen clumsily pulled a body through its back doors. There was a white sheet covering it and the parts touched by the rain turned red and then pink. She assumed the person probably died on the way to the hospital. She lifted her hand and placed it on the window. The glass was not cold. She touched the window sill to compare the difference in temperatures, and then dropped her hand to compare those temperatures to the warm wood and cold metal on her wheelchair. She heard a thumping sound...'No, not a thumping,' she thought, 'a tapping...a tapping in rhythm'. It was coming from behind her. With much effort, she turned the heavy chair around. Standing behind her was a boy around her age. He was wearing a white shirt with red suspenders, short pants and checkered knee high socks. His hands rotated three apples in an 'X'pattern, making the tapping sound she had heard.

'Who is he and why is he in my room jugging apples?' She wondered. She poised these questions to him.

"I'm Leo," he answered, "...and for why? Why not?"

"Because this is my room."

"Not for long."

"What?"

"Is it true you were crushed by an elephant?"

"Maybe...Why do you ask?"

"Just asking." He bit one of the apples and tossed it to her. She refused to catch it and allowed it to hit the ground.

"What do you mean I won't be here long?"

"That's what my dad said."

"Who's your dad?"

"I am," came a voice from the doorway. It was the man who had poked her with the needle. Next to him stood one of the nurses, the one who usually gave her sponge baths. The girl reversed her wheelchair towards a side table next to her bed. In the process, she ran over the apple, smashing it into pieces. "Hello. Do you remember me?" he asked. She didn't speak. She put both hands on her wheels and prepared to escape in any way she could. "...Of course you do..." he said "...How are you?"

Sensing she wasn't going to speak, the nurse answered for her. "She's fine, fine. It's a miracle, that's what we call her—the Little Miracle Angel. Like the good Lord healed her in one night... everything but the legs, but I'm sure that's next."

"Are you sleeping well? Any nightmares?"

She shook her head. The boy walked over to her and started staring at her face.

"WHAT?" she ask defiantly.

"My dad said you're one of them."

"Who's them?"

"LEO!" the man admonished. He turned his attention to the nurse. "Can I have a moment with her? I have to discuss...family matters."

"Oh, of course, of course. Take all the time you need. And once again, sorry for your loss."

"Thank you." After the nurse left, he looked at the girl. She returned the gaze, with suspicion and scorn. "Leo, can I have a moment with her?"

"What?"

"A-lone," he commanded.

Leo slowly left the room. The man walked over to the girl. With nowhere left to flee, she hunched her shoulders. "I'll scream if I have to!"

He stopped and got down on his haunches. "You have nothing to fear. I'm here to help you."

"You poked me with a needle, and it hurt!"

"I know, I know. But it was the only way to save you."

"Are you a doctor?"

"Yes...but not the kind you're thinking of...But, more on that later. Right now, I have more important matters to discuss with you." He looked at the door. The boy was in the doorway, leaning on the frame. "Leo? Do you mind?" Leo rolled his shoulders around the door frame and moved into the hallway. "...Your parents—first of all, let me say how deeply sorry I am for what happened to them. It was a tragic event caused by a colleague of mine. He was that man you saw riding the elephant."

"You're with the circus?"

"Yes...well...was. The circus ended the night of the tragedy. Leo...my adopted son...he was an orphan; he also worked for the circus, but now, like you, has no home to go to."

"What are you talking about? My aunt and uncle are still alive."

He looked down at his shoes. "Your aunt and uncle are spending their days traveling around the country, looking for their lost daughter—your cousin. She was kidnapped by my colleague when you were attacked."

"I can still go with them."

"They said...they said they don't...want you."

The girl was silent for a moment. "You're lying!"

"I wish I was. The nurse can confirm it. She's the one that told me."

"Then SHE'S a liar!"

"Like I said, I wish it were not true. But it is. I don't know why they don't want to take you in, maybe it's too heartbreaking for them to take care of another child right now? But for whatever reason—I'm sure this must be devastating to hear, I want you to know, that I can be of some help." She looked away in the direction of the window, her face was in a stern, slight angry frown. "Just like I took Leo in when the circus ended, I would be willing to take you in as your guard—."

"No!"

"I know this must seem quite odd and a bit fast, but they said that you don't have any other living relatives." He looked at the door then back at her and lowered his voice. "That is why I told them that I am your long-lost uncle. Otherwise, they are going to send you to the city orphanage."

"Then I'll go there."

"Please, reconsider. With my help, you can be walking again. If they put you in that orphanage, I won't have any access to you."

"I-said-NO!" She rolled her chair around him and parked it in her original spot looking out of the window. She heard the man sigh, walk towards the door and pause. "Leo and I are going to be traveling to Mexico. We won't be back for quite a while. I'll do my best to check on you the next time we're in town." He walked out the door.

"We're looking for silver," Leo exclaimed from the doorway.

"Leo!" The man called. The boy walked off to join him.

The girl looked outside and watched the two come out the front of the hospital. The rain poured down on everything, but not the man and Leo. The man held up one hand. The rain curved one foot higher than his hand and fell away from them. She leaned forward in her chair trying to see the umbrella that wasn't there.

10:00 a.m. : Swimming

Sporting a large pair of goggles and a striped bathing suit, for men, Mary traversed cross winds and choppy waves and made her way past a brood of ducks to the Statue of Liberty. The 305 foot, copper coated icon was starting to develop a green patinated hue. Abel followed close behind, in a rowboat with the little Asian girl. The entire swim was almost two miles. She reached the base of the statue, touched it, looked up and took respite in the moment.

"Are you tired?" Abel asked.

"No, not in the least," she responded. "It gets easier every time." She started swimming back to shore.

11:00 a.m. : Piano lessons

Mary played Rachmaninoff's Piano Concerto No.2 op.18 on the music room's Steinway while her teacher Sergei supervised. The little girl sat, quiet and bored. When the teacher went to the bathroom, Mary started playing some ragtime jazz. The girl perked up when Mary played a fast version of her rendition of the Maple Leaf Rag by her friend Scott Joplin.

Mary looked at the girl and winked. "Without music, life would be a mistake...He hates when I play ragtime, so I wait until he goes to the powder room."

12:00 p.m. : Lunch with Thomas

Helga had set out a spread of delights. The table in the back of the lighthouse was adorned with: fruit cocktail, sliced pineapples & bananas, deviled eggs, celery, olives, pickles, salted nuts (almonds, pecans, peanuts, filberts), bread sticks, Parker house rolls, saltine-type crackers, potato chips, Caesar salad, Waldorf salad, finger sandwiches: peanut butter & jelly, ham, turkey, chicken salad, tomato, egg salad, cream cheese fried chicken, baked ham pineapple upside down cake, angel or devil's food cakes, ice cream

& chocolate sauce, chocolate pudding in the back yard on a white table.

In spite of Mary's best pleading for the girl to wear one of the dresses she had picked out for her, she did not change for lunch and wore her same boyish outfit.

Helga and Abel were not joining them. This fact was not lost on Mary as Helga poured the tea. "I wish you and Abel would sit down and have tea with us. There's quite too much food for us to eat."

"No, ma'am, got'a keep up appearances—matter of fact, you come along too, dearie..." Helga called to the little girl. "...Can't have people talking about the little illegal girl on the lawn." Helga guided the girl inside the house. Mary watched how easily the girl went along, letting her know the girl felt comfortable with Helga.

"This is so wrong. I should have the right to eat with whomever I want on my property," Mary complained.

Helga and the girl joined Abel in the dining room.

"You know Mary likes to eat with us, why did you set up outside?" Abel asked.

She grinned. "To give them some privacy."

"You're a sly fox, Miss Pendle," he complimented before sipping his tea.

Mary was still a little angry. "This land of the free—only free for some!"

"Well...things are getting better. We just have to be patient," Thomas countered.

"Don't tell me you're defending her actions?"

"She's just protecting your reputation."

"Harumph!" she protested. "If she cares about appearances, than she wouldn't have us here by ourselves."

"Pardon?"

"Well...you know, us two?...alone...having lunch? What would the neighbors say about that?"

Thomas looked a little angry. "It's not the worst thing in the world."

Mary sensed he was a little miffed and put her hand on his. "Oh Thomas, you know what I mean. You're my dear, dear friend and I love spending time with you."

"Yes, of course...friend." He drank some tea.

Mary changed the subject. "So, how is life in the detective world?"

"Boring. Today I investigated a missing cat, and when I leave here, a break-in at the Flatiron building."

"The Flatiron building? That's where my father's office is!"

"Oh, then I shall make it an effort to stop by and say hello."

"I do hope everything is all right."

"There's a lot of bank business in that building, I doubt they were after his...what is it that he does nowadays?"

"Lately, supplying metals to the British."

"You made a face just then. Do you not support the war against the Kaiser?"

"No! I hate all wars, I detest violence."

Thomas spat out his tea and coughed. "I'm sorry, WHAT? You were arrested for assaulting a man!"

"I know and I am ashamed of myself. It's like there's a part of me that's deplorable. I do everything I can to control it but sometimes it just comes out. I got into a huge argument with my father over his position on the war in Europe."

"Is that why I haven't seen him here in a long time?"

"Perhaps. He also travels a lot and works at the office. I suppose I should make peace with him."

"Then I shall pass that message on to him as well."

Mary laughed.

"Did I say something amusing?"

"Oh Thomas. I just adore how helpful you are."

Thomas was not amused at being called helpful any more than he was at being called a friend.

1:00 p.m. : Fencing

Otto Herschmann was one of the best fencers in the world. So whenever he told Mary to move her legs a certain way or to hold her saber just so, she listened. The two, dressed head to toe in white fencing gear and protective face masks, attacked and parried over and over in the gymnasium level. Otto would usually get the best of her by a mal pare, which caused her strikes or parries to be insufficient, but she was good at disengaging his blade and occasionally causing it to slip out of his hands. Landing a touché or a hit on a fencing champion always filled her with glee, while at the same time making Otto a little more aggressive in his attacks.

Thomas approached the Fuller building, a triangular, 22-story steel-framed landmark in the borough of Manhattan.

He was still eating one of the Parker house rolls from his luncheon when he noticed one of his fellow officers. Detective Douglas, a large, well chiseled man more fitted to be a wrestler than an officer, was also going into the building. The man had developed a reputation for always getting mentioned in the newspaper whenever the press needed a quote from the law enforcers. He slapped Thomas on the back; his hand was heavy and hard-hitting. "Tommy boy!" he bellowed, almost yelling. "What are you doing here?"

"I'm here to investigate a break-in. What are you—"

"Well, it's no longer a break-in, it's a murder investigation. so you can go back to the station. I'm taking over now."

"Wait. What are you talking about?"

"Found two bodies up stairs."

"Oh, no! One of them is not Professor White, is it?"

"I don't know, but you can go home now. This is now my investigation."

"I don't understand. This is still my case."

He put his arm on Thomas's shoulder. "Now there, Tommy boy, if this were a break-in or some old woman lost her teeth, then we can count on you. But this is serious, let the real detectives handle it."

Thomas removed Douglas' arm. "First of all, my name is Detective Vanderbilt. And second this is STILL my case." Thomas walked away.

"Captain's orders, DEE-tective Vanderbilt."

Thomas stopped. "What?"

"The captain specifically assigned me to this case." Douglas walked past Thomas. "Go back to finding lost dogs, Vanderbilt."

Thomas stayed outside fuming for a while, but he wanted to make sure none of the bodies was Mary's. He went inside and upstairs to where the break-in had been reported. Douglas and a few others, including someone who he assumed was a witness, were down the hallway. Thomas breathed a sigh of relief; 'The homicide is down there.' He walked to Professor White's office and knocked on the door. There was no answer. He knocked again and his knock caused the door to not only open but fall off its hinges and collapse onto the floor in a loud crash.

"Vanderbilt! What in blue blazes!" Douglas yelled. Thomas ignored him and stepped onto the door and inside the office. It was indeed a break-in: papers and furniture had been thrown all around and a window was broken.

"My…God," Thomas muttered.

Douglas joined him at the door. "I told you, this is my investigation now!"

"What happened here? What were they looking for?"

"Vanderbilt!"

"This isn't a homicide, your case is down the hall."

"Oh, is that so? Open your eyes, Vanderbilt." Douglas pointed to the wall behind the desk. Thomas was amazed he had actually missed the huge hole in the wall. He walked over to it to have a look. It was burnt and imploded in the direction of the homicide down the hallway. Whatever had crashed through the wall had traveled through two other offices, ending in the third, each time creating a large hole. Thomas ran around Douglas; he had to see the result of the destructive act. "Vanderbilt!" Douglas yelled out. A witness, an elderly, Black cleaning woman guarded the door of the last office. In the last room, two bodies lay on the ground, their large male bodies were twisted like broken rag dolls. Most interesting of all. The wall they had hit, had impressions of human figures in white, surrounded by a large burn mark.

"How did this happen? Was there a gas explosion?" The bodies were much too big to be Professor White. Thomas remembered him as being tall and slim. "I recognize one of those men, he was arrested earlier for an altercation with Miss White. Why is he out?"

"Vanderbilt! I TOLD YOU…" Douglas yelled behind him.

"What happened?" Thomas asked the old woman.

"I heard yelling and a loud racket down the hall, then, like a cannon had gone off, then I see a tall man leap through…"

"Okay! That's ENOUGH!" Douglas grabbed Thomas and pushed him up against the wall. "Go back to the station! And stop interfering!" Thomas brushed himself off, walked away, took out a pen and pad and started taking notes.

2:00 p.m. : Opera.

The song, Un Bel Di Vedremo, or in English 'A Good Day We Shall See' from the opera Madama Butterfly, was performed by Mary in the music room, accompanied on piano by her instructor Louise Homer. A seasoned opera singer, Louise had performed the song in 1907 at the Metropolitan Opera House in the presence of the song's composer, Giacomo Puccini. Mary's performance was not as good as Louise's, but a nonprofessional would have a hard time not enjoying her rendition. The little girl seemed quite enamored by Mary's performance and sat on an ottoman, staring with fascination. Meanwhile, unseen, outside the door, Helga and Abel eavesdropped on the performance.

"Absolutely beautiful," Helga sighed.

In the Bowery neighborhood, a portly, well dressed gentleman made his way to the police station. He is wearing a white suit and carrying a glossy silver cane topped with a winged, golden elephant head. One of the man's eyes was hidden behind a dark monocle. On the sides of his head, a bushy pair of graying sideburns met up with a large bushy handlebar mustache. He looked around for someone to talk to, unconcerned with whoever he might find. A nearby police officer, coming out of the station was chosen for questioning.

"Excusez-moi, officer," he said.

The policeman stopped. "Yeah, what do you want?"

"I was wondering, who are the absolute toughest men you have locked up in your jail, right now?"

"What? Why do you want to know?"

"I am just curious."

"Mind your own beeswax, Frenchie." The officer started to leave but the man grabbed his arm. On the man's hand, a bunch of gold rings were revealed. The policeman shook off his grasp. "Oh, a wise guy, eh?" He took out his baton and prepared to hit the guy.

"*Oo-aid vell ur woove ur aid dwaid!*" the man recited. The whites of the officer's eyes turned red and he instantly became docile. "C'est beaucoup mieux, maintenant(It's much better, now.) Now, I'm going to ask you again: Tell me about the toughest, most dangerous men in your jail."

3:00 p.m. : Volunteer work

Every Monday, Mary liked to strap on an apron and volunteer in a soup kitchen started by her friend, Alva Vanderbilt Belmont, a rich socialite who was also a fellow suffragette. Mary handed out bowl after bowl of pea soup. The little girl, wearing a hat to hide her long hair, helped hand out bread. Big Alice, the woman Mary had shared a cell with, entered the room carrying a very large, heavy kettle full of new soup and set it down. Mary ladled some in a bowl and handed it to a bearded gentleman who thanked her profusely. "You are more than welcomed, my good man." She looked at the little girl and caught her smiling at her. Mary smiled back and handed another bowl to another person down on their luck.

At 3:50 p.m., they returned to the lighthouse. Mary seemed a little down. She spotted Abel in the drawing room. "Abel?"

"Right away, Mary," he complied, putting down the tray of silverware he was polishing,

She followed him into the elevator. The girl followed them by taking the spiral stairs. They ended up on the bedroom level. Mary and Abel entered Mary's bed chamber and closed the door. The girl, locked out, was completely confused about what was going on. She placed her ear on the door. A moment later, there was the sound of Mary moaning. The girl hurried away from the door, unwilling to hear anymore.

4:00 p.m. : Tea with the Suffragettes Women's' Group

Fifteen women, plus Mary and her friend, Alva, filled the drawing room to capacity. They sat, drank tea and ate the delectable spread of crustless sandwiches, jams, crumpets, fruit cake, ginger cake, mincemeat puffs, queen's cakes, scones, lemon curd sponge, currant buns, sables a la poche, pont neuf, eclairs au cafe, small chocolate cakes, Scotch bread, Albert biscuits and Victoria biscuits.

Alva, the head of the group, discussed the recent events and the future of the club. "Mary…" she inquired, "is it true, you were arrested during a march towards city hall?"

"Only briefly, Alva. I pummeled a man who touched my caboose. But it turned out all right."

"And…why is there a Chinese girl sitting over there in the corner?"

Mary looked over at the girl, patiently sitting and drinking tea. "Oh, her. I'm taking care of her until her father gets out of jail."

"Never a dull moment with you, Mary." Alva took a sip of tea, placed her cup down and stood up. "Now, ladies, we need to discuss a way we can capitalize on the protest some of you took part in and perhaps figure out a way to organize a much bigger protest with hundreds...no, thousands of women, marching through the streets of New York." Some women clapped.

"But, how will that happen?" Sarah asked. "...We were harassed and arrested—mind you, thanks to Mary..."

"Sarah," Mary interrupted. "...He who would learn to fly one day must first learn to stand and walk and run and climb and dance; one cannot fly into flying."

"...But how will we succeed on a much larger scale? Besides our group, who will help us?"

Alva looked around the room. "Pray to God. She will help."

Thomas was returning to the station when he saw the most peculiar sight walking towards him. It was the portly gentleman in white. Accompanying him were five large men. He recognized two of them from the illegal fighting ring they had busted earlier, including the Asian man in the fedora who had tried to throw a knife at him.

"What in God's name? Are we letting everyone go, now?" He fast walked towards the group. "YOU!" He yelled at the man in the fedora: "WHY ARE YOU OUT OF JAIL?" The man turned around and when Thomas got close to him, he tried once again to kick him. Thomas was prepared this time and rotated his hips so that the kick ended up missing. Thomas then took the opportunity to plant a perfect right hook on the man's jaw, sending him falling to the ground. The punch hurt Thomas's hand and he tried to shake it to get rid of the pain. Thomas tried to reach for his gun, but someone punched him and sent him to the ground. He looked up and saw the man in white, surrounded by the other released fighters. One of them punched him again. Another was about to punch him a third time but the man in white stopped him. "Gentlemen, gentlemen! Show a little restraint! Who is this man?" Two men grabbed Thomas and held him upright.

The man in the fedora stood up while rubbing his jaw. "He was one of the cops that busted up the fighting tournament. Took my best fighter with him."

"You cur! You speak English!" Thomas accused.

"He took your best fighter?" the man in white said. "Well, it's obvious that you're not the best fighter. He turned to Thomas. So, where is this BEST fighter?"

"I'm a member of the New York Police department and you are all under arrest for—" One of the men punched him in the stomach.

"That is not what I asked you, Mr. Member of the Police Department. I asked where is this fighter he claims you took?"

"I'm not going to tell you that. But I am going to arrest yo—"

He touched Thomas's forehead with his hand with the golden rings.

"*Oo-aid vell ur woove ur aid dwaid!*" Thomas became petrified and his eyes turned red. "Now, that's better. Tell me where to find the so called, BEST fighter."

Thomas struggled not to say anything but it was like the words were coming out before his brain could stop them. "S-She's at-t-t M-Mary's h-house."

"She?" It's a girl?" He almost laughed.

"Yes," answered the man in the fedora.

"Fascinating...L'adresse s'il vous plaît?...the address, Mary's house?"

"Fifth Avenue."

The man hit him in the stomach with his cane. "The whole address!"

"Fifth Avenue...."

"His mind is tough, or perhaps his feelings for this Mary are strong. It doesn't matter—you!" He pointed to the guy in the fedora. "You will find out where Mary's house is and retrieve the best fighter."

"She may not want to join you," he answered.

"She will join us or die." He looked at Thomas. "Par exemple, you may not give us the address of your love, but what about your own safety?" He put his hands on Thomas' head. "Why don't you go walk in front of that streetcar?" He pointed to an upcoming streetcar, noisily rumbling down the middle of the street. "Release him." They unhanded him. For a second he stood still, and then slowly walked away. "Allons-y! (let's go!)"

The group followed the man. Thomas staggered into the street in a daze; he had no control over his body. It was like his mind was in a dream state but his motor controls were off on their own. The street car got closer and closer. The driver of a horse and carriage that barely missed running over him cursed and continued on. Thomas' body stopped so he could time jumping in front of the streetcar. He knew if he stood on the tracks, the driver could stop too early and he would be spared. A part of him tried to fight the urge to kill himself; it was hopeless. It was like fighting a desire to breathe. He had to do it, he had to jump in front of the moving street car. The cars got closer. The squealing metal wheels screamed like a banshee. Thomas took the final step of his life. A hand yanked on the back of his shirt collar and sent him backwards onto the ground. He saw a bright flash when the back of his head hit the ground. He could voluntarily move his limbs again. He blinked and looked up at a face. It was a handsome, young man, about his age, wearing a red newsboy cap. "Wha-what?" Thomas stuttered.

"You all right fella? You're acting a little jazzled."

"Who?"

"Sorry chief, I gotta scram."

The man went away. Thomas picked himself off the ground and looked around. He spotted the man running in the direction of the gang that had assaulted him.

6:00 p.m. : Dinner

Dinner was a formal affair at Mary's underground mansion. Staff and house guests dressed like they were going to be dancing later, except the little Asian girl, who wore the same shirt and pants she had worn all day. Mary showed disappointment in her face, but seemed to quickly get over it by the time Helga bought out the courses of: olives, cantaloupe, Virginia tomatoes and radishes, cold salmon a la Washington, sweet bread, asparagus with vinaigrette, roast duckling, a garden salad and for desert: Saxon pudding and an apple pie.

This time, the little Asian girl took her time eating, and with a fork. She appeared to be studying and listening to the various conversations around the dinner table. Mary looked at her as if she were studying her in return. Mary took her spoon, breathed hot air on it and then proceeded to stick it on the tip of her own nose where it remained without her holding on to it.

"What are you doing?" Abel asked.

"Trying to get a rise out of her."

"Be careful. She's not one to fool with."

"Baloney…" The spoon fell off Mary's nose. The little girl smiled. "… I see nothing in her that I don't see in myself."

Sunday, December 25, 1892

"Merry Christmas!" the boy yelled as he pushed her wheelchair down the snowy hill. The chair quickly lost its direction and tumbled sideways. The girl fell out and rolled alongside the chair, trying her best not to have the heavy chair run over her. Much laughter filled the air. The girl's body came to a stop next to the shore of a frozen pond. There was more laughter.

"Let's do it again!" a boy yelled.

Five children ran down the snowy hill. Two picked up the wheelchair as the others lifted her up and put her back in it. Snow covered her hair and eyelids. Her face held a stern scowl.

"Still being tough, eh?" a boy threatened. "Lets push her down the hill again." The children took her back to the top. A girl pushed her face next to hers. "Nobody likes you!" She gave her chair a huge shove, it made if further this time and crashed onto the shore. Her body rolled out of the chair and ended up on the surface of the pond. Much laughter was heard. "She's on the ice!" Someone yelled and laughed. "Let's break the ice!" The children ran down the hill. She tried her best to turn her body around and crawl to the shore. A rock, was thrown right next to her face to prevent this. She covered her face to protect it, as rock after rock landed around her. A couple hit her on her back. She had to get away from them. She had to get out of their reach. She turned around on her belly and started dragging herself across the ice to the other side.

"Break the ice!" the girl yelled The children started throwing rocks and sticks onto the ice to try to crack it. They were successful in creating cracks but the speed at which it happened was not fast enough. By the time they could break the ice enough for her to fall through, she would already be on the other side. "Break it!" a boy yelled. One of the larger boys, carefully stepped out onto the breaking ice. He stomped on it over and over but it didn't collapse. "Go out there!" The large boy carefully slid his feet closer and closer to the girl, sliding across on her belly.

"Crack it, crack it!" the children chanted. The boy started stomping next to her legs, over and over. The girls face turned from anger to panic. A deep sound of cracking ice echoed under the surface. She looked back and up at the boy. His freckled face was laughing; to him, this was a wonderful game. Two other boys ran out onto the ice to help him complete his deed. With one more stomp, the freckled faced boy caused a chain reaction, culminating in the entire surface of the pond shattering like a pane of white glass.

In a split second, she and the other three went under. The murky green water instantly chilled her to the veins. She waved her hands and was briefly able to come to the surface. All around her were floating chunks of ice. She tried to grab onto them, but they quickly slipped away from her fingers. For a moment, she saw the other three, who were struggling even more than she was: their arms were flapping, splashing the water in failed attempts to keep their heads above the surface. One of them was able to say: "... Can't!..."

She went under again, her legs unable to help her to stay alive. Pushing harder with her arms, she sloppily rose above the surface. Only one boy remained above water. The girl and boy still on the shore watched without saying a word or helping. She wondered what they would tell Mrs. Shue, the leader of the orphanage. Would she be sad? Glad she didn't have to deal with as many children, as she had complained so many times? The little boy on the shore was about to run away, perhaps to get help. The girl, next to him, grabbed his arm and said something to him. He stopped, stood by her side and continued to watch the children slip into the cold dark abyss. Her heart began to race, it was impossible to get air into her lungs. She slowly sunk below the surface of the water. She could see two white forms become engulfed in the murky, green darkness even faster than she. Her vision was fading. She knew this feeling, it was the same as when the elephant stepped on her. There would be no savior this time. Everything went black.

8:00 p.m. : Dessert and port in the 2nd Library

Mary was reading a book titled Tom Swift and His Air Glider by Victor Appleton. The fireplace and the electric light illuminated the curved bookshelf which formed the large room into an oval shape. Some shelves held decorative pottery from Ancient Rome and Greece. Abel brought her a glass of port. She took a sip, sat back and relaxed. She sighed sorrowfully. The brass, candlestick-style telephone rang, startling her. 'Who would be calling at this time?' she wondered. Abel answered the call.

"Hello? Oh, hello, Detective...Of course. Please hold on." He looked over at Mary. "It's Detective Vanderbilt. Do you wish to speak with him?"

"Of course. It must be important." Abel bought the phone over to her. "Hello, Thomas?"

"Hello, Miss White?"

"Mary, Thomas."

"M-Mary. Is everything okay?"

"Yes, Thomas. Why wouldn't it be?"

"I'm afraid I was witness to some strange occurrences, one of which involved your father."

"My father? What! Is he all right?"

"I don't know, I haven't been able to contact him. It seems there was a rather bizarre break-in at his office, crowned by the appearance of two deceased males."

"Deceased? How?"

"I wasn't able to examine the bodies, but if I had to guess I would say some kind of weapon-fire, like a cannon—something large."

"A cannon? How? And no sign of my father?"

"I'm afraid not. That's why I was calling you. I was hoping he would have tried to contact you."

"No, I haven't talked to him for days; God, I hope he's all right!"

"Don't worry. A witness mentioned something about a tall thin man leaving through a window. He could have fled...though I don't remember a fire escape on that side of the building—either way, it sounds like he may be on the lam."

"Well, there's no reason for that. He's not into anything nefarious."

"Are you certain? You said he was working with the British, supplying metals of some sort?"

"Yes, but that's no reason for anyone to want to cause him harm."

"Perhaps...perhaps you're right...Just...just be careful."

"Thomas?"

"Yes?"

"Is there something else bothering you? You seem a bit stiff."

'No…I haven't been drinking…Something…I can't remember, I think I may have slipped and fell…I just feel like you should be very careful."

"I'm more worried about you, Thomas. Are you sure you're all right?"

"I'll be fine…just…I'm having a hard time remembering something that happened, I-I just need to rest a bit."

"Please do."

"I'll say goodnight then."

"Goodnight Thomas, take care of yourself." Mary hung up the phone. Abel waited patiently to learn what the phone call was all about.

"Abel?"

"Yes, Mary?"

"Another glass of port, please."

At 9:45 p.m. the little Asian girl was walking past Mary's bedroom and saw Mary and Abel inside. Abel walked over, loosened Mary's collar and opened the back of her blouse. Mary walked over to the door and slowly closed it. The girl, by this time had run down the hallway to her own room.

10:00 p.m. : Bedtime

Without knocking, Mary opened the door of the little Asian girl's bedroom and walked in. This startled the girl, who dropped the nightgown she wasn't going to wear.

"Oh, hello," Mary apologized. "Sorry I didn't knock. I was trying to catch you doing something that people do when no one is watching." She walked over, picked up the nightgown, examined it and placed it on the bed. "Not to your liking, eh? Guess I'll try again tomorrow."

Mary sat on the edge of the bed. She patted the mattress and gestured for the girl to walk over to her. "Come…what did I hear Thomas say…Lay-lay? Lee lie loo?" The girl smiled and almost chortled. Mary smiled. "At least I can be humorous in Chinese, but I think you understood 'come here.'" Mary did the overhand gesture to beckon someone over to you. The girl walked over, slowly took Mary's hand, turned it downwards and moved it in a downwards scraping motion. "Oh!" Mary marveled, "In China you do it like that? That's the bees knees! What else can you teach me? How do you say your name in Chinese?" The girl stared at her.

Mary raised an eyebrow. "I see, you're not going to fall for that one. It was worth a go. Here, turn around…" Mary gestured with her finger in a circular motion. The girl slowly turned her back on Mary. "Don't worry. I'm not going to hurt you—honestly, what is more important, don't hurt me."

Mary opened a drawer on a side table and pulled out a golden-handled brush. "Now…easy girl…I—sorry, it sounds like I'm talking to a wild horse." Mary cautiously reached out and touched the girl's braided hair. With delicate, calculated movements, she undid the ponytail and let the hair hang down. "You know, I've been almost everywhere in the world except the Orient. I should go one day." She gently and repeatedly ran the brush through the girl's hair and alternatively smoothed it out with her free hand. "It's so soft and thick. You know, I used to have a mother that did this for me every night; '100 strokes,' she would say. She died of the flu a long time ago; sometimes, she would even tell me a story. Do you want to hear a story?" The girl didn't respond. "I'll take that as a yes. Okay, let's see If I can remember one…" she began to re-braid the girl's hair into two ponytails.

"In the wintertime, when deep snow lay on the ground, a poor girl was forced to go out to fetch some wood. When she had gathered it together, and packed it, she wished, as she was so frozen with cold, not to go home at once, but to light a fire and warm herself a little. So she scraped away the snow, and she found a tiny golden key. She thought that where the key was, the lock must be also, and she dug in the ground and found an iron chest. 'If the key does but fit it!' thought she, 'no doubt there are precious things in that little box.' She searched, but no keyhole was there. At last she discovered one, but it was so small that it was hardly visible. She tried it, and the key fitted it exactly. Then she turned it once round…And now you must wait until she has unlocked it and opened the lid, and then we shall learn what wonderful things were lying in that box–good night, darling." Mary stood up and departed the room, leaving the girl seemingly perplexed.

Across town at the New York harbor, a group of passengers were embarking on an Cunard Ocean Liner. The ship would be sailing from New York to Liverpool, England, taking about a week, which made it one of the fastest ways to travel overseas. Mixed in with the regular passengers were a few wealthy ones. This created a small presence of reporters interviewing them before they embarked.

"Mr. Vanderbilt! Mr Vanderbilt!" a reporter yelled. Alfred Vanderbilt stopped before he and his male friend stepped onto the gangplank, and turned to answer questions. His friend appeared not so eager to speak. "Mr. Vanderbilt..." asked the reporter. "... are you not concerned with the warning from Germany that any ship carrying munitions or contraband will be torpedoed?"

"That's nonsense. No one is going to put munitions on a passenger liner full of innocent men, women and children. And besides, they know better than to target a ship carrying Americans. Now if you'll excuse me, we're already late getting onboard."

Ignoring the shouted questions, the two men walked up the plank. Behind them, an older Black man carried their luggage. Alfred's friend tried to grab his own bag but the man refused any help. Alfred's friend nervously turned to him. "Alfred, I can't tell you how much I appreciate you getting me a meeting with Prime Minister Asquith."

"Think nothing of it, ol' chum. After all of the things you have done for my family, I can't repay you enough. But I have to ask, why the sudden urge to leave the country in such a hurry?"

"I can't go into any details. Let's just say it's better if I'm far, far away from New York, right now."

"Didn't you say you had a ship of your own? You could take that?"

"It should stay here...in case it's needed."

"You've always been a very mysterious man, Professor White."

The RMS Lusitania

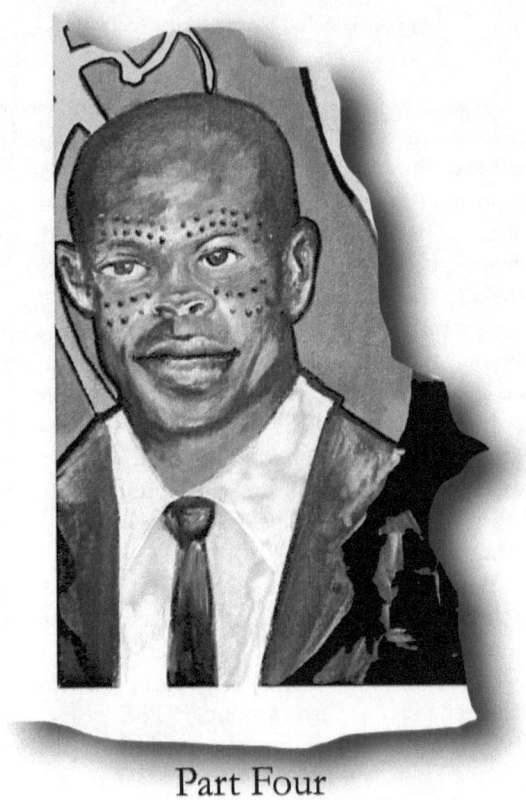

Part Four
ALL DOWN HER BACK

Sunday, January 1, 1893

Her hand was cold. After everything she had gone through, this was to be expected. 'Is this what death is like?' she thought. It was obvious there was no way she could have survived drowning in a frozen pond. Then again, she had survived being stepped on by an elephant. She slowly opened her eyes; she saw red. The red came into focus; it was a curtain; a tiny, open curtain surrounding a tiny round porthole window, the kind you would see on a sailing ship. Outside was dark and green. She stared at the window for a long time, trying to figure out its connection to her death. She heard a low chugging sound, like a quiet steam locomotive. She felt the sound vibrate against her cold hand. She turned her head slightly. Her hand was under the porthole, resting against a wall made of some kind of cold, dark metal. She moved her hand away from the wall and it instantly became warmer. The room was well-heated. She lifted her hand towards a caged, gold submarine light hanging above her head. She could see more red curtains around her. She was lying on a canopy bed, more comfortable than any she had ever been on. The small room was well furbished, with a small wooden chair, an ottoman, and a tiny desk whose legs were carved wooden snakes.

When she turned to her immediate left, she could see her wheelchair, but it was not her wheelchair. The basic structure was there—two large wheels in front, two small ones in rear and the seat—but the wheels were shiny and silver. The seat matched the room's decor and was cushioned, plush, red velvet and behind the chair, a series of sprockets and gears. Connected to the gears on the back was a turnkey, and attached to the key, a note which read: 'Turn me, and tell me.'

"How strange." She reached out her left hand and twisted the key. After three turns she waited for something to happen; nothing did. She remembered the words: 'tell me.' "Okay...tell who?" She looked around in case someone else was in the room. ...Tell the chair? Okay, chair.......Turn around." The gears on the chair whirled and sprang to life. The chair, as though possessed, slowly turned and faced her. She wiggled away as fast as she could without the use of her legs. The thought of ghosts or evil spirits unnerved her. The chair didn't do anything else. She relaxed a little and realized the chair had gears, just like a train, and trains were machines, not possessed by demons. 'Uhh...," she stammered, wondering what else the chair would do. "G-go across the room." The chair rapidly backed away from her and came within an inch of the wall opposite her. "Come back." It returned to the exact position it was before. "Dance." The chair wiggled around the room as being pulled and pushed by two people fighting over it. She laughed at the sight and told it to stop. "Come over here and put me in your seat." It slowly rolled over.

She tried to position herself to slide into the chair, as she had done so many times. To make the chair even more fascinating, her actions were aided. The seat stretched right next to her, using a couple of metal, expandable accordion racks. She easily got into the seat, which retracted and placed her in the chair.

"Leave the room." The chair turned and went to the door. The door was egg-shaped and made of a dark metal. The chair made a bell sound. "Leave the room," she repeated. It did the bell sound again. "Why won't you …" She realized what was wrong; the door was closed. 'Am I a prisoner?' She reached up and grabbed the door latch. It easily turned. The chair immediately backed up, allowing her to pull the door open. When the door was wide enough, the chair quickly entered a hallway.

There were other doors, one of which was open. "Take me to the room with the open door." When she arrived, she peeked in. The room was similar to the one she had awoken in. She assumed the rest were also the same. Down the hall were stairs leading both up and downwards. She hated stairs; they limited her mobility. "Can you take me downstairs?" They zipped to the end of the hallway. She was about to yell 'Stop!' for fear she and the chair would plummet down the stairs, but the chair stopped. The shape of the wheels transmogrified into a more flattened form, not unlike those of a tank's treads. The chair went forward. She braced for disaster. The shape of the wheels allowed the chair to smoothly descend the stairs without the slightest tilt to her chair or any bumping. She smiled with delight.

When she arrived at the bottom, she resisted the urge to go up and down the stairs. The downstairs was all steam-powered machinery: Huge gears chugging along, spitting steam and hissing. In the corner was a smoker box for coal, burning bright with energy, but no place next to it for coal or wood to be stored. In the front of the room was a motor carriage. She was more fascinated with seeing a real car than the fact it was inside this room. The rest of the room was more crank shafts, rods, gears and pistons, all working together for an unknown purpose.

She couldn't wait to try the stairs again, she ascended back to the hallway and then up the second set of stairs to the upper level. More small rooms, but this time, instead of bedrooms, she discovered a fancy kitchen, a drawing room, an office and a bathroom. Each room had a porthole window. This time, the view was bright. She took the opportunity to look through one. There was lots of water outside moving past. 'I'm on a boat? How? Where?' At the end of the hall one more set of stairs ascended to another door. It was already open and bright, grey light filtered down to her. She knew these stairs lead to the outside. Without fearing the chair's abilities, she ordered it to take her up.

May 7, 1915

"Butterfly!" Mary exclaimed looking across the breakfast table at the Chinese girl. "That's what I'll call you!"

"And why, 'Butterfly?'" Abel asked before taking a sip of coffee.

"Well, it's better than calling her: Hey You."

Helga put down her newspaper. "Wouldn't it be better to find 'er actual name? Been 'ere almost a week. Yet, 'aven't got a peep 'outta 'er."

"I'm sure she'll speak when she has something to say."

"Hmmm. 'pose yer right. Still, yeh gotta start earning yuh keep, luv." She nodded at the girl.

"She's a guest, Helga," Mary defended.

"She's a moocher, Mary. Me n' Abel, we don't 'ave to do chores, but we do, because everyone should work."

"But, I don't do any housework."

"I 'ave no idea where'd yuh fit it in yer schedule."

"That's true," Abel agreed, smiling.

"But what can she do?" Mary asked. "You do all of the house things and Abel does the outside things."

"Maybe she could be your chauffeur," Helga laughed, Abel joined her. They looked over at Mary and realized she was not laughing and had an ecstatic look on her face as if Helga had said something brilliant. "Oh, no. No, no, no, luv!" Helga pleaded

"That's the cat's meow!"

"No, luv!"

"We could get her a little black outfit! It'll be smashing!"

"Moe like smashing into everything! 'Ow's that gonna work? 'Ow old is she? Ten, eleven? She couldn't even reach the pedals!"

"A few modifications to the Silver Ghost and it'll be fine."

"Fine? Yeh can't saunter around town with a little Chinese girl driving yuh car!"

"We'll see about that. Abel, can you teach her?"

Abel had a concerned look on his face. Before he could answer, the door chime rang. "Oh, sorry Miss White, I have to answer the door!" With haste, he got out of his seat and ran up the spiral staircase.

Mary took out a notepad and flipped through some pages. She read a sentence she had written: "nǐ zěn me…yàng?" She looked at the girl, who had a blank look on her face. "Hmmm. Thomas told me that means how are you? Either he gave me the wrong words or my accent really is off. I know you're not deaf. Maybe you can't speak at all. Perhaps you lost your voice at some point. Whichever, you poor thing. It must be tough having a parent in jail, in a strange land. Do you miss China? Things must not have been too good for you to risk coming here?" The girl ate a spoonful of her sago pudding.

Abel reappeared at the top of the staircase "...Mary?" He whispered. Mary looked over. Abel had a worried expression on his face, which made her feel a little panicked.

She stood up and walked over to him. "Abel, what's wrong? You look like you've seen a ghost."

"There is a Chinese gentleman at the door. He claims to be the girl's father."

Mary looked back at the girl and then back to Abel. "Let me talk to him. You stay here with her."

Mary climbed the staircase to the ground floor. When she opened the door, there was no hiding the look of skepticism and mistrust on her face; her usual cordial manners were absent. "Yes?" She stated gruffly to the Asian man in the fedora. She made a mental note that he hadn't taken his hat off in the presence of meeting a lady.

"I'm here for girl—I father," he greeted, bowing.

"Oh really?" Mary questioned, raising an eyebrow. "I heard you were locked up in the hoosegow."

"I no understand—hoosegow."

"In jail. I understand you were in jail. Not a very responsible thing to do when a child depends on you."

"Sorry, can I have girl?"

"Not until I am sure she will be safe and well taken care of. Just having her in this country is illegal, meaning you probably smuggled her in for God knows what purpose. And Thomas mentioned you may be involved in some kind of illegal fighting contest."

"I want child, no trouble."

"Well, you're out of luck, because I like trouble, and this morning for breakfast I ate sago pudding with a side of trouble. You see, in the brief time I've spent with her, I've grown quite fond of the little bunny. So, you're going to have to prove to me that you are going to take good care—" Mary's speech was interrupted by the man taking out a large knife.

"Okay. It looks Like we're going to have to do this the hard way," he sneered.

She didn't flinch. "Well, what do you know? Your cute little accent just went away. Proving you're a liar as well as a miscreant."

"Listen you stupid dame. Move out of my way or I'm gonna cut a door in you."

Mary put her hands on her hips. "And YOU listen to me. There is no way I'm going to let someone like YOU take someone like HER. If you do, It'll be over my dead body."

"That makes things much easier!" He held the knife up and started to approach her. Within one step, he found the end of a very large saber pointing at his throat. Mary held the other end of the sword and stood en garde. He raised his hands up and looked cross-eyed at the sword.

"Take no steps, unless they're backwards."

The man smiled for a second and then knocked her blade to the right side with his knife. Mary parried the knife, the man countered upwards. She did a disengage which created a circular movement of the blade removing his blade from engagement. They went back and forth for a moment, him frantically trying to stab at her, and her calmly blocked all of his attempts. She flicked the hat off of his head and when he looked up at it, he was able to witness her cut it in half. This angered him and the speed of his attack increased. Finally, she did another disengage in a circular swoop and sent his knife flying into a nearby tree. The shocked look on his face was enough victory for her.

"There now. You've proven yourself unworthy of being a parent, a guardian, or an opponent," Mary scorned. "Be on your way. I'm sure one of the neighbors have wired the police by now." She looked over at the window of the Astor mansion, next door. She saw a maid on the phone, standing next to a young woman. "Hello Mrs Astor. Lovely day, is it not?" The little Asian girl made an appearance and stood next to Mary. When she saw the man, she clutched onto Mary's side. "Don't worry little lamb. You don't have to go if you don't want to."

"Come here, NOW!" the man yelled.

The girl remained by Mary's side.

"You belong to ME! Come, NOW! Guòlái xiànzài!" He started to walk forward.

Mary lifted the sword at his chest level. "My sword is quicker than your feet."

Abel came to the door holding a revolver hand gun. "Everything all right?"

"Everything is under control, Abel. Our girl's 'father' was just leaving."

"HE'S NOT MY FATHER!" The girl yelled.

There was a silence of at least five seconds. Mary and Abel looked at each other and then the girl.

Mary bent down to her. "You...you can speak....and perfect English, I might say—say it again!"

She pointed at the man. "He's not my father!"

"Who is he? Who are you? Were you smuggled here? Do you like the name Butterfly? How did you learn English? So many questions! What..."

While Mary and Abel were busy interrogating the girl, the Chinese man had snuck over to the tree branch and retrieved his knife. By the time they took notice of him, he was able to bring the knife back and was already throwing it. As though time had slowed down, Abel's first action was to bend down and try to shield the little girl; Mary's was to step in front of them both and raise her sword. She hit the knife in mid flight and volleyed it back toward the man. It landed in his right shoulder, causing him to reel backwards and scream in pain.

"Touché," she bragged. "Did you see that, Abel? My instructor is going to be so proud!"

There was the sound of sirens in the air as police cars from a few blocks away made their way to the disturbance. The man took the knife out of his shoulder and threw it onto the ground. He started to walk forward. The girl took a fighting stance. He stopped and pointed at her. "That girl is Hongdeng Zhao! She's going to kill you all!" he yelled before running away. He disappeared down the street.

Mary looked at the girl. "What does he mean by...whatever he said?"

The girl looked like she was going to cry. She ran away towards the back yard of the lighthouse. Mary gave chase. "Butterfly? Where are you going? Butterfly!" The girl made it to the back wall. Even though it was 10 feet tall, she scaled up in an instant and then jumped over it. Mary was in such shock and confusion at the sight, she stopped pursuing. "My Lord."

The injured Chinese man almost made it to the end of the block before coming face to face with a police barricade of Model Ts. Thomas stepped out of the passenger side of one. "YOU!" he yelled. "What are you doing near Miss White's house?" The man smiled when he recognized Thomas. Thomas looked at him in confusion. "...Wait...didn't I send...?"

"Detective?"One of the police officers asked Thomas. "You all right?"

"Yes, of course...arrest him!" An officer walked over and grabbed the man. He wiggled out of the policeman's grasp and kicked him into one of the cars. Another officer tried to grab him and also received kick, sending him into a back flip onto the ground. "Okay, just shoot him!" Thomas yelled. Without hesitation, two officers took out their revolvers and hit the man with at least two shots each. The man fell and landed on his back, gasping for air. He reached into his vest and pulled out a small, glass vial. "What is that?" Thomas asked. He and a couple of officers approached the dying man. The man bit off the cork and drank a silver liquid. "What is that?" Did he just drink paint?" Thomas' question was interrupted when the man began to convulse and shake like thousands of volts of electricity were flowing through him. A quick jerk later, he lay still, dead.

"Did he just kill himself?" An officer asked. He bent down and took the bottle out of the corpse's hand. He gave it a quick smell. "Doesn't smell like pa..." His words were interrupted when the Asian's body sprung to life and his hand grabbed the policeman by the throat. Everyone jumped back. The Asian guy slowly stood up, clutching the policeman with one hand, dragging his struggling body higher and higher. The Asian had a look of anger and disdain on his face. When he stood upright, he held the policeman two feet off the ground by the neck,. Everyone was so much in shock, they couldn't think of a way to help. With a flick of his wrist, there was a cracking sound as he broke the policeman's neck. He tossed the now lifeless body against a car, where it bounced off and flopped onto the ground, like a large doll. The Asian man smiled at Thomas. He started to move forward but was thrown back by a barrage of bullets. Every police officer available began emptying their guns into him. His body shook and shimmered as the projectiles entered his chest. When there was a lull in the firing, he looked up, raised his arms and screamed. A metallic rain of bullets fell off of his body and landed on the pavement. With a quick charge, he ran forward and grabbed Thomas by the neck.

Thomas felt the life slowly being squeezed out of him. He reached into his coat, pulled out his derringer, put it right next to the man's stomach and fired. The grip loosened around Thomas's neck but the man didn't let go. He looked down at where Thomas had fired and then back at Thomas and smiled a sinister grin. The fact he was still standing was enough information for Thomas to know nothing was going to stop him. He dropped his gun and frantically searched for another weapon—perhaps he had a knife stashed somewhere. He felt something thin and metallic is his breast pocket. He pulled it out. It was a decorative silver fountain pen Mary had given him on his birthday. He wasn't too fond of it because the end was very pointy and sometimes rubbed holes in his shirt pockets. At this time he was glad for its dangerous shape. He grabbed it firmly and with what felt like the final thrust of his life, he stabbed it into the Asian guy's neck. Unlike the rain of bullets, which had been ineffective, the pen caused him to not only scream, but to release Thomas and stagger backwards in pain. A couple of policeman started firing again. The man hissed at Thomas like a cat. His teeth appeared to have turned sharp and his eyes were those of a wild animal. He held onto his neck, took a large 10 foot leap over the barricade and, like a three legged animal, began running on his free appendages at great speed. The continuing gunfire was to no avail. He ran around the corner and quickly disappeared.

"Oh my stars! Thomas!" Mary yelled running towards him. Abel was close behind. "What's going on? We heard so many gunshots."

He rubbed his neck and walked over to the body of the dead policeman. "It was–it was the little girl's father...he..."

"He's not her father. He just tried to throw a knife at us—and Thomas, she ran away!"

"Wait! What? Threw a knife at you? Who ran away?"

"Butterfly!"

"Who's Butterfly?"

"The girl...well, my name for—heavens! Is that officer dead?"

"Yes. That Asian man killed him, with fantastic brute strength. He drank something and next thing you know, bullets bounced right off of him!"

"Thomas, that's impossible. No one can survive being shot, unless he's wearing a suit of armor."

"I know what I saw! What do you mean she's gone?"

"She ran away, right after he called her...let me remember... Hung-den zoo?"

" Hongdeng Zhao?"

"Yes, that's it."

"Oh…oh, my. Well, that would be bad for her."

"What is Hongdeng Zhao?"

"It means Red Lanterns Shining. They were a young female section of the Harmonious Fist, or as we call them, Boxers"

"As in the Boxer rebellion?"

"Correct."

"But what would that have to do with Butterfly? She's at the most, what, 11 years old? The rebellion was 13 or 14 years ago. She would have a hard time being part of that, right?"

"I can't imagine, then again, I just saw a man take hundreds of bullets and run away like a wild animal, so today is not the best day to dispel of anything."

"Thomas, you have to help me find her!"

"I would, but I have a feeling I'm going to be busy here, trying to track down his killer…" Thomas pointed to the body, "…and figure out how a man can be impervious to bullets."

"Very well, then can you give me an idea about where she would be going?"

Down at New York Harbor, the man with the silver cane watched a rowboat containing four men dressed in black like fishermen come closer and closer to the dock. When their boat was near to the so-called 'toughest guys in jail' working for the man with the silver cane, they helped pull the boat next to the dock and bind it to the tie-off pilings. Two of the men stayed in the boat, looking around suspiciously, the other two got out. One of the passengers was a tall, muscular blonde man in his late 30's with chiseled features and a faded scar intersecting his top and bottom lip. He approached the man with the silver cane and reluctantly shook his hand.

"Hello Mr…?" he ask with a German accent.

"It's better I don't give my name. You never know who is listening." The German man looked around, confused. The only witnesses to the meeting were a couple of birds. There was no one else in sight for at least two blocks. "Where is your submarine, Monsieur?"

"Out there." He gestured to the harbor. "It's hidden. Ready to launch a torpedo at us if you try anything."

"There, there my German friend. Pourquoi (why) the sudden mistrust? I gave you all of the information you needed to capture him. Do you know how hard it was to track him to that ship?"

"It was a total disaster!"

"Pourquoi?"

"One of our submarines was able to catch up with him near Ireland. They secretly boarded the boat yesterday and tried to take him alive but something happened."

"What?"

"He must have had help. He killed six German soldiers; the seventh made his way back to the submarine and the captain gave the order to torpedo the ship."

"They did WHAT?" Your people attacked a ship with Americans on it?"

"If we can't have it, then it's better that the British don't have it either."

"You Allemands are so impulsive. But now, there is nothing. We all lose!"

"The Kaiser wants to make sure there are no copies. You must check the man's home."

"He lived in his office. We found no records of any other address, and besides, it can't be copied."

The German sighed and brought his face really close . "Listen, you French schwein! We are paying you a LOT of money to find that thing! As far as I'm concerned, there are three possibilities: YOU already HAVE it, there never has BEEN one, or three, all of this a bunch of hocus-pocus SCHEISSE! So, If you do not present IT, or a copy of IT, or ANYTHING that I can take back to the Kaiser worth more than us destroying a ship full of American's, then I will have to take over the mission and when that happens, what do you think we will do with a lying French schwein and his hunde? VOUS COMPRENDS, MONSIEUR?"

The man with the silver cane straightened his shirt and cleared his throat. "Well...have no fear..." he said calmly "...We'll find out where he lives. In the meantime, let me make one thing perfectly clear. For the record..." he put his hand on one of the German soldier's head, *"Oo-aid vell ur woove ur aid dwaid.* Everything I have told you has been true...Swim back to your ship, please." The red-eyed henchman turned around and without hesitating jumped into the bay and began swimming.

"WHAT DID YOU DO?" The blond man yelled.

"Nothing much. But I hope that your submarine is close by—or he's a good swimmer."

The blond man and the remaining henchman hurried to their rowboat to try to catch up with their swimming companion.

On a nearby piling, a black-and-white magpie was pecking on an old rotten apple. It looked at the men on the dock and then flew away. After soaring over a couple of piers and warehouse buildings, it landed on a bench at another pier, about half a mile from its origin. The man with the red schoolboy cap approached it. The magpie didn't run away as the man fed it a cracker and then picked it up. "There-there, fella," he cooed. "Tell me what you know... *Alad droth.*"

Without hesitating, the bird started repeating verbatim, in a human voice impersonation, the earlier conversation between the German and the man with the silver cane.

Even if he wasn't so tall, the color of Abel's skin would have separated him from the hundreds of Chinese men moving about the streets of Chinatown. Mary, next to him, added even more spectacle. At every opportunity, if anyone seemed to understand English, she would ask if they had seen a little Chinese girl. Even the ones that understood her instantly shook their heads or ignored her and continued on their daily routines.

"Abel, ducks!"

Abel ducked down, expecting something to fly at his head. Mary looked down at him and laughed.

"No, DUCKS, silly." She pointed to a market's window, displaying hanging duck carcasses. Mary laughed for a little more and then sighed. "Oh Abel, we're never going to find her in this."

"I don't understand why we're looking here. Why would she come back to Chinatown?"

"Thomas said that it's the one place where she could hide out without gathering attention...assuming she passes herself off as a boy." They walked for a while until Mary stopped.

"What is it?"

"Thomas said that when he met her, she was part of a raid on an illegal boxing ring at the opium den. Perhaps we should look for her there."

"Now I am confused…besides the fact you know where the opium den is, why would she go back there?"

"Because, if she wishes to acquire funds for survival, she's going to take advantage of her available talents. Everyone has to eat, Abel."

After a long walk, they came to the door leading to the same place the police had raided earlier. Mary knocked on the grey metal door. They waited for almost a minute for someone to answer—no one did.

"Perhaps you mean a different opium den?" Abel asked.

"I'm quite certain this is it. Then again, I was quite tipsy at the time."

"You really should watch your vices."

"Moderation is a fatal thing. Nothing succeeds like excess." She knocked harder on the door. A second later, an old Chinese man slowly opened the door and began to yell at them in Cantonese. Unfazed, Mary talked over him. "Excuse me, my fine man, we are looking for the fighting match. We believe a little man may be involved in it." The man continued to yell.

"Mary" Abel complained, "this is absurd. He doesn't speak English and even if he did, he's not going to tell you about an illegal boxing match."

Mary sighed and turned to Abel. "He's an American. Just, give him some money."

"Pardon?"

"Give him a spot of cash."

Abel reached in his coat pocket, pulled out $25 and handed it to the man. The man immediately stopped yelling, smiled and bowed. "Oh yes, the boxing match, right this way, please." He turned and lead them inside. They walked down a long hallway and then down some stairs to a basement. Abel cautiously looked around for any signs of a trap. He relaxed a little when he could hear the yells and cheers of men behind another metal door. "This way," the man accommodated, opening the door. They entered a noisy room full of men raising money in the air and puffing on fogging cigars. Abel thought his presence among the many Caucasian and Asian faces would create a stir, but no one paid him any attention. Everyone was too busy cheering on the three figures in the ring. Two of the fighters, 18-year-old twin Asian males, focused their attacks on a single opponent, whom Mary had named Butterfly. She had once agin tucked her long hair into a cap. While one of the twins shot finger jabs at Butterfly's throat, the other focused on the girls lower half, repeatedly trying to sweep her legs. Butterfly was always a step ahead of them, and would move her legs in time or brush away the hand attacks. This went on for a while.

"Look! It's Butterfly!" Mary yelled. Abel squeezed them to the front of the crowd for better viewing. The two men increased the ferocity of their attacks and concentrated on face and chest attacks. Butterfly increased her defense speed and started to counterattack. The twins had a hard time both attacking and defending. Butterfly finally saw the opening she had been waiting for and flipped a foot to the side of one's head, knocking it into the other's. Before they could shake it off, she executed a spinning hook kick to the other man, knocking their heads together in the opposite direction.

"Get them, Butterfly!" Mary yelled. The girl looked towards Mary's direction just for one second. This was enough time for the twins to punch her in the chest at the same time. This sent her flying backwards against the line of people. Her little black shoes made a screeching sound. The crowd pushed her back into the ring toward the twins. One did a leg sweep on her and she fell on her back.

"Get up!" Mary yelled. "You can do it!"

Right as one foot and the other's knee were descending to strike a fatal blow on her, Butterfly rolled out of the way, did a leg spin and righted herself to a standing position.

"Thrash them!" Mary yelled, raising her fist.

"Mary?" Abel asked, questioning the barbaric remark.

With lightning speed, Butterfly kicked one of the closest twin's shins sideways, off-balancing him. She kicked his other shin opposite, and he fell forward and dropped onto his knees. She jumped on his back as a springboard and shot her heel out in a sidekick to the other one's face, right above the nose. She put her feet back and grabbed her ankles, her knees pointing downward, and landed them hard on the back of the man on his knees His body hit the concrete and flattened out like a dead frog. The crowd went wild, money was exchanged. The bodies on the ground were splashed with old beer. The twins shook their heads as they were dragged out of the ring. Butterfly walked over to a Caucasian man smoking a cigar. He counted out money to her. Mary and Abel made their way over to her.

"Who's next?" the man smoking a cigar yelled. "Who will fight —The Little Tiger?"

"Butterfly!" Mary yelled.

She looked at Mary and started to stretch her shoulders and arms.

"Butterfly!" Mary yelled again.

"What do you want?" she asked.

"I want you to come home with me."

Butterfly didn't look at her. "Why?"

"Because it's your new home."

"I don't belong there, I don't belong in this country. Didn't you hear what Lo Fang said? I'm Hongdeng Zhao."

"Yes, those were like the young Happy Fist girls, right?"

"Harmonious, yes."

"Butterfly…"

"Min!"

"Pardon?"

"My name is Min…Qing Min."

"Qing Min? That's even more darling than Butterfly!"

"It's also another reason I can't go back to China."

"Butterfly… Qing Min."

"Just Min."

"Min, the revolution happened before you were even born, how could you be Hongdeng…Zoo?"

"My Mother was a leader of all the women in Yihequan. She trained me since I was born."

"And a smashing good job at it—you're brilliant!"

The man with the cigar continued to yell for a challenger. No one seemed to want to fight Min.

"If I go back, I'll be arrested and executed. If I stay here, I'll be arrested and sent back and executed."

"So what are you going to do?"

"Pay to take a boat somewhere else—anywhere."

"Min, stay with me. I'll find a way to keep you here. I'll even talk to the mayor if I have to."

"I can't."

"Why not?"

"Because I'll get you in trouble."

Mary laughed. "Did you not hear what I had for breakfast?"

"I can't...you, Abel, Greta...I won't stay with you."

"Anyone?" yelled the man with the cigar.

Mary looked at him and then Min. "What if I beat you in a fight?"

"WHAT!" Min and Abel yelled, simultaneously.

"If I beat you in a fight, you have to come back home with me."

"What? No!" Min yelled.

"Mary,..." Abel pleaded "...are you out of your—"

Mary interrupted him: "Excuse me, Mr. Fight gentleman!" Mary waved the man with the cigar over.

"Mary, no!" Abel yelled

"What do ya want?" The man asked Mary.

"I wish to fight the Little Tiger." Faster than gossip, Her words spread throughout the room. Pandemonium exploded.

The man spat out his cigar to keep from choking. "Are you a dumb Dora? That kid 'ill clobber you!"

"So be it."

"Nǐ fēngle ma—Are you crazy?" Min asked.

"Like I said: If I win, you come stay with me; if you win, I'll pay for you to hop on the next boat somewhere else."

"I'm not going to fight you!"

"You're not going to fight her!" Abel agreed.

"Don't worry, Abel. I'm not planning to lose...losing is something that happens."

"Nǐ tài shǎle!–You're being stupid!" Min yelled.

"Perhaps. Are you scared?"

"What?"

"Are you scared I'll win?"

"What! You're not going to win!"

"We'll see. How do you say coward in Chinese?"

"Nuòfū."

Mary moved to the center of the ring, wiggling briefly out of Abel's grasp and ignored his yelling, 'No!' She turned around and looked at Min, and then pointed at her. "Nu-ò-fū"

Min's expression became angry and intense. She started stomping toward the center to join Mary.

Abel put his hands on her shoulder. "If you hurt her, I will do everything in my power to hurt you!"

Min brushed his hands off. "I'm not going to lose."

The crowd roared. The man with the cigar approached Mary. "Are you sure about this, you crazy dame?"

"Don't underestimate me. I'm not some milquetoast."

"Okay, then…" he shrugged "…good luck…you're gonna need it—Okay! All bets are in! In this corner…What's your name, doll face?"

"Doll Face, works."

"DOLLLLLLLLL FACE!"

Everyone cheered. Someone yelled: 'won't be doll face for long.'

"And in this corner, our undefeated champion, with 10 consecutive wins…"

"Excuse me," Mary interrupted, "is that total career wins?"

"Naw lady, that's just today, including you….LIIIIIITTLE TIGER!" More cheers and some jeers.

Mary and Min came face to chest. "Okay, you two, you know the rules—NO rules."

"Wait…" Mary complained "…No Queensbury rules?"

"Never heard of her," the man snorted, before exiting the ring.

"Are you sure you want to do this?" Min asked.

"Are you going to honor our agreement if I win?"

"And FIGHT!" The man yelled. Mary lifted up her fist and started to move around like a boxer. She tried to remember everything Abel had taught her and said her lessons out loud: "Now then…keep your gloves up…turn sideways to lessen the strike area…look for an opening…"

Min turned and faced Mary wherever direction she went, she had yet to even raise her arms. "Why are you doing this?"

"I have my reasons. Aren't you going to put up your dukes?"

"I can kill you with just one punch, you know."

"Not if I knock you out, first."

"You're insane."

"And YOU, are getting booed."

It was true, the audience was getting angry from the lack of fighting.

Min looked up and rolled her eyes. "This is ridicul…" Min's words were never finished, as Mary punched her in the face. The whole world seemed to stop and become silent. Mary stopped moving around. Min felt her cheek where the punch had landed. Mary's expression was one of shock, surprise and extreme fear. It was obvious she never even imagined getting to throw a punch, particularly one that would land on its target. Min made a fist. And had an enraged look on her face. Abel started to make a run towards them but was grabbed by people protecting their bets.

"Oh, nuts." Mary closed her eyes and prepared for another concussion. A moment went by. She slowly opened her right eye, then the left. Min was not there. She looked up to see if she was airborne, about to unleash some kind of flying kick. She was not. The crowd broke into a combination of booing and a few cheers. Mary looked down. Min lay on the ground, apparently unconscious. Mary crouched down, believing she had a powerful right hook that could knock out a wushu master. "Min! Min!" she yelled. She shook the little girl's shoulder.

Without opening her eyes, Min said quietly through clinched teeth and a closed mouth, "Shut up and take your bow." Mary stood up and raised both of her fists in the air. Some people threw paper at her, others splashed beer. "Yes!" she belted like a tough person. "Don't mess with the dress!" She pumped her fist in the air and reveled in the booing

As they walked back to the Silver Ghost, Mary counted out all the money she had won. "Wow, there must be at least $200 here. The odds must have really been against me. I didn't hurt you did I?"

"Are you joking?" Min answered. "I should call you Butterfly for your weak punches."

Abel laughed.

On their way back to the lighthouse, they passed the Vanderbilt mansion. There was a crowd of people near the entrance. "What's going on there?" Mary asked. Abel slowed the car down to a crawl. "Pull over Abel." The Silver Ghost was parked near a sea of black automobiles. Instead of waiting for Abel to open the door, Mary let herself out. As she got closer to the crowd, she discovered some of the people were reporters, notebooks in hand. She approached one of them and asked what was going on."

"Where have you been, lady? Didn't you hear? German submarine sank a ship full of Americans."

"Oh my! No! Why would they do such a thing?"

He handed her a newspaper. It read:

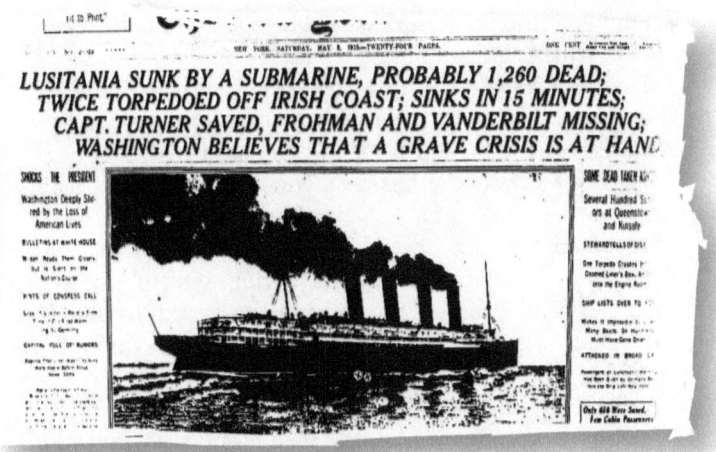

"They warned us they were going to do it, and they did it!" the reporter said.

"Oh God, not a Vanderbilt? Oh, no, poor Alva." Mary pushed through to the front of the crowd. The doorman recognized her and let her and her group pass to the inside. After traversing the many ornately decorated rooms of the estate, Mary, Abel and Min arrived in a large drawing room. Seated inside were Alva and a few member of the women's' group, Sarah and Juliet. Juliet was a middle-aged woman with long features and a pointy nose. When Sarah saw Mary, she left the group, ran over to her and gave Mary a big, long hug.

"Well, nice to see you too, Sarah." When they separated, Sarah looked as if she was going to cry. Mary wondered which Vanderbilt had met a terrible fate. She hurried over to Alva. "Oh, Alva. I'm so sorry. I've just heard. Who was it?" Alva had a shocked expression on her face. "It…it was Alfred."

"Oh dear. Have you talked to Margaret?"

"No, not yet…Mary? Are you all right?"

"Excuse me?"

"How are you?"

"I've been fine, Alva . Why do you ask? We should think about how you are feeling."

Juliet looked at Alva. "She doesn't know."

"I don't know what?"

"Mary, perhaps you should have a seat?"

"Have a seat? What is this all about?"

Sarah burst into tears and excused herself out of the room.

"Alva? What is going on?"

"Mary. Please sit."

"No. Just tell me what this is all about?" Mary felt a bit peeved.

Alva sighed, and looked at Juliet. Juliet nodded.

"Mary? When was the last time you were in contact with your father?"

"My father? It's been a couple of weeks, why?"

"Mary, on the night Alfred was leaving, one of our servants, George, was helping him get his luggage on board the ship. Alfred was traveling with a male companion..." Alva stopped for a moment.

"And? Do go on."

"...The servant told me Alfred called him Professor White."

There was a pause. Mary wondered if she had heard and processed the information correctly. "I...I don't understand."

"Dear Mary...I'm afraid your father was also on board the Lusitania."

Mary slowly turned around. Abel walked up to her. "Miss White?"

She looked through him.

"I'm so sorry, Mary," Juliet whimpered. "...Excuse me." She tried to muffle her sobbing while leaving the room.

"Miss White?" Abel asked again.

Mary slowly walked away from him, towards a very large window. Sunlight blazed through a pair of long, lacy white curtains. The light began to fade, and eventually all turned black.

"MARY!" Alva yelled. "MARY! Someone call the doctor!"

Sunday, January 1, 1893

When the wheelchair exited through the metal door leading to the ship's wooden deck, she immediately came face to face with the tall thin man with the pointy mustache and beard. He was startled as he stood up from a stool. He took a pipe out of his mouth and tried not to let go of a fishing pole. "Oh!" he exclaimed. "Hello." He was wearing a coat with animal fur trimming to protect himself from the cold and the intermittent snow flakes blowing around..

"That's a scream! It really worked!" someone yelled. The girl looked off the port bow. Sitting with his feet dangling over the edge, also dressed in a warm winter coat, was the boy named Leo.

He too sported a fishing rod, dragging a line in the water passing around them. The man started examining the chair. "What do you think? Did it give you any trouble on the steps?"

She shook her head and looked around. They were on a large body of water, but she wasn't sure if it were the ocean. She had heard the ocean was blue but this water was more green. Off in the far distance, she saw a long sliver of land. From the stories she'd read, she believed all land near oceans had palm trees and volcanos. "Where am I?"

The man checked every part of her chair while talking. "You're on board the CSS Virginia, sailing on Lake Michigan towards Chicago. Then, it's off to Great Britain."

"Isn't that across the ocean?"

"It is."

"You can't go from Lake Michigan to the ocean."

"If truth be told, were we to take the Welland canal we could, but we're not going to do that."

"Then how are you—"

"Is it comfortable?"

"Excuse me?"

"The chair?"

"Yes, very. How did I get here?"

"We fished you out of a frozen pond," Leo answered. "You almost died...again." He cast out a fishing line.

"Leo!" The man yelled.

"What were you doing there...How did I get all the way out here? And what is this boat made out of?"

"So many questions."

"Answer me!" The girl angrily demanded.

"Listen: One question at a time. I can't tell you everything all at once because I don't think you'll be able to understand it."

"Then just tell me how you saved me?"

"Also complicated. Let's just say someone told me you would be in trouble at a certain time at a certain place. So, all we had to do was show up at that place at that time."

"I want to get off."

The man sighed. "Dear girl, why? Do you want to go back to that horrible orphanage in that awful town? Mrs. Shue and the local authority—who, by the way, happens to be her brother, were more than happy to see you go so they could cover up the accident. Dear..." He tried to pat her head. She swatted his hand away.

"...When we pulled you out of that frozen hell, there where still two other children in that pond...I'm sorry. As much as we tried, we couldn't revive your friends."

"They WERE'NT my friends! They were trying to kill me!" There was an awkward pause.

"Good thing we didn't save them," Leo scoffed.

"LEO!" The man yelled. "For once, keep your thoughts inside your head!" He cleaned out his pipe. "I'm so sorry for what you've been through...All of it...Every damned minute of it. I'm trying my best to make up for my mistakes. When we get to England, You can stay at my sister's manor. It's a large house with gardens and land—you'll live like a princess."

"It doesn't matter. It won't bring my parents back!"

"True...very true. But..." he leaned in close, "...The man who killed your parents and kidnaped your cousin is somewhere in Europe. Stay at my sister's and receive the best in education and upbringing. I will be hunting for him. And when I find him..." He stood up and lit his pipe.

"How do you know he's there?"

"From the same person that told me about you in that pond."

She looked at Leo, then at the ship. Her interactions with this man were always odd and now he expected her to pack up and travel with him to England. Who or what was he? The prospect of finding the man riding the elephant that had stepped on her father and her was tempting. Would he be able to find him? Would he really kill him?

"Who are you?" she asked.

Part Five
SHE ASKED HER MOTHER

May 22, 1915

Mary, dressed in an all black, Victorian style dress and small hat with a black veil, carried the circle of white flowers to the edge of the shore. She looked at the statue of the goddess Libertas standing tall in the harbor, its flame extending into the sky welcoming all visitors to New York to her shores. Many Americans made the journey across the sea in July, but 1,198 of them will never be welcomed by the statue ever again. Thinking about this caused Mary to tear up. She wiped the tear away with her handkerchief and regained her composure. She held herself together. She was not going to break down in front of the mayor, the Vanderbilts, the Astors and the rest of her father's friends. She would remain dignified and refined. 'He would want that.' She tossed her flowers into the water. They rocked back and forth in the waves, away from her, and joined the others already starting to sink. Others around her silently displayed their grief as the Mayor and a priest gave a speech on a small podium. After the memorial, everyone made sure to tell her how sorry they were for her loss and most made it a point to mention that her father's name was not on the list of the passengers or victims and therefore he could still be alive. She tried not to be too pessimistic about that, but she had thought about it many times already. Alva relayed that when the boat was sinking, Alfred Vanderbilt had attached his life jacket to baskets with babies inside. This act cost him his life. She knew if her father had been on board, he would have been there right next to Alfred, sacrificing his life to save as many as he could.

The young Miss Astor gave Mary a slight hug. Mary almost broke down because Madeleine had lost her husband in a similar fashion three years prior, when their families all sailed onboard the RMS Titanic. "Dear, sweet Mary. Please come to our soiree this weekend. Perhaps it will cheer you up and take your mind off of things."

Mary had no interest in attending, but she remembered her father's words on always attending engagements, even when you didn't feel like it: 'they're good for making and strengthening friendships.'

"Of course, thank you for your kindness, Madeleine."

After conversing with so many offering their condolences, Mary retreated to a bench underneath a tree. She rested and watched the sunlight rippling on the water. Min walked up to her. It was then, Mary noticed, Min had put on a black dress which almost matched her own. "You wore a dress!" Mary praised.

Min looked embarrassed. Mary guided her to sit next to her. When she did, Mary put her arm around her.

"I'm sorry about your father," Min consoled.

"Thank you, dear. I'm sorry we won't be able to do any fun things, today."

"That's okay."

"I wish my father could have met you. He would have loved you."

"What was he like?"

"He was very great man and a great inventor, the things he made were almost like...like magic. He gave me the best life anyone could have ever asked for, and for that, I will eternally be grateful."

"How did your mom die?"

"I don't remember. I was very young at the time. I do know it was peaceful, maybe in her sleep."

"They say my mom died fighting a hundred men."

"Oh, dear, that's terrible, I'm sor…"

"No! It was honorable. She was a legend. They called her Azure Cloud. She saved me from being captured."

Mary squeezed Min's shoulder. She could tell Min was being as brave about her mother's death as Mary was trying to be about her father's. "You're right. She died with honor and bravery. What about your father?"

"My father is probably still alive."

"Probably?"

"My father is a relative of Dowager Cixi."

"You'll have to excuse me. Is that significant? I'm not at all versed in Chinese celebrities."

"Until three years ago, she was the ruler of China."

Mary pulled back. "Y…You mean you're related to royalty? That's fantastic!"

"Not legally. My mother was one of his concubines. She unexpectedly became with child. The royal family wanted me dead; my mother escaped with me and joined the Yihequan—what you call, Boxers. Later, she was put in charge of the women Boxers, or, Hongdeng Zhao."

"So, why do you speak English so well?"

"Part of the plan of the new Hongdeng Zhao, was to blend with the foreigners living in Beijing, gain their trust and then murder them when their guard was down; She killed many foreign soldiers."

"That was a lovely plan," Mary praised sarcastically. "What went wrong?"

"Someone betrayed us and gave away our location. The foreigners attacked us while we slept; many died. I escaped and stowed away on a ship for America…My mother did not."

"So sorry for your loss. You escaped the enemy by coming to their country?"

"Where no one would ever look for me. No one looks for lychees in the dragons mouth"

"That's a brilliant strategy. But why do you trust me? Am I not your enemy?"

"I thought Lo Fang was my friend, but he acts like my enemy and Americans were my enemy, but you, Thomas, Abel and Helga, treat me like a friend."

"We are your friends. And not to worry. From now on I will use every resource to make sure you enjoy the rest of your..." Mary's mind drifted off for a second.

"Are you okay?"

"...Sorry, dear. I just thought I remembered something."

Most of the guests from the Lusitania memorial service had left. Helga, Min and Abel took turns throwing rocks into the bay. Mary sat on the bench under the tree and watched their game. Helga and Abel's rocks would skip the four or five times and Min's would skip numerous times, out of sight. Thomas walked over to Mary and took his hat off. "Sorry I'm late. I was busy looking into your father's case."

Mary stood up and gave him a kiss on the cheek. "Thank you so much for your hard work, Thomas. I really appreciate it."

He blushed and cleared his throat. "Ah-hem, No trouble at all. Anything I can do to help."

"What have you learned?"

"Well..."

"Come, walk with me." Mary took his arm and they began to take a stroll down by the bay shore.

"...From what I could tell, from looking through his papers on my second visit to his office, he was doing a lot of business with the British and there was some correspondence about him transporting something to aid in their war effort."

"A weapon?"

"Unclear. And even if it was, your father was some type of inventor not a shipping mogul, right?"

"Yes."

"Therefore, it was probably some kind of schematic to a new type of weapon. Perhaps it's related to the destruction caused in his office that killed two men."

"Thomas! My father is not a murderer!"

"It could have been in self defense. The two men were very involved in the crime scene. Perhaps they threatened him."

"Leaving in secrecy like he did, could also be explained by having his life threatened."

"That's what I was thinking. Has he ever mentioned anything to you about a secret project or have you ever seen any suspicious characters hanging around him?"

"Never."

Thomas sighed. "...Well, I guess if anyone was after him, it's all irrelevant, now...Sorry. That was uncalled for."

"Not to worry, he's at peace now."

They stopped and looked at a sailing ship passing by. Mary turned to him. "Thomas?"

"Yes, Miss White?" She raised an eyebrow. "...Mary?"

"There's this dance thing coming up next month. I was wondering if you would accompany me?"

He looked like he was about to either burst into tears or happily yell at the top of his lungs. He regained his composure and cleared his throat. "Ah-hem. It's rather unorthodox for a lady to ask a man to a dance. But I shall gracefully accept your invitation. Now, if, you'd excuse me..." He kissed her hand. "...I have to find out more about your father." He turned around and stumbled into a garbage can. He looked back, tipped his hat, smiled sheepishly and continued on his way. Mary grinned and waved slightly.

At the Vanderbilt Manor, Alva watched the woman lift her teacup to her lips. It seemed like every movement was calculated and precise to achieve ultimate grace and refinement. If she made any mistake, it would cause a drip on her all-white Victorian style dress, gloves or shoes. The woman placed the cup down and smiled through blood red lips, her teeth the most perfect Alva has seen. "Thank you Mrs Vanderbilt. It's delicious," she complimented with a French accent. She moved one of her bright yellow, blonde ringlets away from her face. "Your hospitalité has made our move to America very pleasant."

"It is my pleasure. It must be tough for you, escaping all of that fighting on the French border, and you move here and now the Germans are now trying to drag the United States into the fray."

"I am not worried. They will drive the Germans out of Belgium. It is only a matter of time. This will all be over within a year."

"I only hope that the French and British armies share your optimism." The woman took a sip and lowered her tea and saucer to the table. "Your last name, Blanche. It means 'white', right?"

"That is correct."

"I have a friend whose last name is White. You don't have any American relatives in New York, do you?"

She smiled. "No, Blanc was my husband's name. I changed it to Blanche because it is more…feminine. I don't think he has any living relatives, anywhere."

"What do you mean, 'was' your husband's name?"

"Oh, yes. My husband passed away."

"I'm so sorry. Was it related to the war?"

"Yes…a war."

"Which wa…"

"I'm sorry, I'm really not comfortable talking about it."

"You'll have to excuse me, that was rude of me. Let's talk about something else. At the gathering, besides yourself, the Rothschild family are…" Alva's question was interrupted by a butler entering the room and whispering something in her ear. "Oh yes…" she permitted, "…show him in." The butler went to the door and gestured for someone to enter. Thomas came into the room. "Hello Cousin Thomas, how goes the life of the great detective."

"Alva…Miss?"

Madam Blanche stood up and introduced herself. Thomas shook her hand. "She said cousin?"

"Yes…distant cousins."

"Oh! So you are a Vanderbilt as well?"

"Yes…distant cousins," Thomas repeated.

"What can I do for you, cousin Thomas?" Alva asked.

"I came to ask your servant, George, about his last encounter with Alfred and Mary's father."

"Of course." Alva gestured to the butler to take Thomas to George. Thomas excused himself.

After he had left, Mrs Blanche leaned close to Alva and whispered: "So, is cousin Thomas married?"

Thomas met up with George and began to interview him, to see if he had seen anyone suspicious hanging around the professor and Albert Vanderbilt before they boarded the Lusitania. They had barely got through the first question when their conversation was interrupted by the voice of Detective Douglas. "Tommy boy! Fancy seeing you here."

"Douglas? What are you doing here?"

"Came to find out why you were seen coming here." Douglas got close to Thomas in order to whisper. "Thought I made myself clear that you were to stay off of this case, Vanderbilt."

"I'm doing this on my spare time and as a favor for a dear friend."

"Oh, you mean that Mary White woman?"

"Yes?" Thomas didn't like Douglas' tone.

"You know, some rumors are going around about you and that woman."

"WHAT! What rumors?" Thomas felt furious.

"Calm down, no need to concern yourself with that right now. You may have to concern yourself with what the captain is going to say when I tell him you disobeyed orders to leave this case to me."

"What I do on my spare time is my own..."

"Have I mentioned that the captain is currently not pleased with your performance?" Douglas interrupted Thomas. Thomas remained silent. "Yeah, that's right. He blames you for not catching Lo Fang after he murdered a copper."

"Lo Fang was bullet proof."

"Yeah, he believes that, plus, magic, witchcraft and fairy tales." Thomas walked away. "Yes. And don't worry about those fairy tales about you and Miss White. I can't believe that someone like you could ever tame a woman like that." Douglas laughed a little. Thomas felt like hitting him. He instead put on his hat and hurried out of the room.

He felt stupid and angry. 'Why do I put up with that baboon? Why do I put up with any of this? I don't want to spend the rest of my life looking for lost cats and getting in between squabbling couples. I'm far more qualified for better jobs. Why do I go through so much for Miss White?...Well, that is obvious, but she doesn't seem to share in the mutual affection. I guess it's not really me...I've never really seen any man get particularly close to her. Perhaps it's just the way she is. Why was Douglas following me and is so adamant about me not investigating Professor White? Perhaps I should investigate that. Well, Detective Douglas, you have now become the lion following the zebra being followed by the...tiger?' Thomas left the Vanderbilt mansion.

Sunday, May 26, 1895

She told the chair to go as fast as it could and it did. It was nowhere near the speed of a train or automobile, but it was enough to outrun a child chasing after her. The African boy tried his best to touch her chair but it managed to stay just out of his reach. One would think, by the expression of exertion on her face, accented with joy, she was the one doing the running. Not so with the young boy. Exhaustion showed on his face as he chased her around the large hedge maze, constantly turning corners or switching directions. It was quite unfair, as he was running and she was given the luxury of the automatic chair. To make things worse, when the girl and her chair came to a dead end, instead of admitting defeat or surrendering, she commanded the chair to go over the wall. Within an instant, the round wheels transformed into eight, mechanical, spider-like legs. They crawled up the side of the hedge over the top and down the other side with very little effort, keeping her in an upright position. Once she was settled, the legs returned to their normal wheel shapes. This act infuriated the chaser and his complaints could be heard as she smiled and continued on her way.

After a couple of turns, she saw the exit of the maze. Just a little further and she would be crowned winner of their little game. She quickly looked behind her to make sure there were no secret pursuers. She knew it would take him at least five minutes to maneuver around the other side of the maze, but what about the other one? She had not seen him. If she made it outside the maze and he tagged her, it wouldn't be considered fair as you have to do it while the person is inside of the maze. When she made it to the exit, the chair stopped suddenly, right before she exited. "What? What are you doing?" she complained. The African boy ran closer and closer to her. The chair inched forwards and then backwards. She pounded the chair arms with her fists yelling 'GO!' it stood still and made a bell sound. "What's your problem?" The African boy tapped her on the shoulder. "No fair!" she yelled, pointing. "This chair wouldn't go through the exit!" The boy walked to the exit and stopped, as if he had run into a wall. He stepped back and moved his hands up and down. There was something invisible there. "What is that?" she asked him. She reached out her hands and felt something. It had a leafy texture. The two heard the laughter of a little boy. Leo walked around the other side of a nearby hedge wall. He was holding the back half of a very large book which appeared to have been ripped apart. The single back cover was covered in shiny reptile scales. He continued to laugh. "Leo!" The girl yelled. "What did you do?"

"I made the hedge invisible."

"How?"

He turned to a bookmarked page. "This right here." She looked at the words on the page. The African boy also leaned in to see the book. "I don't know why you're looking," Leo teased. "You can't even read English."

"It doesn't matter," she complained, "it's not in English. What does 'sif heed' mean anyway? Where did you find this book?"

"The library. There's all kinds of keen books in there."

"He told us not to go in the library without permission."

"Well, he's not here, is he?"

The invisible part of the hedge reappeared in distorted waves. The girl felt the now reappeared wall again. "I guess it only lasts for a while."

"Oh, well, lasted long enough to catch you."

"That was cheating!"

"No more than using a chair that can climb over walls."

Her brief silence was her agreement. "What else is in here?" She started flipping pages in the book. She couldn't understand the printed text but some words were circled in red ink and, off to the side, notations in English. Words such as: Levitation of Leguminosae, Liquid Metal fit, Enhancement Ferrum de Substantia and other notes which were also hard to understand, even translated.

"It looks like he was translating parts of the book and each thing seems to do something." He pointed to a passage. See, this one, 'Fatuus in oculis Invisibility'? He translated it to, 'Invisibility to fool the eyes.'"

She lifted up her hands to the hedge wall and said the words. "Un-doose-un los...Ahn la-god." The hedge remained visible. "Nothing happened. It didn't work."

"That's because you need this..." Leo took a silver plated fountain pen out of his pocket.

"What is that? A magic pen?"

"Maybe. Nothing seems to happen unless you're holding this pen. Watch." Leo flipped to another page. "Where is that... oh, here it is." He pointed the pen at her wheel chair. "*Urf*-er *caa fael.*"

"What does that mean?"

"You'll see. *Urf uh caa fael,*" he repeated. There was a pause. Her chair then began to shake.

"What did you…" Her chair slowly rose off of the ground and floated slowly into the air. The African boy stepped back in shock. Leo laughed. "What did you do?" she yelled. The chair got higher and higher. She was dangerously getting out of reach of the two boys. The African boy ran under the chair and tried to grab the wheels. They slipped out of his reach, even after he jumped. "Get me down!" she yelled.

Leo stopped smiling and his face became panicked. He frantically started flipping through the pages in the book.

"Put me down!" she yelled

"I'm trying…I can't find anything…" He searched faster; the chair was about 15 feet off of the ground. "There's nothing in…"

"Help me!"

"I'm sorry…I can't."

"Help!"

Leo looked around in a panic. He had no idea what to do. "SOMEONE HELP!"

A dark figure came up from behind him and grabbed the book out of his hands. Leo looked around and saw a middle-aged woman, whose black dress, matched her raven hair tightly tied into a bun and held in place by two silver, raven pins. She pointed to the wheel chair and spoke in a powerful commanding voice: *"Duhc welleg deef thi hav! Duhc welleg deef thi hav!"* Instantly, the chair stopped rising and slowly returned to the earth. The whole time, the woman's hand, sporting at least eight rings; two gold, two copper, but most of them silver, followed it down until it settled onto the grass. Leo ran over to the girl. "Are you all right?"

"No thanks to you," the girl criticized. "Thank you, Aunt Gwenhwyvar."

Leo turned around. "Yeah, thanks Aunt Gwe—" Before he could finish, the woman slapped him across his face. He recoiled, put his hand on his cheek and looked at her with scorn and a bit of fear.

"IMPUDENT BOY!" she hissed, causing her words to echo. "How many times must you be told, NEVER to go into the library without permission? This is a perfect example of what can happen if you do not listen to us! Do you think this is a game?" She held up the book half. "Do you think this is a toy? So many have died for this—my husband DIED so that this doesn't end up in the hands of people who want to PLAY with it as you do, with NO regard for the consequences! Go to your room! There will be no supper for you, tonight!"

Leo gave her a hateful look and then walked away, holding his cheek. They all watched him leave the maze.

May 26, 1915

From her perch at the top of her lighthouse, Mary stared out over the neighborhood as far as the eyes could see. It was a warm, sunny day. But she still wore black. She didn't feel like wearing any other color, at least until the sorrow over her father's death had subsided. She knew when a relative dies, especially a parent, it was customary for one to be in mourning, but she felt something else when it came to her father. Instead of a feeling of loss, she felt she had gained something. She had no idea what it was, but she felt it in her heart; something was just given to her, something she didn't want. This feeling was driving her mad and preventing her from carrying on with her daily activities. No classes or exercises were done this week, nor did she have any interest in meeting with her women's group. Many visitors came by to wish her well, but Abel had to dismiss them all. She turned around and put her hand on the bookshelf running along the wall. One of the books was the bible. She opened it to a random page: Acts 19:19:

...And many of those who practiced magic brought their books together and began burning them in the sight of everyone; and they counted up the price of them and found it fifty-thousand pieces of silver.

Something touched her mind; she felt someone transcendently tapping her on the shoulder. She put the Bible back and looked around. Off in the distance, a man with a red schoolboy cap was walking up the path leading to the lighthouse. She didn't recognize the visitor from this distance and would have to get a closer look. Something intrigued her about him; she hurried down the spiral staircase and arrived just as he rang the chime. She quickly opened the front door, surprising him. He was about her height, rugged and handsome. He smiled. It wasn't the smile you give someone you just met, it was warmer. She nodded hello. His smile faded fast into confusion. "Er-hello…Mary?"

"Yes? Miss White, in truth—do I know you?" She didn't like him acting so familiar with her.

His expression looked a little worried. "Sorry—Yes, hello…Er My name is Leopold…Leopold Bianca."

She didn't know any Leopolds from her past. Her expression turned to stern and suspicious. Was this yet another person come to take Min away? "Well, Mr. Bianca. What can I do for you?" There was an awkward pause.

"Yes…yes. Er-um. I…I was a friend of your father's"

Mary's demeanor softened up a bit. "Oh. You knew my father. So you're here to…?"

"Yes, to offer my condolences." He hurriedly took his cap off and bowed a little.

Abel came up the stairs and stood behind Mary. When Leopold saw him, they both produced surprised expressions. "Hello."

Mary looked back at Abel. "Do you know Mr. Bianca? He claims he worked with my father."

Abel raised an eyebrow. Mary knew he was thinking about the last visitor they had to the lighthouse. "It's possible, I suppose…" Abel admitted, "…your father worked with…many people."

Mary turned her attention back to Leopold. "Thank you for your condolences, Mr. Bianca." She started to close the door.

"Miss White!" he pleaded.

"Yes?" She held the door.

"There's something I need to talk to you about."

"Yes, what is it?"

"May…may I come in?"

She looked at Abel. He lowered his eye lids and slowly nodded. "All right, come along then."

Leopold entered the lighthouse. Mary lead the way down the stairs to the drawing room. Abel bought up the rear. Leopold didn't comment about the lighthouse with its underground mansion, as if he were used to such things. When they sat down, Mary asked Abel to deliver a message to Helga to bring out some tea. He left them alone to talk, but seemed hesitant. "Now then Mr. Bianca. What can I do for you?"

He took a deep breath. "Miss White. Did your father ever talk to you about his work or what kind of business he was in?"

"I know he was into metals and inventions."

"Yes…a simple explanation if any."

"Pardon?"

Leopold cleared his throat. "He mentioned nothing else… anything out of the ordinary?"

"Well, I know he was working with the British, to help them with their war."

"Yes, about that, did he ever mention how?"

"Mr. Bianca, is there a point to this interrogation? If you have an agenda to express, please do so forthwith."

Leopold looked down at the table. "There was something. Something he had that was very important. So important that some men may have tried to kill him over it." He looked up at her.

Mary furrowed her eyebrows. "If that's true Mr. Bianca, it's irrelevant now. Whatever secrets my father carried are now at the bottom of the Atlantic. He was one of the passengers on the Lusitania."

"I know, I know. But…"

Helga arrived in the elevator, carrying a tray with tea and a couple of cookies. Leopold looked at her and smiled. She didn't smile back, put the contents on the table and looked at Mary. "That'll be all Miss?"

"Yes, thank you Helga." Helga slowly returned to the elevator. "You were saying?"

"The people who were trying to harm him. If they were looking for something, his passing won't be enough to stop them from continuing their quest, even if it means coming after you."

"Mr. Bianca, if they were to pursue me for whatever my father could have been hiding, it will be futile. He kept his business life and his private life separate."

"Be that as it may, are you sure there is no way he was hiding anything in your house?"

"If that were true Mr. Bianca, why would I tell you? If he were being harassed by someone, is it not possible that you are one of them?"

"That's true. I understand your point. Be rest assured that I am on your side."

"Nice words can grow flowers…" She took a sip of tea and placed the cup down. "…Just like manure."

He smiled. "Yes…You are right. There is no reason for you to trust me. "What can I do to gain your trust?"

"Simple. Tell me what it is you are looking for and everything about it."

He took a long deep breath and sighed. "…I can't."

"Because?"

"I don't want to involve you any more than I already have. Matter of fact…" He stood up. "…I shouldn't have come here.

I've told you too much....I'm sorry. You'll have to excuse me..."
He bowed his head and walked away from her.

"Mr. Bianca!" she called to him. He ignored her and headed to the spiral staircase. As though she had reappeared out of nowhere, Helga grabbed Leopold's shoulder and stopped his departure. "Excuse me sir," she implored.

"I'm sorry, I'm in a hurry."

"Tis won't take long, sir. I be need'n yuh 'elp."

"My help, with what?"

"I have a large sack of beans in the kitchen that I need, on the top shelf. I was wondering if you might lend me a 'and."

"I'm sorry but..."

"Shan't take but a minute, sir. Please, me back's all knotted up. I'm just a poor weak old woman. Can yeh please 'elp me sir?"

"Could you give her a hand before you leave, Mr. Bianca?" Mary pleaded.

He looked back at Mary and then Helga who had a sad puppy dog expression on her face. "Well, I guess. But then I have to leave. It really is dangerous for me to have come here." Leopold followed Helga down the stairs to the kitchen. She walked ahead of him and disappeared into the kitchen."Right this way, luv," she guided.

When Leopold walked through the kitchen doorway, his nervous system told him to automatically duck. When he did, the handle of a copper plated broomstick swung over his head and smashed a tea cup on a shelf. The broomstick then swung downwards. He twisted his shoulders and the stick hit the ground hard, near his foot. By the third and forth avoided swings at his body, each time smashing into a dish or shelf in the kitchen, he realized Helga was trying to harm him. With calmness and power she jabbed, swung and bought the broomstick down at him as if she had been trained by a Kung Fu stick fighter. He managed to avoid her attacks until one cracked into his right ribs. She followed up to the bottom of his chin, which sent him reeling into a flying back flip on to a cutting board. Unwilling to allow any more hits to his body, he quickly rose and blocked a blow mean't for his head. Using his forearms to counter the stick worked for the 12 or so subsequent attacks she delivered. Leopold realized he would have go on the offensive to get her to stop. He threw a couple punches, but she easily blocked them and countered with two well-placed hits on his shoulder and hip, dispatching him into a cabinet full of teacups, with a loud crash. A jab to the his chest was so powerful, his body slid across the floor to the doorway, into someone standing there. It was Abel. Leopold looked up at him to convey the message: "Can you help stop this?" He punched Leopold, sending his body spinning around just in time for an uppercut to his chin from Helga's staff, followed up by a spin of his body from Abel who delivered another punch, sending his hat flying in the air and him to the ground, onto a bag of flour. The bag exploded into a white powdered cloud. Abel and Helga stood side by side, nodded at each other and readied to deliver the next fatal blow to Leo. He held up his hands. Helga lifted her broom and Abel clenched his fist for another attack.

"WHAT ON EARTH IS GOING ON HERE?" Mary yelled. Helga and Abel immediately stopped what they were doing. Abel ran over to Leopold and helped him up.

"Oh dearie my, Mr. Bianca. All right, sweetie?" Helga consoled like a concerned grandmother. She rushed over to him and started brushing the flour off of him with the broom.

He swatted away the bristles. "Yes, I'm fine. Thank you."

"What happened? It looks like an explosion happened in here," Mary complained, stepping on a broken plate.

Helga looked at Abel. "That's exactly what happened 'ere sweetie. Mr. Bianca was helping me light the stove and next thing ya know–POOF the gas exploded. Miracle 'e wasn't killed."

"Is that true, Mr. Bianca?" Mary asked. She brushed some flour off of his shoulder as Abel helped him straighten his shirt and tie.

Leopold looked at Mary, Abel and then Helga. "...Yes. That's what happened all right. It's a wonder I wasn't killed."

Mary looked sorrowful. "So sorry, Mr. Bianca. I feel just terrible. Is there any way I can make it up to you?" He reached down and picked up his red cap and blew the flour off of it into Abel's face. Abel closed his eyes and sneered.

"No, it's fine. I should be going. He nodded goodbye: "Miss White...Helga...Abel. He headed off to the stairwell.

Mary looked around the room and then at Abel. "That's strange."

"What's that, Mary?" Abel asked brushing flour off his pants.

"How did he know your name?"

Abel looked embarrassed. "I introduced myself before you got here."

"Oh, very well then. I'll go put on some rags and help you two clean up." Mary left to go change. A few moments later, Min came into the room. She looked around with her mouth agape in shock.

"Where were you?" Helga asked. "Could'a used you."

When Leopold stepped outside the lighthouse, the magpie flew up to him and landed on his shoulder. "Hello fella. You got something else for me?" He reached into his coat, pulled out a cracker and fed the bird. "Okay then, what have you got to tell me? *Alad droth.*" Like before, the bird started to recall a conversation it had heard:

Earlier, the magpie had been sitting on a 10th floor stone windowsill outside the New York Hall of Records. The window was open, giving the bird easy access to the conversations and happenings inside. Surrounded by thousands of books, file cabinets and piles of papers strewn about the room, the man who had sent Thomas into the streets to be killed and met with German agents, snipped the end off of a cigar with a gold-plated cutter. Around him, his gang of tough men worked diligently, looking through papers and files. They appeared uncomfortable and unsure, flipping through pages and trying to figure out what they are searching for. One of them became so frustrated, he complained.

"Sir, I don't understand why we have to be the ones to do this. How come you can't use magic to get them to do it?" he gestured to one of two city workers. They were lying dead in the corner of the room.

Their leader rubbed between his eyes, as if he was treating a headache. "For the last time, it is not magic. Magic is a trick—pour tromper les yeux—used to fool the eyes. Seconde, Professeur White obviously forged a spell on the people here so that they will not cooperate in telling us where he lived. They didn't even know about his office—even in death, that man continues to hinder me."

"So how are we going to find his address in all this mess?" The henchman held up many papers.

"Simple mathematics. Success equals work over time, Monsieur."

Shaking their heads and grumbling, they went back to checking all city records involving residents who had moved into New York around five years ago. They were interrupted when a figure burst into the room and slammed the double doors behind him. He had a cloak wrapped around his body to completely hide his features.

"Qu'est-ce que c'es?" their leader asked.

The figure made sure the door was locked, turned around and slowly removed his cloak. It was Lo Fang, but not the one the group was used to—he had been transformed: His teeth were now razor sharp, his eyes were catlike and his ears were pointed.

"Ah, Mr. Fang. So nice of you to finally join us. I see by your appearance that you ran into trouble and had to drink the vial I gave to you."

"What did you do to me?"

"Do to you? What did you do to you? You didn't have to drink it."

"You told me that if I was ever in trouble and there was no way of getting out of it, to drink that stuff...What was that, anyway?"

"It's called ahrion. It's like...I hate to use this word...MAGIC potion. I used it to bring out the inner beast in you...No, to bring out the inner-BEST in you."

"But look at me..." He checked his clawed hands. "...I'm a monster! I'll have to hide my face wherever I go!"

"No, no-no, Monsieur. You are a perfect killing beast. Capable of so much more than you could do before. You can feel it, no? The power rushing through your heart, your soul—like fire. It's like you could rip a normal man in half with your bare hands."

"But...can I turn back?"

"Of course, that kind of ahrion always wears off...when the user has accomplished his task..." He rolled his eyes, walked over and straightened Fang's shirt collar. "...Therefore, I see by your appearance that you were unsuccessful in retrieving the good fighter and perhaps things did not go as according to plan, no?"

"There was a woman."

"A woman?"

"A woman with a sword and that copper you sent into traffic, he was alive. He stabbed me in the neck." Fang pulled his collar opened and revealed a festering puncture wound, still unhealed.

"Stabbed you? C'est impossible. In that form, normal weapons are useless on you. Unless..."

"Unless what?"

"That woman with the sword. She lives at the address with best fighter, no?"

"Yes, her, and a Colored man with a gun."

"And Mr. Copper, who knows...Mary what's-her-name, he happens to have a weapon which can harm you? Was it silver?"

"Yes, I guess. I think it was a knife."

"The shape does not matter, he could have stabbed you with an ink pen if it is made of solid ahrion."

"That magic silver stuff? How would he have that?"

"The same reason he would know the Miss Mary woman with a sword, housing best fighter."

Fang was confused. There was a short pause as he tried to figure out what his boss meant. The boss sighed and looked up. "Only one person in the city could have ahrion...Professor White...That was his house?...You accidentally found his house?...Mon Dieu!" He raised up his hands in frustration. "Gentlemen!" he yelled. "Stop what you are doing. We now know where Professor White's house is." They cheered. "Tonight, we will pay his house a visit. We will kill everyone there and destroy the house if we have to. But we will find that book!"

One of the men looked puzzled. "That Professor guy killed two of your men already. Do we have to drink that stuff to be as strong as him?"

"It won't be necessary. We will strike first with heavy artillery. And I mean REALLY heavy."

Mary stood on the galley deck of the lighthouse and looked down. "Mr. Bianca? What are you still doing here?"

The Magpie stopped talking. Leopold looked worried. "Oh, hello...I was just..." The magpie flew away.

"Was that bird bothering you?"

"Who, Flapper? No. He's my friend."

"That's ducky."

"No, magpie."

"No...I mean—what can I do for you, Mr. Bianca?'"

"Well, even though I'm a little strapped for cash right now, I..."

"Oh, you want money? Abel," she yelled, "go get the green case!"

"No! No, I was about to say, if it would be okay if I could take you out tonight for a bite to eat. But nothing fancy."

"Didn't you say it was dangerous to be around me?"

"I changed my mind. I need to discuss some important things with you about your father."

"...I suppose that would be fine. If it's just dinner–ONLY. You worked with father and perhaps together we can figure out what his big secret was that would cause men to snoop on him."

"Copacetic. I'll pick you up at eight." Leopold departed. Mary watched him as he got on a Harley motorcycle with an attached sidecar and rumbled away.

In the Bowery neighborhood police station, Thomas continued his investigation of the attack by Lo Fang on him and his fellow policemen. He was able to accost Chief O'Riley, who was coming out of the men's room. "Chief, may I have a word with you?"

"What is it Vanderbilt, did your lady friend get arrested again?"

"No sir." Thomas didn't like always being associated with Mary's exploits. "I was wondering if I can have a word with you about that man, Lo Fang."

"Who?"

"That Chinese ruffian that killed officer Peters."

"What about him?"

"Well, if my memory serves me right, Lo Fang was arrested in the afternoon and by early evening he was set free."

"I don't remember that happening, but I'll take your word for it."

"Sir, in order for someone to set him free, they would have to go through you."

Chief O'Riley grabbed Thomas. He looked like he were going to punch him. "What are you saying, Vanderbilt?! That I let a murderer walk free!"

"Sir, if not you, then someone released him from custody."

"Well, why don't you find THAT someone! I didn't set him free–ya got that? You make any more accusations like that and I'll set YOU free. Understand"

Thomas nodded. The chief pushed Thomas away from him like an obstacle and departed. Thomas sighed.

A young policeman approached Thomas. "Psst! Detective," he whispered, gesturing Thomas into a corner of the hall. Thomas obliged and joined him. "What is it…?"

"Peters, sir."

"Peters? As in?"

"Yes, sir. Charley was my brother."

"Sorry to hear that, Peters."

"Thank you, sir. Detective, it's about that guy that murdered my brother."

"Yes, do you have any information for me?"

"Yes, sir…" Peters looked around for eavesdroppers. "…I heard the chief say that he didn't release that Lo Fang fella. But, I saw the whole thing happen with my own two eyes."

"Really? What did you see?"

"This big fella approached the front desk. He leans in close to the chief as if to whisper something in his ear. When the chief leaned in to hear what he was saying, this fella puts his hand on the chief's head and…"

"And?"

"And…I could have just been imagining this, but I swear…his eyes turned red"

"Whose eyes?"

"The chief's."

"Red?"

"Like blood, sir."

"Did he do something to him?"

"Don't know sir. But, next thing you know, the chief orders the release of all of those fighters we busted earlier, and at least four of them walked out the door."

Thomas paused for a moment to comprehend what Peters was saying. "This man, what did he look like?"

"Like I said, big, fancy fellow. Handlebar mustache. Spoke like a Frenchman…"

"One dark monocle on the right eye? Lots of rings on his fingers and a silver cane with a…gold elephant on it?"

"Y-yes sir, that's him! You know him?"

"…No…But for some reason, I feel like I've seen him."

"Sir, I'm okay with the chief occasionally taking donations for his so-called charities to do favors for people, but when he starts setting murderers free…"

"I understand, Peters. I'll continue looking into who that man is. You keep your eyes and ears open for any more information."

"Yes, sir. Thank you, sir."

"And Peters...don't worry. I'm going to find that man and bring him to justice...I swear it."

"Thank you, Detective." Peters tipped his hat and went around the corner. Thomas stayed behind and wondered how he knew what the man looked like. He suddenly had a flash of the man putting his hands on his forehead and saying something. Thomas shook it off with a chill in his spine.

Min carried a cup of tea on a saucer to give to Mary, as instructed by Helga. Mary's door was cracked a little. Min knocked to announce her presence. Her knock forced the door open to reveal Mary with her shirt half down, exposing her back, and Abel standing behind her. Min dropped the cup and saucer onto the ground and was in the hallway before the crashing sound had finished resonating. As she fast-walked down the hall she could hear Mary's voice calling to her over and over. Min quickly went into her room and slammed the door. A few minutes later, Mary knocked on her door.

"Min?" Min didn't answer. "Min? I'm coming in, Butterfly." Mary slowly opened the door. Min was on the bed, facing away from the door. "Min? Why did you run out of the room like that?"

"I didn't see anything!" she blurted.

"You didn't see what?"

"ANYTHING!"

"Butterfly, there's nothing to see."

"Yes, there was."

"I don't know what you think you saw, Min but there really was nothing to see."

"Yes, there was."

"What?"

"You and Abel."

"Me and Abel?"

"Doing...you know."

"Well, I know what we were doing but I want to know what you THINK we were doing."

"You were...you know."

"Come on, out with it."

Min put a pillow over her mouth. "Moo-mer making muve."

"Dear. I'm sorry. I can speak three languages and pillow is not one of them." Mary lowered the pillow from Min's mouth. "Once again, please."

Min was turning red. "You were...you know."

"Min! Spit it out, please!"

In the loudest whisper she could do, Min said: "You were making love!" She then plopped onto her bed and buried her face in the mattress.

Mary thought for a moment and then burst into a raucous laughter.

Min slowly raised her head and looked back at her.

"I'm sorry, dear. That's a real gas. You thought Abel and I..." She laughed some more.

"What?"

Mary wiped away a tear. "Dear, dear Butterfly. Abel and I aren't lovers. I'm not even his type."

"Then why do you do private things with him every day?"

"I can see how you might think that we are making whoopee. But, we're not."

"What else could you be doing."

"He's just tightening my buttons."

"Is that another word for making whoopee?"

Mary laughed again. "No. Here, let me show you." Mary stood up and unbuttoned her blouse.

"What are you doing!"

"Remain calm. I just want to show you my buttons."

"I don't wan't to see whatever you call buttons!" Min put her hands over her eyes.

Mary continued to take her blouse off until she was done. "Okay, go ahead and look."

Min slowly opened her eyes. Mary had exposed just her back. Min felt more comfortable this was all that had happened. She then saw something she did not expect: Running down both sides of Mary's spine, starting at the thoracic shoulder blade area and stopping at the bottom of the lumbar vertebrae, right above her tailbone, six shiny pairs of silver rivets with notched, inverted heads were imbedded in her skin. Min scooted over to Mary and reached out her hand, but stopped before touching them.

"You can go ahead. It won't hurt." Min felt them. They were very well set in. Instead of being cold, they were body temperature.

"What is this?"

"Those are my buttons."

"What are they for? Were you in an accident?"

"No. I was born with them."

Min continued to feel them. "Do they hurt?"

"No, quite the opposite. I guess it was kind of a lie to say that Abel wasn't giving me any pleasure when he tightens them. It does feel quite good...like getting a Turkish massage."

"He tightens them?"

"Yes, every six hours, Abel takes a key..." Mary took a key, attached to a chain from around her neck. It was similar to the music box key Abel used to unlock the doors. "...Abel and Helga both have keys like this one. Every six hours they tighten the buttons for me."

"Why?"

"You know, I've never found out why, because there's always been someone to do it for me."

"So you don't know what happens after six hours?"

"I'm afraid not. I've been very fortunate in that way. My parents and then Abel and Helga have always been there for me."

"C-can I try it?"

"Of course!" Mary handed the key and chain to Min. "Here."

Min held the key. "What do I do?"

"Just insert it into one of the buttons and turn. The ones on the left side turn toward the right and the right ones to the left."

"What happens if I turn them the wrong direction?"

"They only turn in one direction. It's impossible to turn them the wrong way."

Min, timidly inserted the key into the top right rivet. Just as Mary had said, it wouldn't move to the right. She turned it to the left and it easily rotated. There was a quiet ping sound, like a tiny bell had been struck.

"What's that?"

"That just tells you to stop turning and move on to the next one." One by one, Min inserted and turned the rivets. Each one making a pleasant bell chime. When she finished the last one, she wished she had more to turn, she found it kind of fun. "Thank you," Mary praised. She lowered her blouse and redressed herself. Min handed the key to Mary. "No. You can keep it."

"…But."

"It's only fair. You're a member of the household now." Mary took the key and put the chain around Min's neck. "There. Now if I ever need to depend on anyone, I know it can be you." Min looked at the key. She felt very honored and happy that Mary trusted her. Mary unexpectedly hugged her. Min flinched for a second and then allowed it to happen. Mary pulled back and smiled. "Thank you for not punching me."

Sunday, December 20, 1897

Aunt Gwenhwyvar read to two of the children. Leo, the third, looked out the window at the falling snow. He had no interest in participating in any type of celebration. Even the prospect of presents were ineffective on his spirit. Gwenhwyvar ignored him and continued reading:

"…the Fir Tree was put into a great tub filled with sand; but no one could see that it was a tub, for it was hung round with green cloth, and stood on a large many-colored carpet. Oh how the Tree trembled! What was to happen now? The servants, and the young ladies also, decked it out. On one branch they hung little nets, cut out of colored paper; every net was filled with sweetmeats; golden apples and walnuts hung down as if they grew there, and more than a hundred candles—red, white, and blue—were fastened to the different boughs. Dolls that looked exactly like real people—the Tree had never seen such before—swung among the foliage, and high on the summit of the Tree was fixed a tinsel star. It was splendid, particularly splendid. This evening, "said all, "this evening it will shine."

She put the book down and looked at their own fir tree. It was decorated with red and white candles and displayed the little cut-paper nets filled with sweetmeats, red apples instead of green, and walnuts. There were a few dolls, but none of them resembled the members of the household. Gwenhwyvar knew dolls representing real people could be used for dark purposes. "Well," she concluded, "we almost have everything Mr. Anderson describes. Perhaps a star is needed. Dear, could you help me with it?" She handed the girl a large golden star. "Please put this on the top."

The girl knew it was made of one of the forging metals. It was important for her to know types of metals merely from looking at it or feeling them. Yes, ma'am. Chair please go…"

"No!" Gwenhwyvar interrupted. "Don't use the chair. That star is made of pure cop, just like the witches use."

The girl nodded at Gwenhwyvar and then turned her attention to the star. *"Um... Urf...ur caa fael."* Nothing happened. *"Urf ur caa...fael."* There was a pause.

"Do you understand why nothing is happening?"

"She can't say it right," Leo volunteered.

"Silence! Either you help or hinder. I'd advise the first."

"Because I'm not saying it right?" the girl answered.

"Partly, but pronunciation is not as important as you might think. I mean, in the heart of a battle, falling off a cliff or drowning, proper pronunciation would be quite difficult under those conditions, yet many were still able to successfully forge."

"But, how?"

Gwenhwyvar touched the girls head. "Your spirit or your mind..." She touched her chest. "...your heart, your foundation. ..." She touched the girl's right and then left shoulder. "...and your muscle, your will. They must all work together in harmony."

The girl reproduced the movements Gwenhwyvar had done. "Hey! Isn't that what Christians do before they pray?"

"Prayer is just another type of forging."

"Huh? So forging is praying?"

"No. Prayer is connecting with God, forging is connecting with everything else. This time, think of all of those parts in you, working together to accomplish what you want to see happen."

"Yes, Ma'am."

The young African boy walked over to her. "You...can do...it."

She smiled at him and then turned her attention to the star. She thought of her mind: It told her about the star, its shape, its weight, its composition; her heart stressed her desire to accomplish her task; and her muscles were her willpower, her strength. *"Urf ur caa fael."* In an instant, the star rose out of her hands and levitated to her eye level. She had expected this to happen but it still caught her by surprise. She smiled a large toothy grin and looked over at Gwenhwyvar.

Gwenhwyvar nodded but didn't seem a bit surprised. "Now, you have connected with one of God's things; tell it what to do."

She had to remember what her original task was. The star. The star was supposed to go on top of the tree. The star reminded her of Christmas back at her old home: Her parents; the three of them, happy even though they barely had enough money to buy one present; going to the circus; her parents being killed. The star fell to the ground with a thud. She buried her head in her hands and cried. Gwenhwyvar walked over and put her hands on the girls shoulder.

"Happens every time," Leo criticized.

"Be...quiet!" the African boy demanded.

"There-there." Gwenhwyvar said. "That's further than you've ever come." The girl sobbed quietly. "You will learn—"

Gwenhwyvar's speech was interrupted by a loud thump on the front door. Everyone stopped moving. Another loud thump. Gwenhwyvar stood upright and put her hands out, like the letter T. "Children, get behind me!" she commanded. They did as they were told. Leo stayed a little off to the side. Another thump and then the door swung open. A gust of wind and snow rushed into the room. A cloaked figure staggered inside. He fell to his knees. Trickling blood speckled the floor. He was clutching something to his chest. Slowly and cautiously, he removed the object and placed it onto the floor.

"No!" Gwenhwyvar called out. She ran over to the figure and removed the cloak. It was the man who had participated immensely in the girl's life. He was injured. A trickle of red exited from a slash across his abdomen area. He put his hand over his wound. "You're bleeding!" Gwenhwyvar yelled putting her hands over his.

The man laughed in a weak manner. "Yes...but you should see the other fellow." He laughed again but it caused him pain and he winced.

"Leo!" Give me that box over the fire place!" Leo hesitated for a second. "NOW!" Leo ran over and took a small wooden box off of the shelf, decorated with a carving of a two headed snake. As soon as he was within her reach, Gwenhwyvar snatched it from him. Inside was a hypodermic needle and a vial of silver liquid. When the girl saw it, a look of panic came to her face and she physically backed her wheelchair away; she remembered all too well her experience with this instrument. As had been done to her, the same liquid was inserted into the man's arm. He clenched his teeth in pain. Gwenhwyvar put her hand on his chest and said: "*Gwessla orga-na.*" Within a second, his face relaxed. Moments later he removed his hand from his abdomen and sighed with relief.

"Thank you, Gwenhwyvar."

They turned their attention to the object he was carrying. Leo had picked it up. "Is this the second half to that book?" he asked.

"Give me that!" Gwenhwyvar snatched it from him. She handed it to the man.

"Yes, Leo...." The man slowly stood up, with the aid of Gwenhwyvar and the African boy. "This is the top half of that book in my study. This is what was stolen from me...from us those many years ago." The man walked over to the girl. He kneeled down and handed her the book. "The man who took this book from me is the same man who killed your parents."

She looked up at him, full of sadness, then down at the book. It was the same green leather as the bottom half. On the cover was a winged elephant represented in silver metal, and above that, written in shiny golden letters, the words: SIV MYRDDIN.

The man put his hands on hers. "You don't ever have to worry about him ever again."

"Did you kill him?" Leo asked.

He nodded. "Many were killed, we lost two in the raid. Unfortunately..." He looked at the girl. "I never found out what happened to your cousin. I'm afraid he might have done something nefarious to her a long time ago."

Gwenhwyvar put her hand on the girl's shoulder. "It's all over, now. It's a new beginning for you...For all of us."

An etching of the CSS Virginia. Although destroyed on May 11, 1862, the ironclad was mysteriously spotted in Lake Michigan on January 1, 1893

One of the few photographs which may be of
Lady Gwenhwyvar of the House of White.

Part Six
FOR FIFTY CENTS

The golden sunlight was still showing late in the day, casting a yellowish glow on Leopold as he rang the doorbell of the lighthouse. Anyone who might see him would be able to tell, just by his demeanor and his secondhand suit and tie, he was going to be taking Mary out on a date. In his right hand, he held a small bouquet of white daises. He used his left hand to smooth down his freshly oiled and combed hair. When Abel came to the door, Leopold stepped back, expecting to be attacked again. Abel said nothing and appeared to be contemplating obliging Leopold with a punch to the head.

Before said action could take place, Mary walked around Abel to greet Leopold. "Hello, Mr. Bianca." Mary wore a beautiful, Edwardian style red dress with a delicate lace pattern and tiny black roses on the hem, sleeves and neck areas.

"Miss White...You look lovely."

"Thanks, Mr. Bianca. You cleaned up nicely yourself."

ı

"Thanks...I think." He handed her the flowers.

"Oh, African daisies, my favorite. How did you know these are my favorites?"

"Lucky guess?"

"You know, when I was young, traveling in Africa, I have a vague memory of African daises."

"Really? Do go on."

Abel interrupted Mary's story. "Perhaps you should be going, Miss White. You don't want to be late for dinner."

"Yes, quite. Shall we go?"

"Yes." Leopold offered her his arm and escorted her away from the lighthouse.

Abel watched them leave, suspiciously, like peering at a wolf running away from a coop. Helga walked up from behind and stood beside him, she didn't seem happy.

Leopold escorted Mary to his motorcycle and instructed her on how to get into the sidecar. Like a child discovering a new toy, Mary gleefully squealed from her excitement of getting to ride in a sidecar. When Leopold put on a set of goggles and handed Mary her own pair, you could hear her yell: "That's the cat's pajama's!" from across the street. Abel and Helga glared at Mary and Leopold. The couple were loudly transported away, roaring down Fifth Avenue, barely missing a collision with a horse and cart. Abel sighed.

"Who was that? "Min asked.

Abel turned to her and realized she had also witnessed the departure. "Apparently, Miss White has a gentleman caller."

"But...what about Thomas?"

"Indeed."

"We can't let this happen! Aren't we going to follow them?"

"Of course."

Helga turned and headed inside. "Right. I'll give ya some support from the air."

"You mean prayer?" Min asked her.

Helga stopped briefly. "Of course luv. What else could I mean?" She continued on her way.

On their way down Fifth Avenue, Mary and Leopold passed by a large, roofless, red Norwalk Touring automobile with six white seats. Five seats were taken by the man with the silver cane and four other passengers. One of the back passengers was Lo Fang, who kept his face hidden using a scarf and a new fedora to replace the one Mary had cut in half. His anger at her increased when he spotted her and Leopold zoom pass in the opposite direction.

"IT'S HER, IT'S HER!" he yelled.

"It's whom?" his boss asked.

"That dame that lives in the lighthouse, who wouldn't give up the kid."

"Should I turn around?" asked the driver.

"No Monsieur, drop me and Muggsy off at the house. You Three will capture that woman and bring her to me."

"Don't you need us in case someone else is at the house?"

"Not to worry, no one inside will survive this search."

With an exceptional lack of rules and only a vague order of traffic flow which sometimes wove in different directions as if on a whim, the streets of 1915-era New York could be quite chaotic and treacherous at times. Navigating through these streets on a motorcycle was a daring feat that required perfect reflexes and a touch of religion. As Leopold avoided yet another car on the wrong side of the road, Mary grinned from ear to ear as her heart raced faster than it did when she was able to fly in an aeroplane.

"This-is-brilliant!" Mary yelled so she could be heard over the traffic and engine noise. "I've got to get one of these!"

"If you like, you can have this one when I leave," Leopold yelled back.

"Are you leaving soon?"

"Not soon. Not until I finish what I've come here for."

"And what is that?"

"Hold on!" Leopold made a sharp lane switch to get around a pedestrian pushing a wheelbarrow.

"Mr. Bianca?"

"All will be explained…Soon." He revved the cycle's engine and they rocketed down the avenue.

At his desk, surrounded by noise and activity, Thomas flipped through a booklet of black and white photographs. Each set was composed of two shots: one, a closeup of a gentleman's face and a second one of the gentleman standing next to a large ruler, to indicate their height. White hand-written notes next to each indicated each man's weight and name. Thomas felt as though he had examined the faces of thousands of men, but none of them matched the man he now remembered. Next to the photo booklet, sat a larger book listing foreigners who had moved to the city within a year's time. Looking for the man's photo was exhausting, but searching the larger book for one French-accented gentleman among all the visitors, immigrants and refugees listed was frustration personified. He closed the photo book, put his elbows on his desk and rested his face in his hands. "Think Thomas, think!" he mumbled. He leaned back in his chair and put his hands behind his head. "How can you find a foreign male visitor among nine million people?" He thought for a few moments: 'If I were a French, male visitor to New York—with lots of money, from what I can tell by looking at his accessories—where would I spend my leisure time? A bar? But you can go to a bar anywhere. He would want to be pampered and treated well, like in a fine restaurant...' Thomas snapped his fingers. '...Or a brothel! But which one? I'm not going to search every brothel in New York. It has to be specific to his taste...a place where he wouldn't be harassed for being a foreigner, where he can relax and speak his own language. How can I find a list of particular brothels that cater to particular people?' At that moment, Douglas walked past Thomas's desk. 'If anyone knows...' Thomas stood up, fast-walked after Douglas and caught him before he left the room. "Douglas!"

He turned around. "Vanderbilt?"

"Douglas, I was wondering if you can help me with something."

"Sorry, Vanderbilt. I don't have any leads on good horses."

"No, that's not it..." Thomas lowered his voice. "...I was wondering if you have a list of specific places a certain kind of gentleman can go, to meet...particular kinds women?"

It took a while before Douglas understood what Thomas was asking. He cracked a big scary grin and pointed at Thomas. "Ahhh, I see. So you're finally giving up on the Mary White woman..."

"Well, not re..."

"Leave it to me, Vanderbilt. You've come to the right man." Douglas reached into his pocket and pulled out a small black book. He handed it to Thomas. The cover read: 'The Gentleman's Companion'.

"What is this?"

"When I turned 18, my father gave it to me as a present. This is a list of 150 establishments that every gentleman should avoid while visiting New York. It was published as a warning guide."

Thomas read a part of it: *...But we point out the location of these places in order that the reader may know how to avoid them, and that he may not select one of them for his boarding house when he comes to the city...* "This is preposterous. Listing these places and giving exclusive details only encourages the reader to...oh, of course..May I borrow this for a second?"

"Keep it for as long as you like, Vanderbilt. Maybe you'll have better luck with these gals." Douglas winked, slapped Thomas on the shoulder and walked away, laughing.

Thomas almost said thanks but stopped himself. He opened the book to another page. "Now, let's see. Is there a house that specializes in entertaining rich foreigners...What kind of father did Douglas have?"

Mary and Leopold came to a stop to let a trolley pass in front of them. On a nearby telephone pole, Flapper the magpie cawed. Leopold looked up at him and then back over his left shoulder. He noticed the red automobile.

Mary sensed something was off. "Is something the matter Mr. Bianca?"

"Oh! Oh, no. Everything is fine..." he looked back again. The three men in the car quickly turned their heads to pretend they were not spying on Mary and Leopold. "Miss White, we're running a bit late, so if I drive a little...sporadically, please forgive me."

"It's fine, do as you wiiiiiiiillll!" she yelled as the motorcycle jerked her back. They accelerated away at a faster speed than she had ever gone on land.

The henchmen in the red car witnessed the fast departure. The front passenger yelled: "The jig is up, they're making a break for it, after them!" The driver slammed on the gas and the car screeched away after the motorcycle. Abel and Min, riding in the Silver Ghost, five cars back, observed both actions.

"Are those guys following them?" Min inquired.

Abel furrowed his eyebrow. "It seems that way. Let's get a better look at them." Abel repeated what the other two vehicles had done by screeching the Silver Ghost's tires as he set off in pursuit.

If Mary had received a thrill from riding in the sidecar of a speeding motorcycle, then the increase in velocity and the constant weaving around traffic obstacles was like pure ecstasy to her. One minute they were riding right behind a trolley and the next they were on the other side of the tracks and driving towards a horse and buggy coming in the opposite direction. After these dangerous acts, Leopold would look back to check to see it they were still being followed. The henchmen were taking just as many chances, if not more, to keep up the pursuit. Not being as slim as the motorcycle, their car was put in much more dangerous situations: they barely missed getting clipped by the same trolley and they almost killed a woman pushing a baby carriage. To make their pursuit even harder, Leopold turned the cycle into the confined streets of a residential neighborhood. It was hard to navigate the tapered streets, with the onslaught of pedestrians, dogs, food stands and an occasional horse cart created multiple potential crashes. The motorcycle weaved left and right, barely missing anything that wandered into their path. Mary held on for dear life and even had to duck to avoid being struck in the head by a wooden beam being carried across the street. Before Leopold could exit the restricted paths and get back to the wider streets, a horse-drawn milk cart completely blocked the street. Leopold squeezed hard on the breaks and they came to a screeching halt.

"You know...Mr Bianca..." Mary remarked, catching her breath and straightening her hair. "...I'm perfectly okay with arriving late for dinner."

He ignored her and frantically scanned for an escape route; all sides were blocked by cars or people. The red car pulled up not far behind and slowly creeped closer and closer.

"Mr. Bianca?" Mary tried to get his attention. He was too busy looking around and checking back at the red car as it closed in like a shark on an injured fish. "Mr. Bianca?"

A bead of sweat trickled down his forehead. He reached into his shirt and pulled out a silver-chained necklace with a copper crucifix and held it tight. *"Asan-fah!"* he exclaimed.

"Pardon?" Mary asked.

The red car came to a halt. One by one, the henchmen got out, loudly slamming the doors to announce their presence. One of them was carrying a baseball bat with a nail embedded in it, another, a large rusty chain.

Five cars behind the activity, Abel and Min were stuck behind a truck hauling bottles. "They're going to harm Mary!" Min yelled, getting out of the car.

Leopold looked around for an exit. *"Asan-fah!"* he repeated.

"Mr. Bianca?" Mary tried again. "Mr. Bia…" She put her hand on his shoulder. "Leo?"

He quickly turned and glanced at her with an expression of surprise and fear. A second after he looked at her, a strong gust of wind blew into the alley, carrying with it various pieces of paper and garbage. It concentrated mostly on the area off to their side, where a fruit stand was parked on the sidewalk. The fruit stand slowly rolled forward, revealing a narrow alleyway connecting their street to the one on another block. Leopold turned the cycle in that direction and they sped into the alley. The exit was so slender, sparks intermittently flew up when the cycle scraped the sides of the brick wall. At the mouth of the alleyway, they emerged, knocking over a stack of tin cans and causing a cat to scramble out of their way. With one turn to the left, they were back in traffic and many blocks away from the henchmen.

Before Min could catch up to the henchmen. The bottle truck blocking the street finally moved out of the way and the henchmen got back in their car and sped away. Abel pulled the Ghost up next to Min. Without using the door, she jumped up and into the seat next to him and they rode off in pursuit of the men.

The red car zipped around the busy traffic in hopes of catching up to Mary and Leopold. All eyes in the car scanned the area but were unable to spot the motorcycle. The men in the car were too busy to notice Abel and Min slowly pulling up next to their car. The driver gazed over but ignored them. Lo Fang recognized Min and yelled out: "It's her!"

"It's who?" asked the driver.

"That's that kid—she's with our mark— get her!"

Unsure of what to do, the driver sharply turned the steering wheel and swiped the side of Abel and Min's car. The Silver Ghost veered away into the oncoming traffic. Abel quickly regained control and bought it close to the red one. Min stood up on the passenger seat and with one easy leap jumped to the space between the two guys in the front seat, as Abel yelled "Wait! What are you doing?" Without wasting a second, she grabbed the front passenger by the shoulders and swung her knee into his forehead. When his head bounced back from the seat his eyes had rolled up and he flopped forward, unconscious. The driver grabbed a handgun from under the seat and fired at her. His distraction caused the vehicle to swerve as well as him to miss, badly. He didn't get a second try. Min grabbed his fingers and bent them back, producing a cracking noise as well as screaming. The car began swerving even more, as the driver dealt with the extreme pain. Abel had to move his car far to the left to prevent another sideswipe from the red car. Lo Fang swung the bat with a nail in it at Min's head. She leaned backwards and could feel the wind of the nail as it passed one inch from her face. She kicked upwards and sent the bat spinning out of Fang's hand. With a quick switch to the other foot, she kicked him backwards into his seat. Satisfied with her three attacks, she turned her attention to the driver to see if she could figure out a way to stop the car. A hand landed on her shoulder from behind. Realizing Fang was still conscious, she delivered a paw fist to the throat and used a tiger claw technique to scratch across his face. The attack caused his scarf to come off. By the time he hit the back seat again, his face was revealed to be his new monstrous form. Min was taken aback. If the presence of Fang hadn't been enough, his appearance now produced multiple questions. He smiled at her, revealing his sharp teeth. Her distraction was the perfect opportunity he needed to kick her in the chest. The sheer force sent her crashing through the front window and onto the hood.

She sloppily thrashed around to prevent herself from falling over the front of the car and under its rapidly spinning tires. Fang audaciously stomped out onto the hood, reached down and with one hand lifted her up by her shirt.

"Nǐ gāoxìng de kàn dào wǒ ma?(Glad to see me?)" he asked before tossing her to the left and sending her flying through the air. Abel, realizing her body was going to end up in front of his car, hit the gas and accelerated until he made it forward just enough for Min to land in a perfect catch in his passenger's side seat.

"Min! Are you okay?" he yelled, feeling around her head for damage. Min, barely had time to say: "It's Fang!" before Fang jumped from his car and landed on her chest. Min screamed in pain. As quickly as he could, Abel pulled a pistol from out of his coat pocket and fired two shots at Fang's head. Fang recoiled backwards but then slowly stood upright. He smiled a shark-toothed grin at the lack of damage the bullets had done to him. "An anghenfêl?" Abel muttered.

Fang lunged at him, grabbed the pistol barrel and bent it as if it were made of wire. He was about to claw Abel's shoulder until Min kicked him in the chin. He fell back against the passenger door. Min used this opportunity to leap on top of him and deliver multiple punches to his face. Fang lifted both of his feet and kicked her out of the car. She flew high, away from the car, towards the side of a trolley going in the opposite direction and twisted her body just in time to grab onto the sides of the trolley without falling to the ground. Wasting no time in pursuing her, Fang leaped from the Silver Ghost and grabbed onto the back of the trolley, terrifying the passengers on board. The rail car zoomed away down the street.

When a bullet lodged itself into the car door, next to Abel, he was not given any chance to figure out how to handle the situation. He quickly turned and saw the front passenger firing a rifle at him. Abel ducked down as bullets came closer and closer to his head. He turned the car to the right and sideswiped the red car. This halted the gun shots temporarily, as did a horse and buggy that wedged between their cars. When all was clear, the firing continued. Abel knew his most important option was to stop his car and go back to help Min, but he had to find out who these men were. The man with the rifle took careful aim at Abel's head and was about to fire until they all heard a strange sound. It was laughter, but not just any laughter, an insane, cackling. Everyone looked around and up to see from where it had come. There wasn't any sign of its source. The passenger was about to re-aim on Abel's head when something grabbed the henchman and pulled him out of his seat. Within seconds, he was screaming in terror, flying up into the sky and disappeared into the early evening darkness.

While Abel and the red car's driver got further away from the trolly, Min crawled up its side onto its roof. Exhausted and in quite a bit of pain, she had but a second to catch her breath before Lo Fang, leaped from the rear onto the roof and arrived three feet in front of her. He appeared triumphant and energized.

"How does it feel..." he taunted, "...to be the weaker one?" He kicked her in the chest. She slid to the front of the car and rolled over the side. She caught the edge before falling. The trolley's driver saw her, rang his bell multiple times and the motor-man stopped the vehicle. It came to a squealing halt. She waited until it had stopped and let go. Her body plopped onto the ground in front, like a corpse. Women on the car screamed. People surrounded her but none offered any help. Lo Fang jumped off of the car and landed next to her. With one hand he picked her up by the neck, high off the ground, a chorus of complaints erupted from the surrounding witness, who still, offered no aid.

"By the way...I was the one that turned your mother in."

Min became enraged. With a newfound energy, she punched him in the face as hard as she could. Lo Fang staggered back. She screamed in anger and punched him again. This time he let her go. She fell onto the ground. He stumbled for a moment, shook his head and regained his composure with an evil sneer.

"You think that's going to stop me? You think that's going to stop him?" He laughed. "Nǐmen dūhuì sǐ! (You're all going to die!) You, that Colored man, and especially that woman!"

Min was infused with anger. She took the key Mary had given her from around her neck, put it in one of her hands, curled her hand into a fist with the front of the metal key sticking out and punched him in the left eye. Lo Fang screamed in pain. Min pulled her fist back. There was blood present. She was surprised. It wasn't the hardest punch she could have delivered. Lo Fang flailed around, still screaming. He held his face where the key had made contact. Min punched him again with the same fist, each time causing him more and more pain. As she was hitting him in the stomach, he desperately pushed her away from him, ran away through the crowd of people and escaped. Min drunkenly sat down on the ground. She was too exhausted to run after him. She looked at the key. It had a trail of smoke coming from it.

The henchman snatched from inside of the car was flying through the air, far over the city of New York. He finally gained the courage to open his eyes and absorb this knowledge. He screamed in terror and looked around for what could have done this. Looking up, he realized his jacket was being suspended on the front of a metal rod. Further examination revealed, sitting in the middle of the metal rod, a woman dressed all in black, and on the back of the rod, a rapidly spinning propeller pushing them further at a significant speed. He screamed again and wiggled around.

"Best not move around too much, luv, or you'll fall for sure," Helga suggested before laughing.

"LET ME GO!" he yelled.

"Now, luv, don't think you'll like to be let loose 'ere. I was thinking more of the river."

"LET ME GO!" He thrashed around, causing Helga some trouble in maintaining control of the staff.

"Calm down, lest ya want to land on concrete." The man started punching at her feet. Helga rolled her eyes. "OK. 'av it your way." She tilted the front of the rod. He slid and fell off, down towards the ground. "Don't say, I didn't warn ya."

He fell further and further down. He wasn't panicking. He took a vial of the liquid the man with the silver cane had given him and drank it, seconds before his body crashed through the roof of an old car sitting on top of a junk heap in a scrap yard.

Helga levitated above him and witnessed the whole event. "Probably thought I was going to swoop down and save ya. Sorry luv, I'm not Glinda." Helga turned the staff around and was about to head back to help Abel but she heard a metallic rattling sound coming from below. In the scrap heap, pieces of metal moved around. Helga stopped and listened to the noises below. The heap went quiet. The only sounds were the various street noises and the spinning of the propeller on her transport. Just when she was going to turn around again, an object exploded from the heap and something large flew out of it and into the air. This caught her off guard, and she took a second to maintain control and stay in the air. The henchman flew towards her with great speed and then levitated 10 feet away from her. He was being suspended by a pair of ugly, grey bat wings. He looked at his wings and smiled with the same pointed-featured face as Lo Fang.

"Oh, my…" Helga spoke, worried. "…an anghenfêl."

The henchman swung a clawed hand at her. She managed to move out of the way just in time and zoomed away from him before he could try again. As she had expected, he flew after her. Occasionally she looked back to see where he was as she zig-zagged around tall buildings. Each time she lost him he would track her down; she needed more obstacles. She flew down to the apartment-building's level and risked being spotted by the pedestrians. She and her bat-winged chaser raced through alleys, avoiding pipes, wooden fire escapes, and hanging laundry lines. When they were sighted, they were traveling too fast for anyone to even form an opinion of what they had seen. Helga managed to barely make it between two sets of hanging laundry but the demon did not. Just when the lady of the apartment building was about to take the laundry inside, he dragged the clothesline away.

He struggled to remove the twisted white mess of clothes off of his body. By the time he was free of the trap, Helga was gone. On the other side of a nearby building, she levitated, the propeller was now above her head, and she held onto the pole by wrapping her arms and legs around it. There was no sight or sound of the henchman. Helga tilted the staff and slowly moved to the side of the building. She peeked around the corner. There was nothing. She rose, slowly inching upwards. Over the roof of the building she saw nothing. She straddled the staff and was about to leave when something hard hit her in the back. The henchman had run into her at full speed. The force knocked her forwards and sent her and him through the window of the nearest apartment. They crashed through a wall, through a living room, another wall and into a tiled bathroom. Tiles and dust flew everywhere when he embedded her into the wall. He stepped away from her. "I feel so powerful!" he bragged.

"At what price, you wanker?" She shook the dust off of her face and looked over at him. She tasted blood. "...Who...who did this to you?" she struggled to say.

"Sorry, if I told you, I'd have to kill you. No, wait. I'm going to kill you anyway, you witch," he laughed. He lifted his clawed fingers up and prepared to slash her throat open. Something hard hit him on the side of the head. He stopped and looked over at a German American woman holding a frying pan.

"Kommen nicht in mein Haus, ein Chaos, fliegen Sie Hund! (don't come into my house, making a mess, you flying dog!)" she yelled."

Before the henchman could turn his attention to the hausfrau and deliver a fatal blow to her, Helga remotely launched her copper staff into him. It carried him back through the wall to the outside and crashed him into the building across the alley. "Don't call me a witch!" Helga yelled at him. She quickly removed herself from the bathroom wall, and ran towards the hole. "Vielen Dank, luv!" she yelled to the woman. Helga jumped out of the window. Within a second, the staff was under her feet. She squatted down, re-straddled it and flew up and away from the chaos. A moment later, the winged demon was again in pursuit of her.

Abel rammed the Silver Ghost into the side of the red car, preventing the driver from firing yet another shot at him. Using his injured hand to drive and his good one to fire, the driver regained his composure and took careful aim at Abel's head. Right before he could pull the trigger, Abel turned the car into his and forced them both to make a right turn. The sound of screeching tires filled their ears as sparks from scraping metal flew before their eyes. Suddenly, they were surrounded by numerous train tracks and multiple freight trains, all hauling various wares; it was the rail yard. After the slipshod but successful turn, the red car straightened up and again the driver tried to take careful aim on Abel.

Abel looked all around. "Okay, now that there are no Dayfides. around..." He touched a copper medallion with a silver elephant engraved on it, which hung from the steering wheel. "...*Fēv yoth rruist!*" The driver fired his gun. Within the time it took for the bullet to leave the chamber and travel between the cars, the passenger side door of the Silver Ghost had become unhinged, rose upwards and blocked the bullet. Before the driver could come to grips with what had happened, the door pushed outwards, into him, and knocked him back. The gun flew from his hand and out of the car. The door returned to its original position. Abel touched the steering wheel medallion again and said: "*Crafanyo dül lo!*" The right side of the Silver Ghost's outer shell began to waver like mirrored liquid, and ripples began to appear like stones were being thrown onto the surface of a calm pond. An area where one of the ripples undulated pushed outwards toward the red car as a dulled, spiked protrusion. The shape morphed into a hand with a long arm attached. The hand reached out towards the driver, who screamed in terror and turned his wheel away from it. It grabbed the car door and halted the auto from escaping. Another arm stretched out of the Silver Ghost and then another. Each one grabbed onto various parts of the red car. The arms pulled the red car closer to Abel and held on tight. The driver, realizing he had no control over the car, let go of the steering wheel and stood to jump out. One more arm stretched out, grabbed the back of his shirt, pulled him into his seat and held him down to prevent any more escape attempts.

"Well then..." Abel announced. "...Now that I have your attention, who are you working for, and where did you get ahrion?"

The driver didn't answer the questions, instead drawing Abel's attention to their predicament: "We have to stop or else we're gonna get hit by that train!"

Their cars had veered onto a pair of tracks which were occupied by a large steams train coming in their direction at a high speed. If they stayed on the tracks, a train was going to collide into them.

Abel showed no concern for their impending doom. "Tell me where you got the ahrion!" The train got closer and closer without any sign of even slowing down.

"We got to get off these tracks or we're going to die!" the driver yelled.

"Where did you get the ahrion!"

"You're crazy! You're gonna die too!"

"Tell me!"

"You're bluffing!"

"I assure you, I'm not."

"I'm no squealer!"

"Tell me or we'll both die!" A loud train whistle filled the air. Abel looked at the driver and the train. "Last chance!"

"Go to hell!" he yelled.

The train slammed on its brakes. Frustrated, Abel touched the silver elephant again and said. *"Troiy les murgur"* The driver looked over and watched as Abel, the Silver Ghost and the protruding arms slowly dematerialized into a translucent form which then turned into billowing white smoke in their stead. A shocked expression overcame the driver's face. His last act was to turn his head just in time to see the front of the train right before it collided into him. His car was thrown back in a metal-crunching, glass-breaking chaotic spectacle as the train rushed through Abel and his car, passing as effortlessly as through a cloud. The red car tumbled and flipped repeatedly. In the long, squealing moment it took for the train to stop, the red car was a twisted jumbled wreck.

The Silver Ghost rematerialized into its normal form. The watery, motion reoccurred, and in an instant the car repaired the bullet holes and ramming damage which had been inflicted upon it and appeared new again. Abel parked the car and got out to take a look at the wreckage. He was sure the driver was dead, but perhaps he could find a clue in the car or on the man's body as to his identity. The wreckage was at least 10 boxcars away from him. When he made half the distance, the jumbled mess in front of the stopped locomotive started to rattle. Abel stopped. The junk continued to crinkle and move around. A moment of silence followed and then, with a burst of force, the entire wreckage lifted up into the air and flew to the side, 100 feet away. The cause of the uproarious situation, the driver of the red car, walked into sight and showed himself to be not only alive but completely unharmed. Like the others who had drunk the ahrion, he had pointy ears and sharp teeth. In addition, he was bigger than before and sported shirt ripping muscles. Abel started walking backwards towards his car. The driver, now turned beast, smiled, looked over at the ball of car wreckage he had tossed earlier and started walking towards it. Abel turned around and began running towards his car. When he was almost within car reach. The beast had picked up the wreckage and had hurled it into the air at Abel. Abel saw a shadow of darkness and death land on him when the projectile enveloped him and the Silver Ghost.

Above the city, the flying demon chased Helga over the rooftops and around numerous chimney tops. A couple of times, he was not as agile as her staff, and would smash into a chimney, sending numerous bricks flying around. Helga occasionally checked back to see if he was still following her. His wings flapped ferociously, cutting the air like whips. Each time she put an obstacle between him and her, he became angrier and more determined to do her great physical harm. At one point, she was able to accelerate around a large smoke stack of a factory. When he navigated around it, she was nowhere to be seen. Looking around gave no more clues to her whereabouts than when he flew upwards to where a large plume of smoke billowed out of the top of the pipe.

"Where are you?" he hissed. He flew all around the area but could not find her. His accumulated frustration culminated in a loud, roaring scream, which echoed throughout the area. With an aggressive turn, he flapped away, back towards the center of town. The only witnesses to his tantrum was the smoke rising from the stack. The smoke slowly stopped flowing and morphed into a human form, which continued to change until it became the solid body of Helga, holding her staff in her hands as her legs straddled the top of the smoke stack which was, in reality, inactive. She coughed and exhaled a lungful of smoke.

"Well now, Mr. Anghenfêl. Let's see where you came from." She looked off into the distance, at the demon flying away. She activated her staff and within a second was trailing after him, keeping a respectful distance.

Leopold parked the motorcycle in front of a bar in the Harlem neighborhood. Black residents walking down the street stared at Mary as she struggled to get out of the sidecar in her fancy dress. She looked around and realized where they were. "Oh! Why are we here?"

"Well, let's just say it'll be hard for the men who killed your father to follow us here unnoticed."

"As well as us to blend into the crowd."

"There is that. I suggest we get inside as quickly as possible." Leopold led her into a dilapidated building. After climbing some creaky wooden steps, he unlocked a door and they entered a tiny apartment containing a bed, a table near the window with two chairs, and a tiny kitchen area. On a small stove was a sauce pan of simmering liquid.

"Is this where you live?"

"For now."

"It's...cozy."

"No need to be polite. I know it can't compare to your neighborhood. But, it suits my needs."

"Of course. Like Nietzsche said: 'That which does not kill us, makes us stronger.'"

"Huh? True...Who's Nietzsche?"

Mary had a stressed look on her face. "German Philosopher?"

Leopold stirred the contents of the sauce pan, while bringing to boil a pot of water. "Don't know much about philosophy. Never really had much time to go to school."

"That's a shame. You've must have had a rough life." Mary picked up a folded map of New York. On it, various areas were circled and labeled by words such as: elephants, warehouse, and HMS Olympus. She raised an eyebrow.

"Not too bad." He put some dried pasta into the water with some salt and whispered: *"Vetel poi-th."* The pot became red hot and the water came to an almost instant boil. "I like to think that things can get better with just one positive act."

"And what is your positive act going to be?" She noticed there was a small red book on the floor, under his bed. She bent down and picked it up. It was a notebook, bookmarked with a photograph. She didn't understand the language the notes were written in, but by her guess it could be badly written Latin. The photo was of a tall man with a pointy mustache and beard, wearing small sunglasses. Standing in front of him were three well dressed children. One of them looked like a young Leopold. The other was a young Black lad, and the third was a girl in a wheelchair.

"I like to believe that helping you is part of that a—" He looked over at Mary, studying the photograph. He put his cooking utensils down, hurried over to her, closed the book and took it away.

"I'm sorry. I was snooping."

"Not to worry." He put the book in his back pocket and walked back over to continue cooking.

"Is that you in the photo?"

"Yes."

"Who are those other people with you in the photograph?"

"...They are...were, my family."

8:00 p.m., Saturday, February 5th, 1898

Leo walked down one of the many long and elaborately decorated hallways in the manor. Hanging on the wall we're large paintings of angels and demons, such as *Jacob Fighting an Angel* by Rembrandt. A few feet away from him was a ball used for playing various outdoor sports. When he got within a foot's distance from the ball, instead of kicking it and sending it on it's way, he took out his red notebook and turned to a certain page. The page was blank. "Darn it!" he complained. "I thought if I wrote the words backwards, the book would let me copy it." He put the notebook away and tried his best to remember the forge. *"Tro...Tro...Troyo e foof!"* Nothing happened. He tried again and got the same result. *"Troyo e foof!* Oh, wait..."He looked around the hallway. On a wooden side table was a silver necklace with a copper crucifix on it. He picked it up and said the words again: *"Troyo e foof."* The ball wiggled a little. He gestured towards the end of the hallway. The ball hurried away at a high speed towards a wall at the far end. Leo gave chase. On his way to the ball, he heard voices. Two people were having a conversation in one of the rooms off to the side. He stopped at the door, which was slightly open. The man was arguing with Aunt Gwenhwyvar.

"You can't do that to the girl..." Aunt Gwenhwyvar debated "...it's dangerous!"

"It's the only way," he said.

"That's incorrect. You could always leave her the way she is."

"Ridiculous! In that chair that I put her in? Unable to forge?"

"She doesn't have to forge."

"What will you have me do, Gwenhwyvar? Every night she has nightmares, even after I killed Robespierre. You said so yourself, as long as she has that darkness, she will never rise to her full potential."

"She can live a perfectly normal life, like the rest of the Dayfides."

"She's no more of a Dayfides than we are," he scoffed.

"And if you fail?"

"If it fails?"

"She dies."

"Even with success, she dies."

Leo gasped and put his hand on his mouth. They looked at him and realized he had heard everything they said. The man quickly walked over and closed the door. Leo backed away, looked down the hallway and started running. Out of breath, he reached one of the many bedrooms. He opened the door without knocking. The girl was inside. She was staring forlornly out the window.

"Hey!" he yelled, "We have to go, now!"

Mary took another bite of the pasta with red tomato sauce Leopold had prepared. It was not the best Italian food she'd had, but she smiled and gracefully accepted his effort to cook for her. She remembered the original purpose for them having dinner. She wiped her mouth with the towel he had provided for her. "Mr. Bianca..."

"It's okay to call me Leo."

"...Leo. I have to ask, once again, how do you know my father?"

Leo sighed. "Your father and I were members of a secret club."

"Really? What type of secret club?"

"Forging."

"Forging? As in a blacksmith?"

"Something like that. But metaphorically—shaping life instead of metals."

"Like a charity?"

"They can be charitable. There were those who believed in the resilience of humanity and those that believed that humanity was nothing but cattle or sheep, meant to be herded and controlled."

"I do hope you and my father were the former."

"Well...at least I am."

Mary became angry. "You don't mean to tell me my father believed in such things as people are like sheep? My father was one of the most kind-hearted people I know!"

"I'm sure he could be...Let me try again. There are three types of forging clubs or foundries, at least that I know of: Gold, Silver, and Copper. Your father used to be Gold, who believe the poor and weak must be ruled, if not in some cases eliminated, but he switched to Silver, who believe in the resilience of humanity, socialism—all that jazz."

"And Copper?"

"Copper? They can go back and forth. Very neutral and isolationist."

"Why did my father switch?"

"Something bad happened...He felt responsible for it...That's all I can tell you."

"Mr. Bianca, if you don't share information with me, how do you expect me to tell you anything that I may know?"

Leo stood up and walked to the kitchen."Miss White, I'm sorry but there are some things that are hard to explain about the Forgers..." He opened a bottle of Chianti, poured some in a tin cup and took it back to the table. "...Wine?"

"No, thank you."

He sat down, took a sip of Chianti and sighed. "...The Forgers have been around since biblical days. Their influence is... historical. If you can name a significant event in history and the words gold, copper or silver are mentioned, most likely they're involved, somehow.

"Really? And my father was a member of this club? Leo, he had many powerful friends, but I've never seen him wield any power on anyone." She looked around the room. "...And as for you, you don't seem to be a very big egg for a member."

"I choose to live this way because it suits my needs. And as for your father, he was always into inventions. The industrial revolution was about 100 years ago, yet we are still feeling the effect from the Forgers involved in that."

"My friend Thomas said my father could have been working on some new type of invention and maybe someone was after him for that."

"Thomas? Is that your steady?"

"Steady?"

"You carrying a torch for him?"

"Who, Thomas?" Mary playfully scoffed. "Oh my, no." She looked down, picked up the cup of wine and took a sip.

"Uhh, that's my wine."

She blushed, put the cup down and cleared her throat. Leo chuckled.

"Sure you don't want some?"

"No, thank you, I'm fine."

Across town, Thomas came out of his third brothel. A woman of disreputable morals tried her best to entice him back inside, but he remained steadfast in his conviction.

"C'mon fella. Just a little drink, eh?" she begged.

"No thank you." He brushed her hands off and hurried down the street. 'Don't know how many of these places I can take. I'm sure Douglas is a regular patron at some of them.' He opened his copy of The Gentleman's Companion and read another bookmarked page:

No. 105 West Twenty-fifth Street is kept by Mrs. Kate Woods, better known among the aristocracy as Hotel de Wood. This is a three story brown stone house, furnished throughout with the most costly and new improvements. Her gallery of oil paintings alone cost $10,000. Rosewood furniture, immense mirrors, Parisian figures & the house is furnished at the cost of $70,000. She keeps three young ladies or rare personal attractions, and her house receives the

patronage of distinguished gentlemen from foreign-countries. This is the best
house in the 25ᵗʰ St.

"Hmm. The word 'foreigners' sounds promising. Well, fourth time is the charm," Thomas hoped, walking to 25ᵗʰ Street.

At the train yard, Min jogged toward the car wreckage. Many men were standing around examining the damage. She staggered a little and held her hurt arm. "ABEL!" she yelled. She tried her best to run faster but it was too painful. "A-BEL!" she yelled again. As she got closer, she realized the pile of twisted metal was a car on top of another car. "No!" she ran up to the pile and tried to lift the red car up.

One of the men laughed at her. "You crazy rag-a-muffin. You can't lift that."

Min tried again but it was useless. She began to cry. "Abel!"

"Min?" a quiet voice said.

She looked around. "Abel?"

"Min?"

"Abel? Is that you?"

"Yes. How did you find me?

"I just asked and followed the trail of tire marks."

"Stand away from the cars please."

She backed away from the cars. A second later, the red wreckage lifted up in the air, being propelled by extending silver arms coming out from the bottom car.

The men watching this scenario panicked, pointed and some started to run away. One yelled "Monster!"

Three of the metallic arms were covering Abel like a protective cage; he was tucked down between the seat well. The raising arms threw the red car wreckage to the side and the ones covering him retracted. Abel straightened himself up, touched the metallic disk and said: *"Trwsio."* Every dented and bent part of the car bent in opposite directions as the car un-wrecked itself. With loud clanking and pings, the car returned to its former luster and beauty. Abel wiped some dust off of the dashboard and readjusted the rearview mirror. In the reflection, he noticed Min's shocked expression from witnessing such an event. "Oh..." He said. He rapidly got out of the car. Min took a quick step backwards. "Min…" He lifted his hand to halt her from running away. "…I know this may all seem rather extraordinary to you, but I can explain everything…"

"My mother could leap four meters in the air, heal peoples' injuries with a touch and once I saw her block bullets. Tell me something that I can't believe in."

Abel thought for a second. "Quite…I guess explaining Forgers will be a lot easier for you."

Leo cleaned the two plates in a tin tub full of soapy water. Mary offered to help, but he refused.

"Sorry if I don't have any dessert. I can make you a cup'a coffee if you want," he offered.

"Coffee would be lovely." Mary stood up and slowly paced around the apartment, looking at various objects. There were at least two mouse traps on the ground. She nudged one and it sprang to life with a quick snap. She flinched. "Oh, my! Sorry."

"No worries. Plenty more where that came from." He turned his back on her and continued washing dishes. She noticed he had left his red book on top of the bed. She sneaked over to the bed, slowly picked up the book and opened it to the page with the photograph inserted into it. The little girl in the wheelchair looked so sad, as did the young Leo. She ran her finger over the girl's face as if by doing so she could cause her to smile. "Mr. Bianca…"

"Yes?"

"That girl in your photo. Who was she?"

Leo paused for a long moment. "…Like I said, she was family."

"Was? Did you have a falling out?"

"No…she…" He turned around and looked at Mary. "…died…" He discovered Mary was looking at the photo again. A look of fear came over his face. "No!" he yelled. He fast-walked over to her in an attempt to snatch the photo and book away. Caught off guard, she lifted it up and kept it out of his reach. He grabbed at it. In the process, she lost her balance next to the bed and they sloppily fell onto it, with him, landing on top of her. Time stood still as they lay on the bed, face to face. He looked into her eyes. A thousand thoughts seem to run through his mind. She stared at his face. He was so close, she could feel his thumping heart against her bosom.

Mary retracted her lips into her mouth and wet them. He could hear the sound of her tongue click in her mouth. When she said his name, it was like every syllable was drenched in seductiveness. "Mr. B-ian-ca?"

"Yes…Mary?"

"Can you please get off?"

"Excuse me?"

"You're crushing my giblets."

"Oh?…Oh! Right—sorry!" He lifted up, took the photo from her and reinserted it into the book.

"Sorry. I shouldn't have done that," she apologized.

"No, it's perfectly all right," he said nervously. "You want to find out more about your father."

"Does that girl have something to do with my father?"

"No. No, of course not…I mean, in general…"

Mary put her hand on his. "Mr. Bianca…Leo…"

Leo looked down and slowly nodded.

"…That girl."

He looked up.

"My father had something to do with her death, didn't he"

Leo nodded again.

12:00 a.m., Sunday, February 6th, 1898

Leo slowly opened the large creaking door to the darkened parlor room. Satisfied it was unoccupied, he tiptoed inside and then gestured for the girl to follow him. As she had commanded it to do earlier, the chair slowly rolled in Leo's direction.

The squeaky wheels on the chair were not only annoying to Leo, he knew they could jeopardize their mission. "Can't you do something about that squeaking?" he whispered.

"Chair. Walk quietly," she silently ordered. The wheels on the chair rearranged themselves into four metallic crab legs. As her chair walked along the ground, the points of the legs would gently come down, making the minimum of noise. The children continued sneaking throughout the manor, being very carful not to rattle the precious antique china or other items which would make a sound. They succeeded in making it out of the front door. When Leo closed the large door, they both seemed to breathe out a sigh of relief. The bright full moon lit their path and cast everything in a soft blue light. Once they were away from the front and heading towards the gate, the girl felt it was an appropriate time to talk.

"Where are we going?"

"Away."

"Why?"

"Because your life is in danger."

"From who?"

"Whom."

"Whom?"

"Yes. They were discussing killing you."

"What! That's preposterous! He's rescued me on numerous occasions, and Aunt Gwenhwyvar has always treated me like her own daughter."

"If it wasn't for him, you wouldn't be in that chair in the first place."

"Yes, and time and time again he has tried his best to make restitutions."

"Restitutions? That's a big word; you're even starting to sound like them. Why are you defending them? You've seen what they can do."

"And yet, you seem pretty keen at learning to forge yourself."

"So I can protect you." Leo slowly opened the gate. The chair crawled through, Leo followed and slowly closed it without even a click. They began a long walk down a tree-lined dirt road.

Satisfied with their distance from the house, the girl ordered the chair to go back to using wheels. After its transformation, she turned her attention back to Leo. "Protect me from what?"

"Even if they don't kill you, you think that fella that he killed was the last person to come after that book? As long as we live in that house with them, other Forgers are going to keep coming for it."

"Not if they get rid of the book."

Leo scoffed. "Are you daft? Have you read some of the things in there? It makes the Bible look like a nursery rhyme. No, the only option is to get away from those two."

"And go where?"

"Italy."

"Why there?"

"I'm told that's where my parents were from. Figure there might be other relatives there that can take us in."

"And then what?"

"Then what?"

"What will we do? No more large house, no more schooling, fancy food, world traveling. What will we do?"

"We'll live...I'm sure they have schools in Italy."

"Not any that can teach you magic."

"Probably not. But it'll be better. No more worrying. We'll live like regular people, for once."

"Sounds boring."

"Not with me it won't be."

"With you?"

"Of course."

"What, are we getting married or something?"

"Of course."

She laughed. "And why would I marry you? You're like my brother."

Leo got angry and stopped walking. "Fine! Go on back, then!"

"What?"

"If you don't want to be with me than go on back to that crazy house and get yourself killed!"

"Leo?"

He wiped a tear from his face and started walking away. "Go on then. I'll travel on my own."

"Leo!" He kept walking. "Chair, get in front of him!" The chair sped down the road, passed Leo and cut him off. He had been crying even more. "Leo?"

"Just go away!"

"What's wrong?"

"Nothing! Just scram!"

"Leo...you can't go off on your own."

He wiped his face with his shirt tail. "And why not?"

She rolled the chair closer to him. "You said you were going to protect me."

"Yeah, so?"

"If you go...who's going to protect you?"

Leo looked at her face, bathed in the moonlight. Behind her, framing her face was an illuminated field of blue azaleas. "How are you going to protect me? You can't even forge?"

"My Papa used to say: family and friends looks after family and friends."

Leo gazed up at the moon. "Okay. Fine. But the minute I know you're safe, I'm gonna go off and marry someone else."

"What?" she complained. "Just like that?"

"What are you getting angry at? You said you don't want to marry me?"

"Chair. Run over him!" The chair accelerated towards him. He began to run very fast down the road.

"What's your problem?" he yelled.

"Nothing. Now stand still so I can run over you."

"Tell me, what happened?" Mary asked.

"I…I can't."

Mary sighed. "Then I'm afraid there is nothing more that you can do for me. Can you take me home, please?"

"No, please wait for just a while longer," Leo nervously insisted. "I have coffee brewing, remember?" Outside the apartment window, Flapper landed on the sill. "…If you'd excuse me for a minute." He walked over, opened the window and leaned out to look at the bird. "What do you think, Flapper? Is it time for Mary to go home?" He looked back at her and then whispered to the bird: "*Une dio gale?*" The bird cawed and nodded.

"Can I please go, now?" Mary asked, frustrated.

"Sure thing. Let me get my coat."

The guide had given a very accurate description of Hotel de Wood. It was elaborately decorated with very fancy furniture, mirrors, tiny porcelain figurines on shelves and oil paintings. Thomas tried once again to explain to the madam of the house what he wanted. She was an older woman in her 50s, wearing an elegant, frilly black dress usually reserved for balls. Her dress matched a very large black fan she would occasionally wave around. She again said in a French accent: "I'm sorry Monsieur, but I can not reveal the names of any of our clientele. We pride ourselves on protecting their privacy."

"Even if I were to tell you it was a police emergency?"

"Some of our clients are policeman. I'm sure they don't want their identity exposed."

"I'm not asking you to open your books to me. I just want to know if you have seen a gentleman who may frequent this establishment."

"Encore, Monsieur, we do not talk about our clientele."

"What if I came back here with a paddy wagon full of policeman and shut this place down!"

"I'm sure most of them will appreciate the ride."

Thomas was angry. "...Just nod your head, I don't care! An overweight Frenchman, handlebar mustache, one dark monocle, carrying a silver cane with an elephant on it!"

"Désolé Monsieur—Bonsoir." She turned her back on him and exited through a pair of red velvet curtains.

Thomas sighed and pounded his fist on the desk. He walked away and wondered what he could do. He had to navigate around one of the workers, a young woman, exposing more cleavage than one would do, even for bed time. "Excuse me," he apologized, walking around her.

He stepped outside and took out 'The Gentleman's Companion.' He heard a voice from behind him. When he turned around, he saw the girl from inside standing behind him. "Yes?" he asked.

"Monsieur?"

"Yes? Should't be outside dressed like that."

"Monsieur, the man you are describing..."

"Yes? Have you seen him?"

She looked around to make sure no one was listening to them. She nodded.

"Where? Here?" She nodded really fast. He grabbed her shoulders. "Tell me everything that you know about him!"

She looked around again. "He's a terrible, terrible man. He hurts the girls. The girls are all afraid of him. We detest him! I can tell by his accent, he is Belgique, er ah... Belgian. He has a private room upstairs."

"Is he here now?"

"No Monsieur. He comes and goes."

"Can you show me his room?"

"Monsieur, I don't want to get into trouble."

"Don't worry. Just sneak me into his room. If I can catch him, he'll never bother you or the other girls, ever again."

She thought about it for a second and nodded.

Thomas went back inside. This time, escorted by the girl. The madam of the house watched him come inside and head towards the stairwell. "Might as well find out why so many policeman come here," he joked to the madam.

The madam snapped her fan open and smiled.

Leo slowly pulled the motorcycle into a parking spot near the lighthouse. It had been difficult to find a place, because there were so many vehicles and people blocking their way. It was also difficult for Mary to register this was even the location of her house; the lighthouse was actually missing. She disembarked from the motorcycle, helped up by Leo, and pushed her way through the crowd of people. Someone yelled "There she is!"

She made it to the front of the onlookers and had a full view of her parcel of land, minus the lighthouse. Where it once stood, only a large circle of smoldering bricks, which was its base, remained. Mary walked stiffly towards the area leading to the underground stairwell. She constantly muttered: "My lighthouse. Where is my lighthouse?" Over and over. The large iron disk was still intact. This at least gave some hope the rest of the house was still there. She looked up, expecting to see the spire of her house flying through the air like a rocket. A fireman with an Irish accent walked up to her. "We got a call about a kerfuffle going on about your lighthouse. When we got here we found it like this."

"W-where is my lighthouse?"

"Don't know missy. Looks like someone ran off with it. As for how, no idea. Nobody saw a lighthouse traveling down Fifth Avenue. Some of the neighbors did hear a large racket though, but that's all we got."

"I SAW IT!" a voice yelled from the side. Madeleine Astor, accompanied by a maid, walked from the side of the crowd.

"Madeleine?" Mary asked. "Did you see something?"

Madeleine had the appearance of someone who had seen death up close. "T-t-there were two of them, and a man on the ground. They were big...and strong...They flew out from the sky and they knocked it down. One pushed from the top, and the other from the bottom—like birds! And both wrapped their trunks around it, and then they..."

"Hold on. Trunks?"

"E-E-ELEPHANTS! They were elephants! Elephants! They took it—and they flew away into the sky! I SAW IT!" It was obvious telling the tale had put a strain on her. The maid put her arms around Madeleine and led her back to their house.

"So sorry..." The maid apologized. "She hasn't been the same since the Titanic."

Mary looked at Leo. "Elephants? Elephants from the sky, took my house?"

"I wouldn't put too much faith in that story. She seemed a bit fried to the hat."

Mary spread her arms out and backed on top of the iron disk. "It's as good a story as any. I think it's fabulous!" She spun around.

"Mary?" Leo wan't sure if she had lost her mind.

"Just think what the insurance company will say when I tell them: giant elephants from the sky stole my house!"

"You don't seem too upset."

"I think it's the cat's pajamas!"

"You're not mad?"

"Mad? Of course not. I can always buy another lighthouse. The only thing I'm mad about is that I didn't get to see it!"

"You actually believe that story?"

"I believe everything in this world is possible."

Leo looked angrily at her." Un-be-lievable."

"Pardon?"

"YOU! Most people would be upset, confused or even angry that ELEPHANTS flew off with their house; a bunch of baloney, but not you!" he sarcastically praised.

"Mr. Bianca. I'm not sure what Mrs Astor saw is real or not, but why are you so angry with me?"

"It's not you I'm angry with. It's how your father raised you!"

Mary walked up to Leo and without hesitation slapped him. She rapidly turned on her heels and walked to the other side of the disk. The metallic devil head lock which used to be part of the lighthouse wall was undamaged and still in the same place, suspended by a bent iron bar. She placed her key inside the devil's mouth and turned it. The eyes on the sculpture glowed red. The center of the round, metal disk dropped and revealed the spiral stair case. She hurriedly ran down stairs.

Leo ran after her. "Wait!" he yelled. He ran as fast as he could and almost fell down the staircase before it started rewinding back up to reseal the entrance to the mansion. He tumbled off the retracting steps and fell onto the ground of the parlor. He picked himself off of the floor and tried to ignore the pain he had suffered from falling. "Mary!" he yelled. She had made her way to the elevator. By the time he hobbled over to her, she was able to get in the elevator and began to descend. "Wait!"

As she took the elevator downwards, Leo tried his best to keep up with her, using the spiral staircase. With every floor, he tried to apologize and explain himself—First floor: "I'm sorry, I didn't mean to say that." Second floor: "Miss White! I'm sorry for what I said." Third: "Believe me, I had only the utmost respect for your father!" Fourth: "I apologize! Please forgive me, Miss White!" This scenario continued until the elevator arrived at the bottom floor. Leo arrived later than she did. He paused briefly to look around the unfurnished room. Mary stood in front of the large, metal vault door with the silver engraving of a winged elephant. Leo limped over to her and tried to apologize again. "I'm so sorry for what—"

"WHAT IS IN THERE?" she pointed at the vault.

"Excuse me?"

"Stop pretending like you're trying to protect me from someone! You know exactly who took my lighthouse, you know exactly what my fathers secrets are, and you know EXACTLY what's behind this door!"

"...Miss White..."

"NO MORE GAMES! Mr. Bianca! Tell me what's behind this door!"

"I've never been here before."

"JUST TELL ME! NOW!"

The look on her face scared him. She had gone from light to dark. "It's a book."

Her face transformed from angry to confused, to happy and then back to confused. "...A book?" Leo nodded. "...A book... My father was killed over...a book?"

"I'm afraid so."

"Must be one bloody good book."

The stairwell of the three-story brothel was just as elaborately decorated as the rest of the house: more paintings, figurines and mirrors adorned the walls, each, Thomas supposed, averaging in price to more than his yearly rent. The young courtesan lead the way down a red furbished hallway past many rooms, each producing various noises, from laughter to what may or may not be anguish. Thomas focused on the job at hand but could imagine how tempting giving in to being pampered by an attractive young woman with a French accent would be. She stopped at a room near the end of the hall, handed him a skeleton key and gestured at a door. Before he could ask any questions, she was already down the hall and heading towards the stairs. After a quick look around to make sure he wasn't being watched, Thomas unlocked the door, took out his derringer and stepped inside. The room was dark. Thomas struck a match and lit the mantle of the gas light. "Hello?" he called. No one answered. The bedroom was what one would expect in a fancy, yet at the same time seedy hotel: Canopy bed with a sordid history, a very large window, framing a nice view of the city as well as a crime-ridden alley, and early Victorian furniture including a desk and chair. "Why would anyone need a desk and chair in here?" he wondered. "…Unless it's to write a letter of confession to their priest."

He first searched a closet to make sure no one was inside. He found changes of clothes, various suits, all in the same size and shade of white Thomas had seen the man wearing. This confirmed for him the occupant's identity. There was nothing else of significance in the closet offering any clues to the man's itinerary, not even luggage. Thomas went back to the bed chamber and searched the desk. This produced better results. Inside were various pamphlets and maps about New York. "Understandable if he's a newcomer." On one of the maps, the docks near the 100th area next to the East River were circled. Next to the circle, the words: *Le loyer est bon marché ici* were written. Thomas took out his notebook and wrote down the observation. More rummaging through the drawer revealed silver coins with engravings of a two headed snake on one side and a winged elephant on the other. "Not sure if I recognize this country." He did a quick sketch of the coin. The last item of interest was a list on a piece of stationary. He recognized from the letterhead that it belonged to the house of Vanderbilt, as he had received many notes on such paper from his cousin. On the stationary, in the same handwriting as the map, he read the words 'Liste de 400', and underneath, the names: Vanderbilt, Astor, Carnegie, Rockefeller and numerous others.

"What is this? And how did he get Vanderbilt stationary?" Thomas noticed something wrong. When he had been in the Army, fighting against the Boxer Rebellion, his peripheral vision had become very keen and sensitive to sneak attacks. This skill came in handy as he was able to notice something approaching from the outside of the window. On closer inspection, he realized it was something flying over the buildings towards him. "An eagle?" he wondered. "No, bigger, much bigger." The winged gargoyle landed on the ledge outside the large window. It's wings retracted until they were inside of his back and out of sight. Thomas thought about running but it was too late to run—the demon had spotted him.

With almost graceful yet nefarious movements, the anghenfēl opened the window and stepped inside. "Well, well, well, look at what we got here," the demon hissed. He turned, slowly closed the window and locked it.

"Put your hands up." Thomas pointed the gun at him.

He laughed. "You really think that's going to harm me?" He approached Thomas.

Thomas fired and, as he had been warned, it was as effective as an insult. The demon knocked the gun out of Thomas's hand.

"Who...What are you?"

"You can call me..." His sharp teeth extended out of his mouth. "...DEATH!" He reached out to grab Thomas, who punched the demon's cheek, which only made it madder. "Always wondered what people meat tastes like."

Thomas remembered the last demon, and how it had reacted to his pen. He took it out and swung it at the beast. The anghenfēl blocked Thomas' attack with his hand, he had a smug look on his face announcing he thought Thomas's attack was futile. It changed to horror and surprise when he saw the pen imbedded through his smoking hand. He screamed and backed up.

"I'm going to rip out your—" His threat was never finished. Something large came crashing through the window, slammed into the demon and pinned him into the door. Thomas was thrown back towards the bed and onto the floor from the flying glass, wood and force of the commotion. The sound of a propeller filled the air as did the screaming of the anghenfēl. He was impaled in his chest by a copper staff. Helga dismounted the staff and noticed Thomas.

"Oh. Evening Detective Vanderbilt. Fancy seeing you 'ere," she greeted him calmly.

"Helga?" Thomas picked himself off of the floor. "What the…"

There was a knock on the door. Someone yelled "What's going on in there?"

"One moment please!" Helga yelled.

"I'm going to kill you both!" yelled the anghenfēl.

"Tsk, tsk" Helga said, walking closer to the monster to have a better look. "Where did you come from? Is this your flat?"

"Helga! What is that thing? Did you come flying in on a broom?" Thomas yelled. There was more knocking on the door. Someone tried to open it but the force of the demon being pushed against it stopped any attempts.

"Don't you worry, officer, all will be revealed as soon as I find out where this bugger came from." She came too close to him and his hand almost clawed her face. A second later, his wings expanded and knocked over any loose items caught in their wing span. "Hello? You're full of vinegar aren't ya? Tell me. Who's yuh boss, slag face?"

"How do you know I'm not the boss?" he hissed.

"He's not," Thomas said.

"Oooh" Helga said " 'ear that? Says you're not the boss. Now, out with it, who ya working for?" The knocking on the door got louder. " 'old on a tick!" she yelled. "We haven't got much time, mate," she addressed the anghenfēl. "Don't like to expose ourselves to the Dayfides for too long."

"What's a Day-fide?" Thomas asked.

"That's you dear. You and that lot behind the door. Which reminds me. I guess I'm going to have to do a mind scrub on yeh. Don't want yeh being thrown into the loony bin." Helga walked over and put her hand on Thomas's head.

"Helga" What…"

"Don't worry dear, won't take a sec. Than I can deal with that anghenfēl. Let's see here…*Ang hofio.*" There was a pause. The silence was broken by the demon screaming, knocking outside and someone trying to push the door open. "Just one bloody minute! I said! There, officer, 'ow's that feel?"

"Helga? What's an anghenfēl?"

"Pardon?" Helga looked shocked.

"What's an anghenfēl?"

"Detective Vanderbilt?"

"Yes?"

"You remember what's going on right now?"

"Helga? There's a gargoyle pinned to a door and you just came flying in through the window on a broom and pinned him! How could I possibly forget that?"

"Oh dearie my. It didn't work."

"What didn't work?"

"The mind forge."

"What's a…"

"Detective Vanderbilt. I think your brain might have been welded at one point."

"Pardon?"

"Hypnotism dear, someone hypnotized you. Once that happens, it can't be done twice on the same person."

"I don't remember anyone hypnotizing me…" Helga looked at him and raised an eyebrow. "…Right, I wouldn't remember, would I?"

"Quite." Someone from the outside was trying to ram the door, over and over. "Blimey. Guess I better wrap this up, eh? Detective Vanderbilt, you wouldn't 'appen to have that pen that Miss White gave you on yuh birthday?"

"Strangely enough, yes. It's in his hand." Thomas pointed to the demon. "Seems to be the only thing that works on these beast."

Helga turned around and looked at the thrashing anghenfêl. "Hmm. Guess he's not gonna give up that pen so easily…Let's see what I can do." She walked over, grabbed her copper staff and stuck out her hand. "*Do ha toth*" The pen wiggled out of his hand causing him to scream in pain. It flew across the room and was grabbed by Helga.

"Helga. How did you do…"

She ignored his question. "Now then, what were those words?…Ah yes: *Eh-ha-gu avuh .*" The small pen which Helga held in her hand, suddenly elongated and thickened. Within an instant, the pen formed itself into a saber sword, complete with an ornate silver handle and various inscriptions carved into its blade.

"Helga! What in God's name?"

She ignored Thomas again, walked up to the monster and put the sword hilt against its neck. "Now then. Let's make this quick. Yeh got 10 seconds to tell me every thing yeh know, or off with yuh 'ead." She looked at Thomas. "yeh may want to avert yuh eyes, luv…10!"

"Shut your yap," said the beast, "He told us if we squealed, he'd do more damage to us than you ever could!"

"...9..."

"When I'm loose, I'm going to rip off your head!"

"...8..."

"I can't wait to sink my teeth into the both of you!"

"...7..."

"Give it up, you old witch!"

"...3-2-1!" With a swift back-hand strike, Helga swung the sword at great speed. The facial expression on the anghenfēl went from anger to surprise. Then, like an apple rolling off a table, his head separated from his body. And hit the floor. There was no blood present.

Thomas, who had borne witness to this violent act, was about to say something but was interrupted when the entire body of the anghenfēl, including his dislocated head, dispersed into miniature sparkling fragments and, within one second, shone as brightly as fireworks, illuminating the room, and then dissolved into blowing, black ashes.

"Don't—call—me—a—WITCH!" Helga yelled.

Thomas backed up and sat on the edge of the bed. He felt like he was in shock. "Helga?"

She turned around and directed her attention back to him. "Yes, officer?"

"During the war, I saw Boxers do stuff that I thought were only illusions, but this week...You...you killed him."

"He was dead the minute he became an anghenfēl, Detective." She walked over and pulled Thomas up with ease. "No time for resting, we have to go before that lot calls for backup."

"You're very strong, what are you?"

"I'm a Coppersmithian—a Wiccan...or that other word."

"And Mary and Abel?"

"Abel's a Stryker."

The door was starting to give way as a hat rack, being used as a battering ram, was thrust into it.

"And Mary?"

"Mary's just a normal lady—Detective Vanderbilt, we have to go!"

"Go where?"

"Away from all this..." She looked around. "...Hop on."

"Hop on that? That broom?"

"It's not a broom, it's a teclyn. Now get on."

"How?"

"For the love of…" She sighed, lifted him up and sat him on the staff. He winced at having something metal hit him between the legs. "Sorry, luv. Teclyn, do you mind? *Kefor-dis.*" Within a second, the bar between Thomas' legs formed into a soft seat cushion with gold tassels.

"Thanks," he breathed a sigh of relief. Helga jumped on behind him, grabbed his waist and then held the sword against his neck. "Er–Helga?"

"Since you can't be charmed to forget everything, the only other option is to kill you to keep our secrets."

"Helga? I would never betray your trust."

"And how would I know that?"

"I would never do anything to harm Mary. You and Abel are very important to her and I would never do anything to disrupt that. You have my word as an officer of the law and as a gentleman. I will take your secrets to the grave."

"That's what I wanted to hear…*Dückweh luhg.*" The sword shrunk back into a fountain pen form. She put it in his breast pocket. "I think this belongs to you. Now, 'old on luv!" She backed the staff away from the door. It flew backwards out of the window and zoomed upwards into the air.

Behind the door someone was yelling: "1-2-3!" With much more force than was now necessary, the door was easily bashed open by the hat rack, and four people, two of them courtesans and the other two bouncers, fell onto the ground on top of each other.

2:00 a.m., Sunday, February 6th, 1898

"Leo! When can we rest?"

"I think there's a train we can catch to Cardiff, and from there we can get a boat to Italy."

"I'm tired."

"Why are you tired? You're not walking?"

"I'm tired and sleepy. It must be three o'clock in the morning. Can't we rest?"

"Rest where? Who knows what's in those woods? Could be anything."

"Then we should rest there." She pointed to a glowing orange light off in the distance. As they got closer and closer to it, it was revealed to be a campfire. "It's a fire."

Leo held out his hand to halt her. "Careful. It could be rabble-rousers. Let me take a look-see." He went ahead to scout who would set up a campfire on the side of the road in the middle of nowhere. He slowly sneaked closer and closer to the flame and peeked his head through a thicket.

A small black cauldron was suspended over the fire. Tending to the pot was a girl in her late 20s dressed for a funeral, all in black. Her dark attire was offset by her snow white hair, braided into two long ponytails. She opened the lid to the cauldron, took a spoon and tasted the ingredients inside. Her face winced from its bitterness. Leo looked back to see if the girl was all right.

"Yeh can come out now," the young woman in black said. Leo was startled. He tried not to move. "Listen, mate, either yeh come out now and enjoy the fire, or hang out in them woods and enjoy the hogweed."

Leo looked around. He didn't see any hogweed, but he jumped out into the opening just to be sure. He took a defensive stance. "Who are you?"

"Yuh know, it's customary for the attacker to give 'is name first."

"I'm not an attacker."

"Sneaking up on people in the woods at this hour? Sounds like a ne'er-do-well to me."

"I was only scouting?"

"For who? That lass in the wheelchair?" Leo looked back to make sure she was okay.

"Yeh know, the first law of protection is to never leave the ones yuh protecting, unprotected. While yuh here chat'n with me, I could have had some bloke sneak up on 'er and cut 'er throat."

Leo ran back to the girl. She had a surprised look on her face, wondering why he had come back so soon.

"What?" she asked.

"Nothing. Let's get out of here." When he turned around to leave he was startled to find the young woman standing in front of him.

"Sorry about that. I didn't mean to startle yeh. I was just pointing out the dangers of two kids being alone by themselves with no planning."

"We have a plan."

"Really? Where are yeh sleeping tonight?"

"We-we have a place."

"Do we?" the girl asked.

"Do yeh?" The young woman asked. "Come on then..." She gestured back to the fire. "...Rest by the warm fire until the sun is up. Better than risking the throat cutters." The young kids looked at each other. "...Come along then, safety in numbers." The girl nodded and the children followed the young woman back to the camp fire.

"What's in this book?" Mary asked.

"It's like a list of instructions."

"For what?"

"Everything."

"Everything?"

Everything!"

"Really. So If I wanted a recipe for shepherd's pie...?"

"Okay, I stand corrected. Let's just say it contains secrets that whoever has the book can use to dominate the other foundries."

"I see. And why does my father have this?"

"The book made it's way from Wales to the Americas in the late 1600s. When its location was uncovered, your father and his brother, Robespierre, traveled to..."

"Wait! I have an uncle?"

"Yes, he's deceased...I'm sorry. He had no children."

Mary looked sad. "Continue."

"They made it to the Americas and tracked the book from Salem, Pennsylvania to Chatsworth, Illinois where it was being held by a foundry of Coppersmiths."

"Wait, Salem? Isn't that where the famous witch trials were?"

"Yes. It's kind of related, but let me continue. They stole the book from the Coppersmiths but instead of returning it back to the foundry, they decided to keep it for themselves."

"Why would my father do such a dishonest act?"

"The book seduces all that possess it. Like I said, with the information in this book you can rule all of the foundries."

"No wonder they were harassing him."

"Correct. Your father and his brother studied it and knew that eventually the other clubs would pinpoint their location. To hide their activity, they took a job working with the Berkeley Brother's Circus."

"Why a circus?"

"A circus is a great place to hide for two rogue outsiders, and it constantly changes locations. But, as history tells us of men that possess great power; power can never be shared as long as greed exists. Your uncle betrayed your father, he tried to take the book, a fight took place and the book was ripped in half. He was able to get hold of the bottom half. In the confrontation, there was a…was a fire. Many people were killed and injured. Coincidentally, five years earlier, when the circus first passed through this town, a train wreck occurred and many more people perished. I'm not sure if that's connected, but it's strange that all of these events happened in that town."

"Why didn't my father ever mention any of this to me?"

"Why would he? Your father's goal for you was to give you the best of lives. Why would he burden you with his sordid history?"

"Perhaps you're right. Please continue."

"Your father quit the Gold foundry and joined the Silver because he felt that the Goldsmithians were too addicted to power and greed. He spent many years looking for his brother and the top half of the book. He tracked him down in Belgium. Your uncle was living a very lavish lifestyle there. Gaining procession of the top half of the book was like a war, requiring many members of each foundry fighting to the death."

"To the death, over a book?"

"Like I said, not an ordinary book."

"But still. Risking your life over a silly little book. And to think, someone would run off with my lighthouse over it!" Mary put her hands on her head in frustration.

"Miss White, I think it's important to understand—if we could find the book, perhaps we could understand more about what was so important that your father risked his life to protect it."

"More and more you seem like a greedy member of the Gold foundry, trying his best to find the book and gain all of that power for himself."

"Believe me, the only thing I want is to give you a normal life, like he did. But it's impossible as long as that book is somewhere in this house."

"Well, I fear to tell you your ship is out of luck. I know every shelf in this household and have read every book on it, including the library, which was apparently stolen by elephants. There is no secret book unless it's behind that door." She pointed to the iron vault.

Leo walked up to the door and felt around it, looking for a knob. "Is there a key?"

"There is always a key to a locked door. Do you have the key? is a separate question."

"Do you have the key?"

She walked over to him and moved her face within three inches of his face. "NO!"

He hit the door. "Damn it!"

"His secrets will die with him. Now, if you don't mind, it's been a long evening and I wish to retire."

"No, wait! You don't have a key to this? Did he have any secret stashes of keys—or have you ever seen anything like that in his office?"

"Mr. Bianca, I've tried for many years to get through that door. There is only one key that opens all doors to every lock in this house." She pulled out her necklace with the music box key on it. "This skeleton key not only lets you inside the house, it also starts our automobile, and opens every door inside the house..." She pointed to the vault. "...except for this one."

He walked over to her. "May I have a look at that?"

She handed it to him. "I've tried that key Mr. Bianca. There's not even a key hole for it."

He examined the key and then the door. The only place where anything could be inserted was under the winged elephant medallion. Instead of a hole, it was more of a one inch slit.

"You see? Theres not even a keyhole. I've looked all over this room for one and never..."

"It's a clo keffin." he interrupted.

"Excuse me?

"It means: 'reverse lock'" He rotated the key so that it was handle first. "See?"

She rushed over to him. He handed her the key.

She looked at him and then the door. Slowly, she approached the door. She looked at him again. He nodded. She inserted the key into the door. "...*She tried it, and the key fitted it exactly. Then she turned it once round...*" she recited. The key fit perfectly in the reverse lock. She turned the key to the left.

" 'Ow yeh doing, Detective Vanderbilt?" Helga asked.

"Terrified..." he answered, looking at the sprawl of buildings passing 100s of feet below, as the wind whistled pass his ears. "... But I have to say, this is quite thrilling."

"Let me know if you see Abel and Min in the Silver Ghost. Last I saw of 'em, friends of that anghenfēl were giving them trouble."

They flew around the tallest building in the world, the 60-stories Woolworth building.

"Helga?'

"Yes, Detective?"

"You're a Coppersmithian?"

"Correct."

"Also known as a wit..."

"We don't like that word, officer. Witch is a term invented by Dayfides to persecute other Dayfides."

"And you think the boss of that anghenfēls is a...Goldsmith?"

"Of course—*Gold is for the mind and soul.*." she sang

"Pardon?"

"Little song we used to sing at the smithing school. Although, as you saw with me and your ahrion pen, Forgers can alloy different spells, but we try to master one type."

"Mary gave me that pen. Does she know about any of this?"

"No, and we plan on keeping it that way–Hold on. I think I've spotted them."

Far below them, Abel and Min were traveling in the Silver Ghost back to their home. Abel was explaining Forgers to Min, as Helga had been doing with Thomas. "...As a Stryker or user, I can use magic weapons, but I can't forge like the Smithians."

"And anghenfēls are beast men?" Min asked.

"Worse. The stuff legends are made of—soulless slags..."

Thomas fell from the sky and landed in the back seat startling Min.

"Hello," he gasped. "I just flew through the air like a bird."

"Evening, officer," Abel said. "I assume Helga informed you about our current situation."

"She told me what you are. But she didn't explain why you were attacked."

"We were actually following Miss White and a gentleman suitor, and some ruffians started following them. Two of them turned into anghenfêls and…"

"Wait a minute! Gentleman suitor? WHO?"

"He only heard that part," Min said.

"It's a man named Leopold Bianca. We suspect he's after a special book hidden in the White manor. We lost track of them during the chase. Hopefully, we can make it back before he finds it."

The door of the vault swung open with a rusty whine. The inside of the vault was all black but for a single light. It illuminated a green, leather-bound book sitting on a black stone pedestal. The book's top and bottom halves were held together by red twine. On the cover was a winged elephant representation, embossed in silver metal. Above that, written in shiny golden letters, were the words: SIV MYRDDIN. Mary walked over to the pedestal.

"It's the book." Leo looked around the room. He seemed uninterested in it. She picked up the book and read the cover: "Siv Myrddin?" What does that mean?

"It means, Book of Myrddin."

"That's a cute name for a book of club secrets…" She turned around and looked at him. "Mr. Bianca? You seem preoccupied?"

"I'm sorry, I'm looking for something."

2:40 a.m., Sunday, February 6th, 1898

"So, why are yeh running away?" The white-haired girl asked.

"He claims our guardians were going to kill me," the girl answered, looking slyly at Leo.

"It's true. I heard them talking about it," he said defensively.

"Why? Were they abusing yeh?"

"No, not really," he answered.

"Not really? It's either yes or no."

"It's not that simple."

"I think what he means to say…" the girl interrupted. "…is that you only got disciplined if you did something dangerous or wrong."

The young woman looked at Leo. She lifted one of her pony tails and pointed it at him "Let me guess, <u>yeh</u> got disciplined <u>all</u> the time?" He didn't respond. "Where I come from, they used to punish yeh by dunking yeh in water or setting yeh on fire."

The girl gasped. "Oh my Lord! That sounds like murder!"

"They called it 'God's divine retribution'." A long moment of silence followed. "But, I'm guessing yuh guardians must be better than that."

"Quite," The girl said. "They've been nothing but sweet and accommodating: They've taken us to exotic lands, fed us extraordinary foods, and this Christmas, they gave me..." She looked over at Leo. He was angry.

"Then why are yeh 'ere?" asked the young woman. "Sounds like yeh don't believe a word he said about yuh life being in danger, do yeh?"

"I...I think he may have heard something, perhaps he misunderstood."

" 'ear that?" She said to Leo. "...Why are you dragging 'er out here with the cold and the throat-cutters in them woods?"

"Stop trying to scare her with danger!" Leo yelled. "Mind your own business, you witch!"

The young lady looked angry. She stood up and slowly walked over to him. "It's not nice to call someone that, mate! Especially after they've offered them a warm place to sleep and food."

"What food? leg of toad?" he joked.

She walked over and pulled the small cauldron away from the fire, using a long rod and placed it on the ground, "No..." She took off the lid, dug a spoon in and picked out some kind of eyeball. "...Eye of newt." She ate a spoonful. "Needs salt." Leo backed away really fast. She put the lid back on the kettle and started walking towards the children.

Mary picked up the book off of the pedestal. "This is interesting leather, what is it?"

"Some say dragon's skin," Leo said running his hands along the walls and looking around for something.

"Flying elephants and dragons? What a darb. What's next, unicorns?" She opened the book and tried to read it. "I don't recognize this language."

"It's the language of the ancients."

"Your clubs sure have a flair for the dramatic, don't they?"

"You have <u>no</u> idea."

"I can't believe my father was harassed for this...this..." She looked over to the pedestal where the book was displayed. There was an inset space under the book housing; something was inside. "What's that?"

Leo stopped what he was doing and ran over to the pedestal. He slowly reached his hand inside and pulled out a black, glass sphere. He held it up to the light to examine it. The blackness inside seemed to move around, like liquid smoke.

"Something new? What is it?" Mary asked.

"It's truth." He looked at her and then the sphere. "Stand back."

"What?"

Leo threw the glass sphere to the ground.

'Outside, Helga came in for a landing on the top of the iron disk "Oh-My-Gods!" she muttered. She ran over to the devil-head lock. "Hope I'm not too late," she said fumbling for her key necklace.

3:14 a.m., Sunday, February 6th, 1898

As the young woman with the white hair approached the children, Leo put himself in front of the girl in the chair. "Now, if I were going to kill yeh and sell that fancy wheel chair there, 'ow would yeh stop me?"

"Stay back!" Leo yelled. He grabbed the crucifix around his neck.

" 'Ow are yeh going to stop me?"

As Leo backed away, so did the girl in the chair.

"Yeh 'ave no plan and no future except for dying on the streets a pickpocket or a poor street rat, and as for 'er, the good lord knows what the big city will do to a pretty little thing like 'er—wheelchair and all! Maybe a quick death is the most charitable thing someone can do for yeh."

"Stay back! I'm warning you!"

"So yuh said."

"Roe arden!" Leo yelled pointing to the fire. Everyone stopped moving and looked at the fire. Nothing happened.

The young woman looked back at Leo and smiled. "Cover yuh throats, luv."

Instead of breaking, the black sphere bounced across the room like a rubber ball. Leo chased after it.

"Mr. Bianca! What on God's earth are you doing? You almost broke it!"

He picked it up. His facial expression looked quite confused. "But it didn't—Why?" He picked up the ball and examined it again. "It's been forged."

"Excuse me?" Mary asked flipping through pages in the book.

"The glass. It's not normal glass…" He looked at the book. "…Unbreakable glass…unbreakable glass…I remember that one… What page? What page?"

"Mr. Bianca, you're rambling."

"May I see the book for a moment?"

Mary looked suspiciously at him. "Why?"

"I just want to look something up."

"Perhaps you can tell me what you're looking for? I fancy I can find it."

"Miss. White…Mary: I know you don't trust me, but I just need to look up one phrase."

"It's Miss White, and NO! I don't trust you no more than those chaps which were chasing after us earlier."

"Y-you saw that."

"Of course I did. I'm not completely daft. Now, either you leave, or I'll get my saber and make you leave."

Leo sighed. "Sorry."

"Excuse me?"

Leo touched her chest. *"Vin din óll!"*

Mary started to protest, but her body was suddenly sliding backwards towards the wall.

The elevator started going upwards at a fast pace. Leo looked over at it, grabbed his crucifix and pointed at the shaft. *"Ah-rohs-fah!"* The elevator ceased operating.

Upstairs, Helga pressed the elevator button over and over. Realizing it was now out of order, she ran as fast as she could to the spiral staircase.

3:15 a.m., Sunday, February 6th, 1898

The girl and Leo backed away from the young woman. The girl was frightened, which made Leo even more afraid. Thoughts raced through his mind for his next plan of action. If he could only remember some forging words which could help them, but not many of them would be enough to actually hurt your opponent. Their guardians had, by choice, left these lessons off the child's forging classes. The best plan he could think of was get close enough to the trees and then try to find a stick while the girl got away. He turned around and checked the path he would be running toward. He spotted a body walking towards them. The young woman saw it too and stopped approaching the kids. It was a large man, dressed like a vagrant. He stepped out of the woods and slowly approached the kids.

"Help!" Leo said. She's trying to kill us!"

The man looked at the young woman. "Don't you worry kids. I won't let her harm you."

"He's dangerous, step away from him." The young woman warned.

"I don't believe you!" Leo yelled.

"Bloody hell…" she complained. "…I thought I could get to the kids before yeh did. I was wondering when yeh two would show up."

"Two?" Leo said.

She gestured backwards. "I'm sure yuh smelly brother is somewhere back there, am I right?"

The man smiled. "Come on out, Charlie." Another large man in similar attire, came out of the woods where she had gestured to. Charlie had a knife in his left hand.

"I told yeh two, back in Cardiff, if I ever saw yeh again I would set yeh on fire."

"Sorry…." the first man said. "…gotta pay you back for Charlie's scar. Ain't that right, Charlie?"

"That's right, Dudley." Leo could see Dudley had an 'X' shaped scar on his cheek.

The young woman put her hands on her hips. "The first slash was for touching on me bum. The second was for beating up on yuh wife."

"Figure we owe you a scar as well; guess where we're going to put it?" He smiled with a mouth full of crooked yellow teeth.

"Sorry..." said the young woman. "...that scar was especially designed for weedy, idle-headed louts like yeh two."

"Bricky girl, got a mouth on 'er." Dudly said. "I'm gonna enjoy sewing it shut."

"Guess I'll start with yeh this time. Maybe I'll but an 'O' on yuh forehead so I can play tic-tac toe." The young woman started to approach Dudley but stopped when he placed his own knife against the neck of the young girl. Leo gasped at the sight of the blade.

"Not so fast..." Dudley warned, "...Don't think yeh want to be doing yuh fancy fighting moves when I got these kids so close to me knife, now do you?" The young woman crossed her arms, and backed away.

"Yeah, that's right," Charlie agreed walking closer to her back. "What do you think we should do with them, Dudley?"

"Don't know Charlie. With 'er, it's easy. Not much we can do with the boy and a gimpy girl. Legends says there are witches in these parts. Suppose we can sell their livers and hearts to them for a favor or two." He laughed.

"You don't know anything about witches," the young woman interrupted. She uncrossed her arms and slowly started wiggling her copper-ringed, left hand fingers in the direction of the fire." *Vetel poi-th,*" she whispered and looked at Dudley's knife.

"What did you call me?" Dudley asked.

"I said, you think witches eat human body parts, ride wooden brooms and are all ugly..." Small amounts of jellied air heat waves traveled from the fire to the direction of Dudley's knife. "...but animal parts are closer to nature than human, and therefore more pure. And witches don't ride brooms—wood isn't very sturdy at high speeds..." The blade on the knife started to glow red from heat. "...And as for ugly, if truth be told, only the most powerful elder witches get ugly, It's a sign of high status."

Charlie smiled. "Well, at least we know you ain't a witch You're not ugly."

"I'm also not an elder."

Dudley screamed and flung the red hot knife out of his hands and onto the dirt.

The little girl looked at the knife on the ground and then at Dudley. "Chair! Back over him!" she yelled. Before he could ask her what she had said, Dudley felt the back of the chair bump into him, knock him to the dusty ground and a tire run over his legs. While he screamed in agony, Charlie approached the young woman and bought his knife down to stab her in the back. She rotated her body so his plunging knife arm came down in front of her, over her shoulder. She grabbed his arm and pushed the blade hand away from her as she pushed her back into his body. With a quick reversal of her position, she turned his wrist upside down, forcing him to go down on one knee in front of her in a submissive pose. Before he could yell in pain, she kicked him in the face and sent him backwards onto the ground.

Dudley got up fast and started to run toward the girl, who had just commanded the chair to go towards Charlie and run over him as well. Leo jumped on Dudley's back. He flipped Leo over his shoulder and stomped twice on his chest, Leo screamed. Before he could do it again, a metal leg knocked Dudley forwards. The chair walked over him with its metallic crab legs.

The young woman walked to the fire and pulled out the metal rod, which earlier had been holding the caldron over the flames. "Curious thing about a teclyn…." she informed Charlie as he stood up and looked around for the knife. "…it doesn't ever heat up. Makes a perfect broom and a pot holder." She held up his knife. "Yeh looking for this?" She threw it into the fire. "Go get it, yeh sheep fart." He ran towards her. With very little effort, she rotated her body and forced him around her and straight into the fire. He landed on the blaze and screamed in agony, when he tried to get out of the fire, she pushed him down with great force with the teclyn and prevented his escape from the hellish death. "Stay in! Yuh not done cooking!" Witnessing his brother's horrible fate, Dudley, lifted himself off of the ground, picked up his knife and started walking towards her, screaming: "I'll kill you! I'll kill all of you! I'll kill you, you horrible witch!"

She pointed to the fire with the teclyn, said "*Roy are don!*", then pointed it towards Dudley. Like a fire magnet, Dudley's body started to heat up and was soon covered in fire, which was transferred in a blazing stream from the camp fire to him. He spun around, screamed and eventually collapsed onto the ground, creating a second campfire. The young woman looked at Leo: "I think that was the forge you were trying to do earlier, am I right?"

Leo didn't respond. He looked over at the girl. Her chair slowly transformed back to normal. "Are you all right?"

She had a look on her face which he didn't expect to see. Instead of fear or horror at all they had gone through, she was... smiling, but this was not one of happiness.

"Are you all right?" he asked again. She rolled the chair away from him towards the young woman. Leo joined her.

"All right?" the young woman asked them. The young girl nodded.

"You killed them," Leo complained.

"Devine retribution," she responded. "...And what are yeh complaining about? I saved yuh arses, and she did mo' to save herself than yeh did—Saved herself, she did. Yeh'l never be able to protect 'er."

"YES-I-WILL! Leo covered his nose. He looked upset. A horrible smell was coming from the fires.

The young woman looked over at the burning bodies. "Blimey. I'll never get used to the smell of burning flesh."

"There they are!" a young voice yelled.

Everyones' attention turned to the sight of the African boy, leading Aunt Gwenhwyvar and the man towards them

The young woman stood in front of the kids to protect them. The young girl put her hand on hers and said: "It's okay. It's my family."

"Are you two okay?" The man asked.

"Yes,"the girl answered. "She saved our lives."

The man looked over at the two smoldering bodies. "Thank you."

"It was no problem. Are yeh their father?"

"Guardian...You're a Coppersmithian."

"Yes...How'd yeh know?"

"Those markings on your teclyn. You're with the House of... Pendle?"

"Yes, sir. And who might yeh be?"

"We are with the House of White."

"Sir!" The young lady got on one knee and bowed her head. "My name is Helga of the House of Pendle. I was sent by the foundry to serve and aid in yuh protection of the Siv Myrddin."

"No, please…" He walked over and helped her up "…No need for that, I have always had a good relationship with the house of Pendle. I would be honored to have you, Helga of the house of Pendle."

Gwenhwyvar walked over to the kids. She looked first at Leo and then the girl. They stared at each other without speaking. Gwenhwyvar had a sad expression on her face. The girl broke down and started crying. Gwenhwyvar bent down and hugged her.

"I'm sorry for running away. I didn't want Leo—"

Gwenhwyvar cut her sentence short. "Shh! I know. Let's go home."

Everyone started to roll and walk to a large, two-horse carriage. Leo turned his attention to the African boy: "You stool pigeon! You ratted us out!" he accused.

"She's my sister…" he responded. "…And I thought you were my brother."

Before they went any further. Gwenhwyvar stood in front of Leo and blocked his path. Leo looked at her and then turned his head, shut his eyes and prepared to be slapped. There was no slap. He slowly opened his eyes and looked back at her. She stared at him, first with the same sad look she gave the girl, then a stern and angry look. "What?" he challenged.

"You want to run away and no longer be part of the House of White? Then you should run away and no longer be part of the House of White." She turned around and walked towards the carriage.

As the carriage pulled away, he heard the girl yell: "No!" He knew she was protesting him being left behind. He didn't run after them. He kept hearing Helga's words echoing in his head: 'Yeh'l never be able to protect 'er.'

Leo found the page in the book he was looking for. Mary was astonished. She wasn't able to move away from the wall; invisible arms were pushing on her. "What is this?" she asked.

"Just a restraining forge."

"How are you doing this? Is it magnets?" He didn't answer. "I knew I shouldn't have trusted you! How foolish of me to believe you were working with my father when in reality, you're working with the elephant people."

"I'm not with them!"

"From where I stand, pinned against this wall, looks like you're one of the bad eggs."

"I'M NOT WITH THEM!" he yelled.

"Of course..." she sarcastically agreed. She tried to struggle and release herself. "...SOMEONE! HELP!"

"Please...be quiet...Oh, here it is." He pointed to a passage in the book.

"MARY!" Helga yelled. They looked at Helga at the top of the stairs.

"Helga! Help!"

Leo held the book in one hand and the black orb in the other. Helga started to run down the staircase. *"Calon Breagus!"* he yelled, tossing the sphere into the air.

Helga pointed her teclyn at him and yelled: *"MELLT!"* A bolt of blue lightning flowed out of her staff and hit Leo in the chest. He was thrown backwards. The second he was struck, Mary was released from her invisible bonds. There was a shattering, breaking sound throughout the room, like ten chandeliers had hit a concrete floor, an almost musical resonance filled the air. The black orb shattered into thousands of tiny black fragments once it came in contact with the floor. An eerie, black smoke flowed out of it and snaked its way around the room. First it approached Helga, then Leo. It ignored them and turned its sight on Mary. As though she were the easiest path to take, the smoke entered her nostrils and mouth until it was completely inhaled. Mary's eyes widened. She appeared to be in shock. She then exhaled white smoke which quickly dissipated in the air.

Helga ran over to her. "MARY! Are you okay? MARY!"

Leo lifted himself upwards into a sitting position. Helga looked at him and then the book. *"Crafanyo dül lo!"* Sections of concrete floor elongated, deformed and stretched until a cage of arms and hands had surrounded the book. Abel, Thomas and Min ran down the staircase.

"Mary?" Abel yelled.

"Protect the book!"Helga yelled pointing. Min jumped from the stairs until she was in front of the arms and hands sculpture.

Abel ran up to Leo and picked him up, ready to punch him. "WHAT DID YOU DO!"

Thomas ran over to Mary to try to revive her, she appeared to have fainted. "What happened to her? Is he after that book?"

"You can...have the...Book," Leo struggled to say. Abel punched him.

"You cur! I knew I should have killed you the minute I saw you!"

"I've seen him before...Who is he?" Thomas asked.

"Parts of the past, best forgotten," Helga informed, rubbing Mary's head. Mary's eyes fluttered and opened. She looked surprised to see Helga.

She looked at Thomas, and seemed confused.

"Mary? Are you all right?" he asked.

"Thomas?" she asked. She looked at Helga. "Helga?"

"Yes, Miss." She and Thomas helped her stand up. She looked over at Abel and Min. "Abel, Min?"

"That's right Miss." Helga smiled. "Yuh gonna be all right, Miss."

Mary looked at Leo. He shook off the punch Abel had given him and wiped the blood away from his mouth.

"Is that...Leo?"

"Yes, Miss. Back again to cause calamity."

A thought entered Mary's mind:

...A large sign announced their arrival into the area currently occupied by the Berkeley Brothers Circus. The little girl is ecstatic, as if magic has happened in her own town. "Mama! Mama! It's a circus!"

Mary shook off the memory and then looked up at Abel:

...Tribal scars formed intricate patterns across their faces. Many in the audience gasped, and some sensitive women fanned themselves to prevent fainting. A young West African boy, around the same age as the two girls, looked over at them.

Mary looked at Min. Min waked over and put her hand on Mary's shoulder. "Are you all right, Mary?" Min's key dangled from her neck. Mary looked at it:

... The dad screamed in pain and tried to protect his daughter, spreading his arms and legs over her in a push-up position. The weight of the beast won

and he collapsed onto his daughter. There was a horrible crunching sound. The little girl saw a flash of bright red, and her body went numb.

Mary screamed: "MAMA!...............PAPA!" Tears ran down her cheeks. She looked up and stared for a long time at the ceiling. Her eyes closed and she fainted away. Helga and Thomas caught her.

Abel grabbed Leo's collar and prepared to punch him again. "You bastard! You killed Mary White!"

"He smiled through bloody teeth. "No...I saved Mary Black."

The Lighthouse which was on Fifth Avenue from 1912-1915, until it mysteriously disappeared

*Photo believed to be of the person
simply known as Professor White.*

Part Seven
TO SEE THE ELEPHANTS

10 p.m., Sunday, February 13, 1898

Young Leo looked around, in case the House of White had hired guards or were using dogs to keep him from returning. There were none. He touched one of the large stones on the eight foot tall wall which ran around the manor. Stone protrusions transmogrified into arms and hands and elongated outwards. As the hands started to grab at him, thick, thorny vines grew out of the ground and over the top of the wall and began to wrap themselves around his head, legs and back. The hands painfully gripped his shoulders and head, while the vines worked their way towards his neck and became tighter and tighter. He knew his time was limited. "Don't you recognize me anymore? It's me, Leo, Leopold of the House of White!" The hands and vines stopped moving. Everything went quiet. The hands retracted back into their normal block form and the vines released him. He rested for a moment and rubbed his neck and arms to alleviate the pain of being strangled. Using the same vines which has previously tried to kill him, he scaled up and over the eight-foot wall and landed in the courtyard behind the mansion. He knew her room was the third one from the left, on the second floor. As luck would have it, that was the wall where the ivy grew the thickest, which would make it easy to climb. He ran toward the wall and went up as fast as he could. As he did, he practiced what he was going to say: "...Hi, Mary, I'm back. I found a captain who will take us to Italy, but he's leaving soon, so pack your things... Don't you worry... I'll be able to protect you." He reached her balcony and crawled over the rail. Mary was asleep in her canopy bed. Leo looked around for her wheelchair. It was stationed in the corner. He silently opened one of the French doors and entered. She appeared at peace. The half moon cast a beautiful blue light over her face, causing her to look like a sleeping porcelain doll. It reminded him of her and the field of blue azaleas. He crept over to her and slowly tapped her shoulder. Mary stirred. He tapped her again. She slowly opened her eyes. "Mary!"he whispered loudly. She turned her head and looked at him. "Hi! Mary. I got us a boat. Pack up your things, I'm going to get you out of here."She lifted herself up and looked at him. It wasn't a look of happiness, more one of confusion. "Hi, get your —"

Leo never finished his sentence. Mary let out an ear piercing scream. "Mary, what's wrong?" She couldn't hear what he was asking because of her continual screaming. "Mary I..." He heard someone coming down the hall. "What's—" Unable to take any more screaming and in fear of being captured, Leo backed away from her. The quick footsteps outside the door and someone yelling: "Mary?" caused Leo to make a hasty retreat. He grabbed onto the ivy vines and lowered himself over the balcony. Halfway down, the branches gave way and he fell on the ground. He quickly got up and ran to the hedge maze. The screaming had stopped. Leo looked up at Mary's balcony to see who had come to her aid. Professor White appeared and looked over the balcony. Leo ducked down. The Professor stuck out his hand and said: "*Headvan Tân !*" In an instant, a glowing light the size of a firefly, but much brighter, appeared from his palm and then another and another. The lights flew off in different directions like search lights. One of the lights shone on Professor White. "Are you all right?" he asked the girl.

"...Yes," she answered as she walked out onto the balcony.

"Mary..." Leo whispered silently. "She's walking?"

"Maybe it was a nightmare?" Professor White said, comforting her.

"It wasn't a nightmare, I saw a strange boy in my bedroom!" she protested.

"Okay, why don't you get some rest? I'll search the grounds."

"Yes, Father."

"Father?" Leo muttered. He sat on the ground.

"What were those little lights, Father?"

"Just an invention of mine, now, lay down and please rest."

Leo turned his back to them and sat on the grass for a while. "She called him father…She was walking…Father?…What did he do to her?"

One of the fireflies flew near Leo's face and illuminated it. To prevent discovery, he swatted at it and it dissipated into tiny sparks. There was another one above him. It illuminated another object, the stern face of Gwenhwyvar.

Many more fireflies flew near them and illuminated their scene. Leo looked at the necklace around her neck with a snake on it. Without thinking twice, Leo grabbed his necklace and pointed at the one around hers. "*Vetel poi-th.*" Her necklace started to glow red hot. She ripped if off of her neck and threw it onto the grass where it started a small fire which quickly went out. Before he could forge another spell, this one on her rings, Gwenhwyvar pointed to his mouth and shouted. "*Sel-yo!*" In an instant, Leo's lips tightly came together. He was unable to open them no matter how hard he tried. He stood up and tried to hit her in the chest. His fist felt like he had hit a brick wall. Gwenhwyvar back-handed him and sent him flying onto the ground.

"You know…" she explained, while walking over and picking up her necklace, the fireflies tracked both of their movements. "… if you had studied longer, you would know how to quench the mouth seal without having to speak…*Droo-so!*" Her necklace fixed itself and she put it back around her neck. "You would learn how to mend broken objects…" She walked over to him, grabbed one of his legs and lifted him up in the air. "…And you would know one of the rules of forging is to <u>never</u> forge against anything living, unless you intend to: draw, shrink, bend, spread, taper, upset, punch, or weld." She carried him into the hedge maze.

"Now, considering you did not mean to change me into something or help me in any way, I can only conclude that your intention for forging on me was to use a punching forge, which includes cutting, slitting, and drifting, in other words: An attack! I believe under the rules of engagement, I now have permission to counterattack in an equal manner. So, what shall it be? Shall I use Copper forging and turn you into a rat?" Leo panicked and tried to yell through stuck lips. "Shall I use Gold and make you forget who you are or forget you ever knew Mary?..." Leo tried to grab at the grass. "...Or shall I use Silver and instantly turn your necklace into metal hands to choke you to death?" Leo quickly took the necklace off and held onto it. "No...I won't do any of that. You know why..." They arrived at a well in the center of the maze. "You see, Leo, in spite of all the trouble you've caused me, there is a part of me that says: One day. One day this impertinent lad can blossom into an honorable man. But until then, until he has suffered just the right amount and learned from his mistakes, he shall aways be a thorny rose bush. But you're not a rose, Leo. You're a dandelion, a weed." She held his leg over the well. Leo screamed as best he could. "You wanted to see Italy? How about starting with the canals of Venice..." She dropped him into the well.

A bucket of water splashed Leo on the face and awakened him. He coughed and sputtered. Helga put the bucket down. "Morning, Leo! Breakfast is ready!" Leo did the best he could to shake the water away from his head. He didn't have access to his hands as he was still held tight by concrete limbs pinning him to vault room's floor. He didn't remember falling asleep. Perhaps Abel had punched him asleep or the fatigue caused by all of the preparations and time to get to this point had finally allowed him a moment to relax. Helga set a plate of sago pudding next to him. "Eat up."

"I don't like pudding."

"Sorry luv. Would yeh like some bangers and mash or toad in the 'ole?"

"Sure?"

"Fine then." She pulled a plate from behind her back containing the ingredients she had just named and set them on the ground, next to the other dish. " 'ere ya go."

Leo's face lit up at the sight of his favorite breakfast. He remembered his predicament. "I seem to have a problem eating it. My arms are a little restrained. If you don't mind?"

"Oh, I'm sorry. 'ere, let me give yeh a hand..." Helga squatted down and held a fork for the bangers and mash and a spoon for the pudding, scooped up a sample from each plate and held them close to his face. "...This hand..." She lifted the fork with the bangers and mash. "...is for when you tell me something that I like to hear..." She held up the other spoon of pudding. "...And this one is for when you tell me something I don't like. Are we clear?" Leo nodded. "Now then...Question: Are you working for the man that destroyed our light house?" He shook his head no. Helga tilted her head sideways and fed him the pudding. He tried to refuse it. "Either this or nothing, mate." He made an awful face after taking a bite of it. "Want to answer that one again?"

"I worked for him back in Europe...briefly on the premise that I would help him get the book...But I couldn't care less about the book, all I wanted to do was return Mary back to normal." She fed him a piece of sausage.

"So, that's what this is all about. All these years, you've been plotting 'ow to take your revenge."

"It's not revenge! It was wrong for them to do that to her! They turned her into that...that pip!"

Helga fed him the pudding. "That pip, as you call 'er, is happy. Been happy for 17 years."

"But it's not real! Her—this—none of this is real! He tried to give her a normal life! We're not Normalu! We're Forgers! That man is coming after that book; they'll always be coming after that book!"

"And you lead him 'ere!"

"I did nothing of the sort! I followed him here! He thinks I'm dead. After I got the information I needed to find out how to break the forge on Mary, I gave him some false information about where the book was. When he found out, he sent some men to kill me. I barely managed to escape. I followed him here to get to the book first! How was I to know he would go to such extraordinary measures to get that damned book?" She fed him the pudding. "What! I'm telling you the truth!"

"I know. I just don't like what yuh saying." She fed him more pudding. "By you pretending as yeh say to help him, yeh really did help him. He's a Gold, Leo. He probably did a weld on yeh and found out what Professor White looked like, worked at. They sank an entire ship of innocent souls just to get to him, yeh know that?"

"The Lusitania? That's a coincidence. You don't know that!"

"They did the same thing three years ago when we bought the book to New York. That time, they used an iceberg."

"He...he didn't do a weld on my mind!"

"How would yeh know?"

"Because...Be..." Leo looked down.

Helga set the utensils down on the plates. "Yeh should have stayed away, Leo…Should have stayed far away." She stood up and took the two plates of half eaten food out of the room.

Helga met Abel in the kitchen, He was holding up different knives and examining them.

"Well?…" he asked. "…Did he tell you anything significant or shall I try it my way?"

"Don't think those will do yeh any good." She slid the food into a garbage pail and the dishes in the sink. "What's done is done. His whole mission was to get one line out of the book to break Mary's bend."

"And you believe him?"

"I do. He had many opportunities to grab the book and run but he stuck around looking for just the right words to release her coal."

Abel sighed and put a knife down. "So, what do we do now? Remember what she was like before?"

"I do. But you know…sometimes there's a part of me that misses that girl."

"But she was so sad sometimes."

"I know. I love the way Mary White is. But Mary Black…when she had those moments of brief happiness, it was…It was more powerful."

"Perhaps. What do you suppose we should do now?"

"Well, I'm going to take her breakfast…You, you should either let Leo go…or kill him. I won't 'old either against you." Helga started preparing breakfast as Abel left the room.

Mary sat upright in her canopied bed, looking at the view from her large window. The view was of the outside front, facing the park. Occasionally a pedestrian would enter and leave the scene as would a horse-drawn cart or an automobile. She sighed, got out of bed and walked over to the window. She touched it. When she waved her hand around, the visuals rippled and distorted, similar to an image in a pool of water. She sat down in a chair next to the window and continued looking at the projection.

There was a knock on the door. She heard the voices of Thomas and Min having what could be a mini argument. She investigated by slowly opening the door and peeking out.

"I'm not going to harm her," Thomas told Min.

"I'm sure that's what that man said," Min countered. She was holding a large Chinese spear called a qiang and blocking the door.

"Where did you get that spear?"

"Chinatown."

"Min! I...Mary?" Thomas looked at her worriedly."...Are you all right?"

Min looked at her with equal concern. Mary appeared saddened to see them both. She turned around, reentered her bedroom and closed the door to them.

Min turned her attention back to Thomas. "Until she says so, nobody gets past me!" She held the qiang up to Thomas's neck. He didn't show fear, only mournfulness.

Thomas went outside and sat in a chair on top of the metal disc which used to be the lighthouse. Next to his feet was a rifle which he had borrowed from Mr. White's armory. He took out a pipe and spent a significant amount of time trying to light it. When he had finished, Helga appeared up the spiral staircase, bringing him a tray of the same ingredients she had offered Leo. "ere yeh go Detective." She set it on his lap.

"I love sago pudding. Thank you, Helga."

"Not at all, Detective."

He started eating the food. Helga looked at the real version of the view which Mary was staring at earlier.

Between bites, Thomas asked Helga some questions. "So... Helga...who is Leo?...Is he with the Belgian?"

"Name's Leopold Bianca. He, Mary, Abel and eventually I, grew up together."

"Really? Like in an orphanage?"

"No...Well, Mary did spend time in an orphanage, had a terrible time there. No, Professor White adopted them all. I came along to help protect the book. Lot o' good that did, eh?"

"Well, the book is still here."

"For now. Those men will try again once they figure out there's nothing in that lighthouse but books of ancient erotica."

"Erotica? I thought they were all religious studies?"

"You ever read an uncensored version of the bible? Blimey, lot'a cheeky devils in that one."

Thomas cleared his throat. "Is he a Forger or a Stryker?"

"Leo had the potential to be a Silversmith, but 'e was exiled. 'e didn't get along too well wiff our leader."

Thomas handed Helga his empty plate. Helga took it and started heading back down.

"So...who is Mary? Really?"

Helga turned around. "In due time, Detective. I'd rather she tell you herself...Yell if you see anything."

Helga returned to the underground and Thomas took out his notebook and reviewed the section pertaining to the Belgian: A map marking an area near the docks and the words, '*Le loyer est bon marché ici*',and a list of some of the richest families in New York under the words, 'Liste de 400'. "Helga!" Thomas called. Within two breaths, she had run back to the top and was holding her teclyn.

"What is it?" She appeared ready for battle.

"I'm sorry, Helga, I didn't mean to alarm you. I simply have a question."

She relaxed and lowered her staff. "' 'ere, let me make it easier for me." She gave him one of the coins with a two headed snake on one side and a winged elephant on the other.

"I saw some coins like that in the Belgian's room."

"They're very convenient for forging on the spot. Made of pure ahrion and eyve." She cupped the coin between her two hands.

"What's eyve...Actually, you never explained what ahrion is."

"Ahrion is a purified and blessed form of silver and eyve is the same for gold." She closed her eyes. "Forging should only be performed using pure metals. All others and you get terrible results......*Aufheav fuh vave, Aufheav fuh fee.*" She handed the coin back to him. "Right, 'ere ya go. Just keep this coin with yeh, for good luck."

"Okay...Thanks." Thomas examined the coin to see if it had changed in any way. As far as he could tell, it was the same; the only difference, it felt warmer.

"So, what did yeh need when yuh called, Detective?"

"Oh, right...Do you speak French?"

"Of course. You live in Britain, gotta talk to yuh neighbors."

"Good. So what does..." he checked his notes. "...Le loy-yeah es bon mar-che e-c and list de 400 mean?"

"Le loyer est bon marché ici? That's means rent is cheap here and liste de 400 means what it sounds like, the list of 400."

"Hmm. The Belgian wrote that and circled the docks near the 100th block area next to the East River. Why would he care about cheap rental prices?"

"No idea sir, wish I could help."

"No matter. For now I'll find out why he had my cousin's name on a sheet of <u>her</u> stationary on <u>his</u> premises." Thomas stood up. "Can you get Abel to take my place?"

"Of course. Just be careful, Detective. This Gold Forger is right powerful. It's one thing to control elephants, it's another to make them fly and be strong enough to lift buildings."

"Right." Thomas put on his straw boater hat and departed.

Min knocked on Mary's door. Mary didn't respond. Min entered without permission, carrying a tray of food which Helga had prepared. "Helga made you breakfast. I tasted it all to make sure she wan't trying to poison you."

Mary smiled a little. "You don't have to worry about Abel, Helga or even Thomas harming me. I trust them...at least when it comes to physical harm."

Min set the tray down on the bed. "Do you want me to get you anything?"

"No. Thank you." Before Min could leave, Mary called to her. "Min...stay with me." Min walked back over and sat on the edge of the bed. "How are you?"

"How am I? You should be more worried about yourself. What happened to you?"

Mary sighed. "I was killed."

Min gasped. "You're dead?"

"No. I was dead, and now I'm alive."

"That's good, right?"

"It is neither good nor bad...Much like myself."

"I don't get it."

Mary grabbed Min's hand. "The Mary White you knew is dead, Min. She never really existed"

Friday, February 11, 1898

Young Mary walked down the hallway with a large book balanced on her head. The other members in the House of White waited in the music parlor. Near the window, Helga played the song 'Gymnopédie', by French composer and pianist Erik Satie on a large golden harp They watched Mary's entire journey as she walked along the carpeted path, the perfect model of grace and poise. When she entered the parlor, it was like the entire room exhaled in relief.

"I did it!" she exclaimed. She took the book off of her head and re-shelved it.

"Well done, Mary." Gwenhwyvar praised. Mary walked over to Professor White and hugged him.

"Looks like you'll be running by the end of the week," Helga joked.

"She still won't be able to beat me!" Abel teased.

"We shall see," Mary bragged.

"Now then," Gwenhwyvar insisted, "shall we continue your lesson?"

"Yes."

Gwenhwyvar held up a silver stick. "This is what Forgers call an anvil or a teclyn, but the Dayfides call a magic wand. Throughout history, anvils take on many forms: magician's wands, the staffs of biblical figures leading tribes out of Egypt, scepters of great leaders, magical swords embedded in stones—any story involving a magical weapon is all based on forging. But to forge, you only need a personalized object made out of ahrion, eyve, cop, aviv, deave or hiyaguh, with which to focus your smithing. To the Dayfides, an anvil has to be in stick shape..." She held up a pen. "...But, Helga's teclyn, made out of cop, is a harp at the moment. This pen is ahrion, as are my rings, my necklace and now, your spine."

Mary felt along her back. It's ahrion?"

"Yes, dear. It's in actuality an alloy, a mixture of ahrion, eyve and cop

"Does that mean I can forge whenever I wish?"

Whenever you wish."

"May I?"

"Of course dear. What is it that you wish to forge?"

"I...I want to do a location forge. I want to find out if Leo is all right."

Gwenhwyvar and the Professor White looked at each other. "... I understand," she concurred. "Go and retrieve something personal of his."

Mary hurried out of the room.

"Are you sure this is okay?" Professor White asked.

"Yes, it'll be fine. Better to put this whole matter to rest."

Mary returned with a fishing rod. "I found this. He loved fishing."

"Okay, dear. Inveniet can only be used to locate loved ones, which is good because you don't want your enemies to be able to find you. I want you to hold onto that fishing rod and concentrate. Think about Leo. Not what he looks like but who he is, your relationship, what's in his heart and finally his place in this world." Mary closed her eyes and did what Gwenhwyvar had said. "Now… repeat after me… *"Doe-doe he da meed."*

"Doe…Doe…"

"Doe-doe he da meed."

"Doe-doe he da meed." The fishing rod became warm in her hand. She thought about Leo. Who he was: her friend; his relationship to her: brother; what was in his heart: care, bravery and love; and finally, his place in this world: a great Silversmithian.

I see him!" Mary exclaimed. "…He's in a town, it's…Cardiff. He's…down by the docks, asking a question.…It's…He asking ship owners if they'll take him to Italy…He's…"

"He's what?" Gwenhwyvar asked.

"He's leaving…He's leaving…He's going away…Without me.… Just like my parents." Mary began to cry. Helga stopped playing the harp.

Gwenhwyvar put her arm around her. "It's all right, dear."

"IT'S NOT!" Why do people always go away from me?"

"Dear, Leo chose to leave."

"Then he could choose to stay!" Mary began to cry more. Gwenhwyvar held Mary tighter. She looked at Professor White. He was sad, for more than one reason. He put his hand on Mary's shoulder. "This…this is always going to get in her way," he complained.

"You shouldn't!" Gwenhwyvar pleaded.

"As long as the coal is in her heart…she shall always live the life of a heart-broken Dayfide."

"We don't know that."

"Yes, we do. You said so, yourself."

"What I saw was a road with many paths. Two of them lead in that direction, but the third…"

"The third can give her a chance."

"The third will require removing her coal along with other memories…It's too broad."

"But it's better than a lifetime of…this!" He gestured to Mary, still crying.

"I won't allow it."

"As the head of our foundry, I will accept your ruling…but, shouldn't you ask her?"

"She's just a child."

"I'm not a child!" Mary yelled. "Stop talking about me as if I'm not here!"

"I'm sorry, dear, you're right, this does involve you," Gwenhwyvar apologized.

"What are you talking about?"

Gwenhwyvar and Professor White looked at each other. Gwenhwyvar stood the girl up and looked her in her eyes. "There is an old Gold forge from ancient Rome called Calculus Remotio, or 'coal removal'. What this does, it moves the most painful memories from your heart and places them in a vessel. The problem with this forge is that you may lose other memories which although painful, are significant in your life, if the forge turns into Damnatio Memoriae, or 'condemnation of memory'. He wants to do this to you because as long as you have the painful memories of your parents dying, you will never be able to forge.

"He wants to remove my bad memories?"

"Yes."

"Then do that."

"Mary, It's too dangerous! If you go through with that, you could lose more memories than you expect. The bad and the good memories could be affected; not only your parents dying, but every Christmas you've ever had with them as well. Is that what you really want?"

Mary shook her head no.

"Then it's settled."

Saturday, February 12, 1898

Gwenhwyvar came downstairs for breakfast. There was laughter coming from the dining room. When she entered she was surprised to see Mary balancing a spoon on her nose, entertaining Abel and Helga. Professor White sat across from her, smiling.

"I told you I could do it!" Mary exclaimed before laughing.

"I stand corrected," he relented.

Mary put the spoon down. "You know what I want to do today?" she announced.

"What's that?" Abel asked.

"I want to build a boat!"

Helga laughed. "Are you off yuh onion? Why would yuh want to do that?"

"I was reading this jolly good book by Mark Twain. In it, the main characters, living in the colonies, sail down the Mississippi river in a boat and I thought, wouldn't it be smashing to do that down the River Taff, all the way to Cardiff?"

"So you can find Leo?" Helga asked.

There was a long pause. Mary looked at her with confusion. "Leo?...Who's Leo?"

Abel and Helga looked at each other and then Professor White. He turned his gaze to Gwenhwyvar. Her face was one of extreme contained rage, like a bonfire.

"Anyway, wouldn't that be fun, father?" Mary asked.

"Y-yes. Yes, quite..."

Gwenhwyvar turned around and started walking fast through the hallway. While she walked, all doors automatically slammed shut behind her.

"I can't believe your father would do that," Min bemused.

"He's not my father."Mary corrected.

"Oh, right."

"My name is Mary Elizabeth Black. I grew up in Chatsworth, Illinois, the daughter of Noah and Mabel. My...parents...My real parents..." Mary started to cry but held it in. "...d-died in an attack by a Forger on a circus in 1892. I was taken in by the House of White and raised overseas with Abel, Helga and Leo. Without permission from our leader, he removed the memories of the attack on my parents, along with any memory of them or Leo. In order to fill the gaps, he replaced the memory hollows with Mary Elizabeth White.

"Why did he do that?"

"He felt responsible for my parents' death, for all the deaths that occurred that day. I was now his daughter, born and raised in Great Britain. My mother...her mother, died of an illness when she was five...I've now lost two mothers..." Mary wiped away a tear.

Alva Vanderbilt Belmont hit the red ball with her mallet. Instead of traveling through the hoop, it stopped short by a few inches. Alva cursed her luck in the most polite and silent way she could. Madam Blanche took her turn on the course and hit her own white ball. It traveled fast and strait. It knocked Alva's ball off the course and still managed to travel through the hoop.

"My word." Alva exclaimed. "Are you sure you've never played croquet before?"

"Mais non, this is the first time. Perhaps it is the luck of the beginner, non?"

"I suppose so. It's your turn again."

Madam Blanche walked over to further thrash Alva in the game. Thomas made an appearance in the yard behind the manor. He said hello to George, the servant, and made his way over to Alva.

"Cousin Thomas, nice to see you again. Two times in one month," Alva joked.

"Alva, Miss…" Thomas tipped his hat to Madam Blanche. She bowed her head to him.

"What can I do for you, cousin Thomas…unless this is a social visit…croquet?"

"No, thank you, I can't stay long, I need to get back to Mary's"

"How is she? I heard her lighthouse collapsed, is that true?"

Thomas cleared his throat. "A good explanation as any—she's fine, little under the weather."

"Poor dear. She's really taking her father's death hard. I guess we all mourn at our own speed."

"Yes…Yes we do. Anyway, I have a question for you."

"Of course, ask me anything."

"Have you ever seen this?…" He unfolded the paper with the list of 400 on Vanderbilt stationary and handed it to her. She looked at it with a furrowed brow.

"This is…this is our house stationary. Who wrote this?"

"That's what I'm trying to find out. Did you?"

"It's not my handwriting, and it's in French."

"But you went to a French boarding school, did you not?"

"Yes, that was years ago. But I would remember writing this. Where did you find it?"

"In a…in a hotel."

"How strange. Why does it have the list of 400 on it?"

"Perhaps you can tell me."

"Cousin Thomas, I didn't write this!"

"Then perhaps you can explain how your stationary ended up in a hotel."

"Thomas! I'm not one of your irrefutable lowlife reprobates! When I tell you I have no idea how my stationary ended up in whatever flophouse you are talking about, I mean it!"

"Sorry, Alva, I didn't mean to insinuate. It is possible someone stole your stationary; for what purpose I am unsure. But can you tell me if you know what: Liste de 400 means?"

"As a Vanderbilt, surely you know who the 400 are?" Thomas shook his head. Alva rolled her eyes. "Do you ever read magazines? Thomas, Caroline Webster Astor created that list over 40 years ago. It lists the top 400 richest and most influential families in New York. It's also the number of people Mrs. Astors' ballroom can accommodate during a party. Speaking of which, are you coming to the soirée tonight?"

"Is that tonight?"

Madam Blanche walked over. "Cousin Thomas, are you playing?"

"I am not."

"Oh." She had a sad look on her face. "Oh, you will show me how to hit the ball, non?"

"Pardon?"

"I do not know how to hit the ball correctly."

"I don't think that's true," Alva countered.

"Non, Cousin Thomas. Show me how to croquet."

"Well…"

"Show me please." She positioned herself until her back was against his front, she took his hands and put them on hers in order for him to guide her. "Like this, non?"

Thomas blushed. "Uh, yes, that's fine…" He helped her hit the ball and quickly backed away from her. The ball traveled perfectly through the next hoop. "…I think you have the hang of it."

"Thank you, Cousin Thomas. Are you coming to the party tonight?"

"I was just discussing that with him," Alva added.

"I'm not sure. Mary was supposed to go with me, but she's not feeling well."

"Oh?" Madam Blanche asked. "This Mary, would she mind if you save one dance with me?"

"I'm not sure how that would go."

"Please try to get her to come, Thomas." Alva pleaded. "It'll be good for her. They'll be lots of socialites from all over Europe."

"European socialites?"

"Yes. All recently moved here because of the war."

"Hmm, including from Belgium and France?"

"Of course."

"Well...All right. I guess it couldn't hurt."

Abel was pretending to clean the Silver Ghost, but in reality he was guarding the front of the house. Within easy reach on the front seat was a shotgun, a revolver and a dagger. He polished the car's finish until he could see his reflection in the hood. While looking at his face, another face appeared next to his. Abel jumped back and took a defensive position. The other person was Min.

"Min! You scared me half to death. Don't sneak up on me like that!"

"Sorry. I've come to let you know that Mary wants to see you."

"Oh. She must be feeling better! Tell her I'll be right in."

Abel was not the only one Mary had called. Helga was already by Mary's bedside when he arrived at the bedroom.

"Mary! How are you?" Abel exclaimed, running to her side. He grabbed her hand.

She patted his hand and slipped out of his grip. "I'm fine."

"I'm so sorry we let Leo do this to you. I never thought he would come here for that. I really thought he was here for the book."

"It's okay," Mary sadly remarked. "No one is to blame."

"Still..." Helga said. "...e's lucky I didn't get to him first."

"Please don't punish, Leo."

"But Miss..."

"No! There is to be no more pain. No more hurting, there's been enough."

"If you say so Miss."

"STOP CALLING ME MISS!" Mary yelled.

Abel and Helga were shocked. Min peeked inside from the hallway.

"Sorry...Mary," Helga apologized.

Mary looked down. "All these years...all this time...you two worked for me as if you were my maid and butler...Why?"

"It was our choice," Helga answered.

"But why? You gave up your lives, for what reason? To guard that book?"

"No, Miss...No, Mary. We did it because we wanted to protect not just the book, but you."

Abel interrupted. "When you were changed to Mary White, we made a decision that you should have a normal life and we could handle all of the occult activities. That way, you could help us keep one foot in the world of the Dayfides. By being with you we could be grounded to the rest of the world. Professor White decided not to train you in forging or even talk to you about it any more. We agreed and took on our new roles."

"For 17 years?"

"We've enjoyed every last minute of them," Helga rejoiced, putting her hand on Mary's. Abel nodded in agreement.

"No!" Mary yelled. "I won't have it! You two missed out on falling in love, getting married, having kids! All for what?"

"Mary, Coppersmiths don't get married or have kids. It's a coven."

"And I simply keep my love life to myself," Abel added.

"It doesn't matter. You two need to go out there and live without having to worry about me or that God-cursed book."

"But I'm bound to protect it," Helga stated.

"Then as the elder member of the House of White..."

"No Miss, don't do it!"

"...I hereby relieve you of your duty."

"No!...No!...No...." Helga looked down and put her hands on her face.

"Now that you are relieved. You may go about your way. Go back to the coven. Be happy."

Helga cried. Abel put his hand on her shoulder.

"As for you, Abel...you're dismissed as my butler."

Abel sighed. He stood up and helped Helga stand. "Thank you for your years of employment...Miss White. I would appreciate a letter of recommendation."

"Of course..." Mary's lips quivered to prevent herself from crying.

Abel walked Helga out of the room.

12 a.m., Sunday, February 13th, 1898

Gwenhwyvar threw Leo into the well. He fell a lot longer than he had expected, until he hit the water at the bottom. He immediately tried to swim to the water's surface, but it was difficult to do. The water was pulling him down, as if he had a rope tied to his legs. The more he struggled, the more it pulled on him until he reached what he was certain was the bottom. 'She really is killing me!' he thought. He looked down and saw light. Moonlight shone from the bottom of the well. He looked up and saw darkness; he was upside down. He quickly did a somersault and righted himself until the moonlight was above him. He quickly swam upwards. Feeling his oxygen starting to give out, he swam faster. The moment he broke through the surface of the water, the very last bubble of air left his body. There was no stone wall around him, as he had expected. He was not deep in the well but on the surface of a canal. Surrounding him were buildings pressed right up to the water, connected by bridges. Boats filled the sides of the canal and a few traveled through the middle. A gondola made its way over to him. The operator, upon seeing Leo, stopped paddling and began to reach out his hand.

"Bambino, perché sei in acqua?" he asked.

"What?"

"Nuoto?"

"I don't…?"

"Sei inglese…You, English?" He lifted Leo out of the water.

"Yes. Where am I?"

"Don't you know?"

"No."

"You hit you head? You in Venezia."

"Venezia…Venice?"

"Si, Venezia."

Leo laid down inside the bottom of the boat and looked up at the moon.

Another bucket of water splashed Leo on the face and awakened him. He coughed and sputtered. He was still on the floor of the White household. This time, Mary held the bucket of water.

"You have got to find a better way to wake someone up around here." He realized another change—he wasn't bound by concrete arms anymore. "I'm free?"

"My conception of freedom—The value of a thing sometimes does not lie in that which one attains by it, but in what one pays for it—what it costs us. Nietzsche said that; such useless information."

"Didn't sound useless to me." Leo sat up

"Not what he said; he was brilliant. It's the fact that I know so much about him...about a lot of things. All part of Mary White's life. A life that was a lie."

"I'm sorry you had to go through that."

"What's done is done." She carried the book into the vault, returned and then shut the door.

"They're going to come back for that, you know."

"I know. It won't do any good. Even if they completely decimated this entire neighborhood, this safe wouldn't have a scratch on it. Its been forged.

"And the key?""

Mary held out her hand holding two copies of her key she had collected from her former housemates. "You mean these? I plan on throwing these into the deepest parts of every ocean."

"If they can't have the book, they'll just kill you."

"I've died three times already."

"What about all that knowledge in the book? You could help the Dayfides evolve."

"I'm–going–to–end–THIS!"

The door chime sounded upstairs, Min activated the spiral staircase to the outside. It was Thomas. He noticed how sad Min looked. "Min? What's wrong?"

"Abel and Helga left," she sadly moaned.

"What?" Left where?"

"Mary told them to leave."

"What? That's absurd, why?"

"I don't know."

"Where is she?"

"On the bottom floor with that guy."

Thomas took off his hat and stomped inside.

Downstairs, Leo still sat on the floor, drying his hair with a towel

Mary looked at the two keys. "My whole life was created as a facade to hide the unusual activities of everyone else—like a distracting debutante!"

"Even I'm not sure if that's what their motivation was."

"Even so, it's the result. And now that I'm back, I can stop all this socializing and galavanting around like a happy dingbat."

Leo started to stand up. "Well…Starting over is hard to do. I know—had to raise myself after they dumped me in Italy, didn't even know Italian…" When He stood up, he lost his footing and started to tumble forwards "Whoa!" Mary caught him before he could fall. "Sorry, legs fell asleep." She held onto him. They looked at each other in the eyes.

Thomas stood at the top of the room's spiral staircase, witnessing the accidental embrace. "Ah-hem," he intervened, clearing his throat. Mary quickly pushed Leo away. "I hope I'm not interrupting anything."

"No, of course not," Mary stammered, nervously.

"Hey! I know you," Leo said.

"Pardon?"

"You're that fella I pulled away from that trolley car."

"Trolley car?"

"Yeah, you were almost killed. You must have really been half seas over."

"I'm sorry, I have no recollection of that event."

"I bet you don't," Leo laughed.

"How may I help you, Thomas?" Mary asked.

"Did you send Helga and Abel away?"

"Yes, I did?"

"Why?"

"Because my whole life with them was all a ruse. Created by my fa–Professor White to protect me from the people that attacked us."

"I don't fully understand what you're talking about, but from what I've seen of Helga, she's the best protection you can get from the monsters I've seen."

"Don't have to worry chief, I'm not a bad Forger, myself," Leo bragged.

"Leo…" Mary turned to him. "…you're going to have to go, also."

"What?"

"Like I said, I'm going to end this."

"Whatever do you mean?" Thomas asked.

"Just what it sounds like, Thomas. I'm going to get rid of the reason anyone would ever want to hurt me, you or anyone else I l...care about."

"Mary," Thomas said, "I want to protect you, as well as bring these people to justice."

"He'll kill you."

"Not if I can get him first."

"She's right, old boy," Leo scoffed. "These are not your run of-the-mill Forgers."

"You seem to know a lot about the man I'm looking for. Care to share some of that information?"

"Sorry, can't help you. The more you Dayfides are out of harm's way, the better."

"There's that word again...what's a Dayfide?"

"Sheep..." Mary answered. "...It's an insult. Forgers don't consider regular people on equal grounds."

"Well, this sheep is going to find the wolf on my own, without your special hocus-pocus. I'll be arresting him at The Astor's party tonight."

"Thomas!" Mary call out. "Please, just forget about all of this. I don't want anything to happen to you."

"Sorry, Mary. It is my duty as an officer and as your friend."

"But..."

"Now, if you'd excuse me, I have to go iron my waistcoat." Thomas climbed the stairs.

"Don't take any wooden nickels!" Leo called out. "That Dayfide is either brave or very stupid."

"He's not stupid. He's the bravest, sweetest man I know!" Mary corrected.

"Ahh, are you sweet on him?"

"Leo...you need to leave."

"What?"

"You've done your duty...You can go."

"Mary, we have years to catch up on."

"Leo, the Mary Black you knew is no more real to me than Mary White."

"What! That's the real you!"

"How do you know?"

"Because I knew you when we were kids."

"And now, I am a woman. Do you understand?"

"I said I was going to protect you, and I will."

"Leo."

"Do you want me to throw him out?" Min called from the top of the stairs.

"That won't be necessary. Good day, Leo, and I guess I should say thank you for releasing me. But you need to go far away from me, now."

Leo looked at Min and then Mary. He nodded and slowly climbed the spiral staircase.

Min knocked on Mary's bedroom door and then entered. Mary was laying down with her back to the door. "Mary?" Min asked.

"Hello, Min."

Min slowly walked over to her. "I was going to make you some food but I didn't see any rice in the pantry."

"Oh, I'm sorry. Do you wish to go buy some?"

"Yes, I could do that."

"There is a green, crocodile-skinned brief case in the library if you need money. There is always money inside of it."

"Is it magical?"

Mary thought for a moment. "I guess it is. I never thought about it...I never thought about anything," she lamented.

Min walked over and almost patted Mary's shoulder but stopped. "I'll be back soon to make you stir-fried rice. Will you be okay here?"

"Yes. Please, go."

Min exited and closed the door. A second later, Mary heard the pinging sound her buttons made when it was time to tighten them. "Min?" Min was already out of earshot. "I guess it can wait."

The second ping woke Mary up. She sat up in bed and felt her back. "Min?" she called out. "Min?" there was no answer. Mary wanted to get out of bed. She wanted to move her legs but something was wrong. 'Did I sleep wrong? Are my legs asleep?' She used her hands to move her legs over the edge of the bed. Her limbs felt weak. 'Perhaps I need some blood in them.' She used her arms to push herself up. Clumsily she stood up. "What's going on?" She took a step and then another. The third was impossible; her legs gave way and she collapsed onto the floor; her legs didn't respond anymore to her brain's command. "Min!" she called out. She crawled across the floor to the nearest chair. It was hard. All of her weight was on her arms. "I can't walk!" She made it to a chair and tried to pull herself up. Usually, she would have no trouble doing gymnastics but it was like her energy was half of what it usually was. "I can't pull myself up. What's wrong with me?" After trying and failing twice to pull herself up to the chair, Mary rested for a moment. She took the key from around her neck and tried to tighten her buttons herself. She was only able to do the lower four, but the others required too much contortion. "Blast!" she yelled. It was then, she noticed the thumping sound. "What is that? Min?" The thumping sounded like something hitting a door down the hallway over and over. "Is someone trying to get in?" the thumping continued over and over until there was the sound of someone crashing through a door. "Oh god! Who is that?" Mary looked around for somewhere to hide. 'Under the bed!' She started crawling towards her bed. A squeaking metallic sound came down the hallway towards her bedroom. Mary was in a panic. 'I've got to crawl faster!' She pulled herself along the floor with great difficulty, her energy level got worse and worse by the second. The squeaking sound arrived at her door and stopped. Mary stopped crawling to keep them from knowing she was inside the bedroom. There was a long silent pause. She looked at the door and tried her best not to breathe too hard. Her rapidly beating heart was making the most noise in the room.

Suddenly, there was a great banging on her door. The person was ramming themselves against her door repeatedly. Mary screamed and covered her mouth, realizing the mistake of making a noise. It took an extreme physical effort to make it under the bed. The crashing continued and increased in aggressiveness. She made it under the bed frame and had to pull her legs in to keep them from being spotted. Within seconds, the door was forced open with a loud crash, knocking over a bottle of perfume on her vanity. Mary tightly closed her eyes and clinched her fist. 'What can I do? Should I try to punch him? I haven't got any more strength! I shouldn't have let anyone leave the house! I've doomed myself! I've doomed the world. I can't let it end like this. Please, someone help me! Abel! Helga! Min, Thomas, Leo,——anybody!'

Tuesday, February 8, 1898

Professor White held a needle in his hands. It was filled with ahrion. "This is going to be excruciating, but only for a second." The girl lay on her belly on a white, cloth-covered operating table. She was in a laboratory in the basement of the manor. She had never been in this room before. She wasn't sure if it was because there had never been a need to use this room, or if the large number of beakers, test tubes, electric devices and small caged animals would provide a dangerous playground for a 10-year-old girl.

Aunt Gwenhwyvar was there also. Like Professor White, she was wearing a white outfit for surgery, including a mask. He walked over to Mary and with a gloved hand felt along her spine. "Usually this procedure could be done with only one injection. But we waited so long to get hold of the forge from the second half of the book, now, it will take eight." He took the needle and screwed it into a large metal device hovering above the girls back. Seven other needles, all filled with ahrion were lined up parallel to her back. Above the needles hung a spherical, copper-colored device; below, a series of gears, small pumps and rubber tubes, all twisting and expanding up to the ceiling in different directions. "With this, we can get the whole thing done in one, without repeatedly putting you through more injections."

Professor White nodded to Gwenhwyvar. She walked over and applied iodine to the girls entire back. She used the back of her hand to stroke Mary's head.

Professor White walked over and grabbed the Siv Myrddin off of a pedestal. "Now, after we inject you, I will say the words. If all goes well you will be walking by the end of the day."

"And if not?" Gwenhwyvar asked.

"If we have waited too late, the ahrion will be unstable and will have to be adjusted every couple of hours."

"For how long?"

"For the rest of her life, I suppose. But, it will still be better than being in a chair all of the time."

Gwenhwyvar thought about what Professor White had said. She bent down to Mary's ear. "Are you sure you want to go through with this, dear?"

"Yes. Yes, I do."

Gwenhwyvar put a wooden spoon in Mary's mouth, between her teeth. "Here, bite down on this if it hurts." Gwenhwyvar stepped back and put her hands on a large lever. She nodded to Professor White. He nodded back. Gwenhwyvar pulled a lever. The tubes flexed, swelled up and moved, as air was pumped through them. It reached the needles and all at once, the needles inserted into her back. The girl bravely gritted her teeth on the wooden stick and bore the pain. Ahrion slowly moved down the valves and injected itself into her spine. The last thing she remembered before passing out was the sound of the wooden stick breaking and a sorrowful Gwenhwyvar saying: "be strong."

She opened her eyes to see what her future assailant's feet looked like. There were no legs. She looked around and saw no one, anywhere. "Is he flying?" She looked around the floor of the room, the only thing she saw were wheels. 'Why are there wheels here? Is it someone in a wheel chair?' No movement was being made by her nor the potential assailant. Suddenly, there was a bell sound. It seemed familiar. It rung again. 'I know that sound!' She crawled to the edge of the bed and slowly peeked her head out to look up at whoever was making the sound. Her investigation revealed shiny, silver wheels on the side of a red velvet seat and behind the seat, a series of shiny sprockets and gears. "My... chair?" She pulled herself all the way out. The chair remained still. Mary was about to grab the foot hold and pull herself up, until she remembered the special properties of the chair. "Pick me up, please." The chair made a bell sound. It turned in her direction and the seat expanded to the ground in front of her. She crawled onto the seat and it immediately lifted her up and off the ground. After a little bit of twisting around, she was sitting in her old wheelchair. "Where did you come from? Were you in this house the whole time? And how did you know I would need you? Can you show me where you've been for 17 years?" The bell on the chair rang. The chair immediately turned around, sped out of the bed room and headed down the hallway.

At the end of the hallway was a new expansion. The wall which used to be there had become an open door, revealing another hallway made of metal. The wall door looked like it had been forced open.

"That would explain the racket down the hallway. You must have sensed that I was on the floor and needed help." The chair traveled through the metal hallway and came to a metal door. It was locked. Mary felt around and noticed it was a clo keffin. Repeating the solution to the vault containing the Siv Myrddin, she reversed the key, inserted it and opened the door. She immediately heard the sound of rushing water. "What in the world? Go in slowly," she commanded. The chair rolled inside the dark room.

She was on a long, iron walkway with metal handrails. As the chair moved along, some caged lights automatically came on. She was in a cave. This was understandable, considering the house was already underground. What didn't make sense to her was the sound of the waterfall. "Where is that water coming from?" After reaching the end of the walkway, the chair changed its tires to stairs mode and rolled her down three flights. She screamed briefly. At the bottom flight was a large underground pond. The chair rolled onto a small wooden dock. It went a little further and when the next set of caged lights cut on, illuminating her destination, the chair stopped and rang a bell.

Unveiled in front of her was a large, black, metal ship.

"What is that?" yelled Min from the top walkway.

Startled, Mary jumped in her seat and then caught her breath. "Min?"

Min ran down the flights of metal steps and met Mary on the bottom. On each of her shoulders, She was carrying 50 pound bags of rice. She set them down. "What is that...what is this room? Why are you in a wheelchair?"

"Many questions, one answer: Professor White."

"Your fa...the man that raised you?"

"Yes." Mary looked at the ship. "This used to be the CSS Virginia It was an ironclad warship built by the Confederates during the Civil War. It was destroyed over 50 years ago by its crew after it got stuck in a river in Virginia. My father discovered the wreckage and used forging to raise and change it into this." Mary rolled the chair next to the ship. She rapped twice on the metal hull. "We used to travel all over the world in this, before they took away my memory. From then on, it was by conventional methods. It could travel from New York to London in only two days."

"What? That's impossible."

"This is no ordinary ship."

"What's it doing down here?"

"He must have been using it…Curious…why didn't he take this instead of the Lusitania? He'd still be ali…" She turned her back to Min and regained her composure."…If you'd please do me the honor…." Mary pointed to her back.

"Your back! Is that what happens when you don't tighten them?" Min took her personal copy of the key from around her neck and walked behind Mary.

"Appears so…" Min opened the back of Mary's blouse and started turning the buttons.

"…Apparently, I lose the use of my legs if I don't reset these every six hours. This is going to make getting rid of the keys harder to deal with."

"You won't be able to walk again."

"I know, but to save the world from that book, I'll gladly spend the rest of my days in this chair." Min tightened the last button. There was a bell sound. Mary moaned in pleasure.

"Are you all right?"

"Yes, dear. It feels great…" She stood up and stretched out her arms. "…I will miss that feeling, though." Min was about to hand the key to her. "Do you want this back?"

"No, hold on to it, for now."

Mary and Min ate the stir-fried rice Min had made. They ate at the small servant's table in the kitchen, Mary felt eating at the fancy table in the dining room was too formal, when it was just the two of them. Her silence while eating prompted Min to enquire about her thoughts.

"Pardon me?" Mary asked, breaking free of her concentration.

"I said, do you like the food?"

"Oh! Yes, quite! Sorry I didn't say anything. No, it's quite delicious. How did you learn how to make this?"

"My mother."

"It's tasty. Thank you for making it. I'm afraid my culinary skills were never as developed as my other attributes."

"Because Helga did all of the cooking?"

"Yes."

"I miss them."

"They've only left hours ago."

"I know. I still miss them."

"It is for their own good and safety."

"What about me?"

"Pardon?"

"What about me? Are you going to send me away also?"

"I haven't decided. After all, you're still a child."

"I can defend myself better than you can."

"True. But wherever you end up, I want it to be a safe environment where you can learn and live and laugh—a place far away from danger."

"And what about you?"

"What about me?"

"Once you get rid of the keys and me. What will you do?"

Mary thought for a moment. "I guess I haven't really thought about it. I've never had the opportunity to do anything for myself in a long time. There is a possibility the bad people will catch up to me one day."

"Which is why you'll need me, for protection."

"I'm sorry, no. I told you, I will use every resource to make sure you enjoy the rest of your life, far away from all of this."

"Why are you trying so hard to get rid of me?"

"Min, I'm not trying to get rid of you."

"You acted like you wanted to take me into your house and take care of me! Was that a lie?" Min began to get upset. "I should have stayed on the streets of Chinatown! At least there I was taking care of myself!"

"Min, that was dangerous…"

"Danger doesn't matter when you have family looking out for you! I'd gladly face any danger if it meant seeing my mother again! But not you! You send everybody away without asking them how they feel!"

"Min I…"

Min stood up from the table and took her plate and chopsticks out of the room. "…I thought you liked them…I thought you liked ME!"

"Min!" Mary called out. She didn't follow her. She didn't know what to say. "I'm doing this for them…I'm doing this for you…" Mary started to cry.

Thomas was alone in the armory of the police station. He had deduced he would need stronger firepower than a derringer to bring the Belgian to justice, especially if he encountered gargoyles. He picked up a rifle off one of the many shelves containing various weaponry. "I guess I can't go into Alva's party holding this." He put the rifle back on the shelf and grabbed a revolver. "Truth be known, if he's like those monsters, my pen is the best weapon." He chuckled. "...The pen really is mightier." He took out the pen and held it. 'Hmm, what did Helga say to turn it into a sword?' He retrieved his note book and turned to a page. 'Let's see...Here it is...' The notes he had taken were missing the words for the forge but still had his crude illustration of the anghenfél. "That's odd, what happened? Did I not write it down? I never forget to take notes; people make fun of me for writing everything down. Let's see if I can remember the words.' "Dück weigh lug." Nothing happened. "No wait, that's the other one. "EE-ha-goo ...Ah-ha-who gu ave ...*Eh-ha- gu avuh."* In an instant, the pen converted into a sword and embedded a hole into a brick wall. "Great Scott!" Thomas yelled. He quickly looked around to see if anyone else had witnessed this. He pulled on the sword; it wouldn't budge. He heard footsteps coming down the stairs. "Come on!" he yelled pulling harder to no avail. "Why won't you budge!" The foot steps were getting closer.. *"Uhhhhh* Dück leg? Duck web luhg Dückweigh luhg...*Dückweh luhg!"* The sword retracted and turned back into a fountain pen just when Douglas reached the last flight of steps. He rounded the corner and looked at Thomas. Thomas quickly picked up the pen and put it away.

"DEE-tective Vanderbilt," Douglas said.

"Douglas?" Thomas said hoping he didn't notice the hole in the wall. "What can I do for you?"

"What's the matter, Vanderbilt? Catch something at one of the brothels I sent you to?" Douglas laughed.

Thomas fake laughed. Hoping that would move Douglas away, faster. "No, I'm fine, thank you."

"Good. Listen, Vanderbilt, let me ask you this: your cousin and that Astor dame are having some kind of shindig tonight, ya know about it?"

"Yes. I was planning to go "

"Oh." Douglas looked surprised and a little concerned. "You wouldn't happen to be bringing that Mary White woman, would you?"

"I'm not sure. She might be feeling under the weather."

"Good."

"Good?"

"No, I mean, sorry she's not feeling well."

"But…it is a possibility she and I would go together."

"Oh." Douglas seemed unhappy.

"Why do you ask?"

"Just asking, Vanderbilt. Still, find it weird that a woman like that likes a guy like you."

"Eats you up, doesn't it?" Thomas said a little mad.

"What?"

"Does it make you cast a kitten thinking about her and me? Or …" Thomas got close to him. "…is it the fact that she doesn't like …you?"

Douglas got angry. He grabbed Thomas and pushed him against the wall. "You listen to me, Vanderbilt, and you listen good! Keep her far away from that party, you hear me!"

"What? Have you lost your mind?"

"Far away, you hear me, or else you'll regret it!"

"Are you threatening me, Douglas?" Douglas punched Thomas in the stomach. Thomas doubled over and dropped to his knees.

Douglas straightened his tie and coat. "I don't make threats, Vanderbilt." He left the room and climbed the stairs.

In the marble-tiled Roman bathroom at the White household, Mary washed her red hair under the spitting cherubim statues, the water reveal the truth of how long her hair actually was. When she laid in the tub, her strands stretched down to the middle of her back. She closed her eyes and tried to enjoy the therapeutic effects of the warm water. The water helped a little, but various thoughts still swam around her head, more numerous than the ripples on the water's surface. Mary sighed. 'What am I going to do with Min? She was probably safer fighting in that opium den.' She felt a slight tug on her heel. It pulled her foot to the bottom of the tub. 'Is the water draining?' "Drat. Did I accidentally pull the plug?" she felt along the bottom of the tub with her foot, looking for the drain. She found where the water was draining out. There was no plug to be replaced.

"Where is that plug? This water is draining fast. The tub will be empty by the time I find it." She looked at the water level and noticed something. "Why is the water staying the same? Shouldn't it be getting less and less?" She pulled her hand away from the drain. The suction increased and pulled her hand back in. "What's this?" She pulled harder. The harder she pulled the stronger the suction increased. She started using two hands and then tried to stand up. The suction increased and became stronger and stronger. "What in the…Help! Someone! He…" Her legs were dragged into the drain and her head went under the water. She grabbed onto the side of the tub and tried with all her might to pull herself out. Her legs went into what was now expanding into a large whirlpool. "Help! Anybody! Help Me…"the force of the whirlpool was too strong to fight. She was dragged into it and was sucked into a spinning watery vortex. A wall of water and bubbles spun all around her, and her body rotated in the same direction as the liquid tornado. She felt the pulling take her down to at least 10 feet.

As fast as it started, it ended. She was now suspended in a blue pool of calm water. She felt the pressure of holding her breath start to become laborious. 'I have to get to the surface!' She looked up for the surface; it was dark. 'Where is this light coming from?' She looked around, panicking as her oxygen ran out. The light was coming from underneath her. She tumbled and righted herself in the correct orientation. With little time to spare, she swam upwards and broke through the surface. She took a life-sustaining gasp of air. She treaded water and kept breathing hard until she was calm enough to access her situation. 'Where am I?' She looked around. The sun was low, indicating it was late in the day. She was in a pond surrounded by tall trees. She recognized this pond. When she rotated around, a fire on a beach revealed itself. It was a campfire. Next to it were a table and two chairs. The table was set for some kind of meal. Draped over one of the chairs was some white cloth. Knowing if she stayed in the pond, she would eventually tire and drown, she started swimming toward the shore. "Hello?" she called out. No one answered. She reached the point where her feet touched the muddy bottom and she was able to stand up. The white cloth was a robe of some sort. Mary looked around to make sure no one from the woods was staring at her naked body.

Satisfied she was alone, she slowly exited the pond and walked up on the shore.

She was cold and wet. After one more look around, she grabbed the cloth off of the chair. It was indeed a robe. In addition, there was a white towel. She put the robe on and dried her hair. "Hello?" she yelled. No answer but the sound of frogs and a few crickets. "Is this...is this the pond near White Manor?" Unsure of what to do, she felt a need to rest. She sat down in one of the chairs. Within a few seconds of sitting down, a figure emerged from the woods. Mary stood up, fast. "Hello?"

It was a short, elderly maid. She was carrying a tray with a complete silver tea set on it.

"Hello? Is this White Manor?" The woman didn't answer. She went straight to the table and set up two cups and saucers, sugar, cream, spoons and a large pot of tea. "Excuse me? How did I get here?" Once finished, the woman turned around and headed back into the woods. "Am I dreaming? Should I follow you?" The woman disappeared into the thicket. Another figure emerged soon after, a tall woman wearing a long black dress. Mary recognized her, looking exactly the same as she had seen her years ago. "Aunt Gwenhwyvar?" Gwenhwyvar now wore an eye patch over her right eye. "Aunt Gwenhwyvar!" Mary risked walking on pebbles and sticks on bare feet and ran over to her. They embraced for a long time. "Am I dreaming?"

"No, dear."

How did I get here? What happened to your eye?"

"I used a forge called Vorago."

"Whirlpool?"

"Yes. I'm sorry for bringing you here without a warning. But my eye told me it was time."

"Your eye? What ever do you mean? What happened to your eye?"

The elderly maid reappeared carrying another tray. This one contained a plate of sandwiches, cookies and a small silver sphere sitting in an egg-serving cup. The items were set on the table. Gwenhwyvar sat down and took the small sphere out of the egg cup. She lifted her eye patch and inserted the sphere into an empty eye socket, and after massaging it in, she removed the eye patch and blinked a couple of times. She looked up, down and finally at Mary at what now appeared to be two normal eyes.

"Aunt Gwenhwyvar, what happened to you? Did you loose your eye?"

"I've never had two, dear."

"Pardon?"

"I was born with only one eye. The replacement was stolen from three Coppersmiths by the same man that wrote the book everyone is after."

"Myrddin?"

"Yes. Have a seat, dear." The maid poured them some tea.

"Why am I here? Is it late afternoon? It was nearly 2 p.m. when I left."

"Time change, dear, you're in the United Kingdom. Please, have a seat. Greta has made tea."

Mary sat down. "Who is Greta?"

"She's my maid, Greta, of the House of Samlesbury."

Mary looked at Greta and bowed her head. "Why are the Coppersmiths still helping you? The book hasn't been in your possession for three years, you don't need protection."

"On the contrary. We're all going to need protection."

"There are some Forgers trying to get hold of the book in New York. Do you mean them?"

"I'm afraid this is much bigger than them." Gwenhwyvar prepared her tea and took a slow sip before putting it down. "There is a war coming."

"The Germans?"

"The Germans are just pawns, like the British, the French and, very soon, the Americans."

Mary looked down. "The Germans...they killed my father." She shook her head. "Why do I keep calling him that?"

"Because he was your father."

"No he WASN'T! My father's name was Noah Black! I'm from Illinois, I'm NOT British! Yet I'm stuck with this bloody accent! You changed my memory! You took me from my home and turned me into Mary White! Why did you do that to me? You're not even my real Aunt? Do I have any real relatives?" Mary started to cry.

Gwenhwyvar put her hand on Mary's. "You have every right to be mad at us. It was wrong of us to take away your memories. We did it for purely selfish reasons and I would understand if you we're to never speak to me again. But know this, our love for you is real, and Mary White is about as real as Mary Black."

"I WILL NEVER BE MARY WHITE, EVER AGAIN!"

"You're understandably upset. You've been through a lot. And you shall go through an abundance more. What he–we did to you was wrong, but it was the only way we could save you."

"Save me? From what? Elephants killing my parents? Children trying to drown me in a frozen lake?"

"...And the train wreck?"

"Excuse me?"

"The train wreck."

"I wasn't in a train wreck."

"Your other parents must have withheld this information. It was on August 10th, 1887, in Chatsworth, Illinois, your home town. A terrible train wreck occurred, 85 people died, many more were injured."

"That has nothing to do with me. I wasn't even born."

"You were still there."

"That's impossible."

"Your mother was on that train. She was with child—you!"

"She...but, she obviously survived."

"Obviously. But, guess who was also there?"

"My Father...Professor White? But how? What was he doing there?"

"Searching for the book with his brother. It was onboard that train, guarded by some Coppersmiths from the House of Salem; there was a confrontation, and the results were many dead. He actually saved your mother from the wreckage."

"Train wrecks, elephant attacks, drownings—it's like I'm cursed. This proves that this book brings death and misfortune wherever it goes. It must be gotten rid of!"

"I haven't figured out if the drowning was connected to the book, but I did send him back to pick you up when this event revealed itself in your fate. Your lives seem to be intertwined. The fighting between Forgers sometimes spills into the world of Dayfides, and it's only going to get worse once Germany gains possession of that book. My eye also sees this in the tomorrows."

"The Germans?" Mary scoffed. "What are the Germans doing in America? The English will defeat them before the year is done."

"They now have help from a group of rogue Forgers called the Followers of Myrddin. Somehow, they've made an alliance with the German Emperor."

"Doesn't matter. They won't get the book. I'm going to get rid of the keys to its clo kefin, or, I will lock the keys and book inside the vault itself."

"The clo kefin forge prevents the door from being locked when the keys are inside. Once The Followers of Myrddin discover where it is, even without the key, they will try everything in their power to get inside of it."

"But they can't. They'll try and fail."

"They will try again and again and they will try everything! Including destroying New York city, just to open that vault."

"But how could they destroy an entire city?"

"If the German's aren't stopped, they will one day develop a terrible weapon using the help of the Forgers—it will catch the sky on fire. When they join forces with an army, Forgers can do significant damage: Gaius Julius Caesar, Alexander of Macedonia, Arthur Pendragon, Napoleon Bonaparte—just to name a few."

"Some of those names you mentioned are considered conquering heroes."

"But of course. The victors rarely cast themselves as villains in history books. But I know from firsthand accounts, Arthur Pendragon was a tyrant who had to be stopped."

"Then I will destroy the book."

"You already know you can't. Unlike it's cover, the pages are indestructible."

"Then I will separate the pages to a thousand places around the world!"

"And they will search for a thousand years to find each page and a thousand years of conflict will result as they do."

"What do you want me to do!" Mary yelled. "I can't keep the book, I can't discard it! What can I do? I'm not a Forger! I can't spend the rest of my life fighting those people! They have flying elephants! What do I have?"

"You have your friends and family."

"I will not let them die because of me."

"It's their choice."

"No. It's mine. I will not let them get involved."

Gwenhwyvar laughed. "Do you not think they are involved already? Your coils are so entangled right now, it reveals a spider web. No, dear. Where your fate takes you, theirs will follow. If you fight, they will fight. If you give up and die..."

"I only want to protect them." Mary looked down.

"Then do so. You say you're not a Forger? This is why he had your coal removed. He thought it would remove the barrier to keep you from forging and give you a fighting chance."

"And it didn't work!"

"It did! If you wanted, Mary White could have been a right powerful Forger."

"Then why was I not trained? Why the flippant lifestyle of a socialite?"

"I wouldn't call your life flippant. You've grown to be a wonderful woman, well-loved by many and socially active in justice."

"Which makes taking my memory useless, unless if it was so I could be a Forger!"

"Because Mary White changed his mind."

"Pardon?"

"I've told you many times. He felt bad for the trouble all this has caused you. When Mary White was born, he saw how you could live a long, wonderful life, away from all this uproar."

"And you allowed it!"

"I did. I saw what he saw. I know I could have easily broken the sphere and released your coal, but I saw it too. The nightmares had stopped. You were so positive, you were like a contagion of joy. My eye always gives me three possible paths for subjects. Believe me when I tell you, as hard as your life was and as hard as it's about to get, what you've been through was the best choice I could make."

"Then you should have chosen another path for me! Because I want nothing more to do with this!" She stood up and walked toward the pond. "Is the Vorago still there? I wish to return home!"

Gwenhwyvar sighed and stood up. "Mary. I see three paths not just for you, for all of your friends and family members...Including a little Chinese girl."

Mary turned around. "Min?"

"I don't know names. But I can tell you this without revealing too much of her three paths, she dies at the ripe old age of 200, happy, surrounded by generations of loved ones."

"200? That's impossible."

"Do you not know how old I am?"

"She's special...Hongdeng Zhao."

"All of your friends are special. Do you know what her other paths predict? One is mixed. But the other...You give up...You die, I die, she dies…everybody you love dies, terribly and soon."

Mary buried her face in her hands and cried. "But, I–I can't…"

Gwenhwyvar walked over and embraced her. "The forces of depravity are numerous and powerful, but they have only one weapon, fear. This is what kept you from forging. It is what they use to enslave and concur." She looked at Mary in the eyes. "Be brave, Mary. If you don't want to be Mary White, then be Mary Black. They are both powerful." She let go of her. "Now go. Stop them on your side of the world and we will stop them on ours."

Gwenhwyvar turned to the water and gestured with her hand. A small whirlpool formed not far from shore. Greta took off Mary's robe and towel. Mary walked back into the pond. When she got within one foot of the swirling water, she turned around and looked at Gwenhwyvar. Gwenhwyvar nodded. Mary dove into the water and was immediately sucked down into the abyss.

Mary was waiting on the bottom level, looking at the closed vault door. She was wearing only a spa robe and her hair was still wet. Min descended in the elevator and got off.

"What does this say?" She realized Mary wasn't responding and was staring blankly at the door. "Mary?"

Mary sighed, looked at Min and reached out her hand. Min gave her the note. "I tried to write 'come to bottom floor'."

"You used the wrong word for 'bottom'. This is 'rear end'."

Mary chuckled. "Sorry, I guess the Chinese dictionary in the library was wrong." She gave the note back to Min. When Min took it, Mary grabbed her hand. They stayed like this for a while until Mary spoke. "They'll never give up trying to get the book," she sadly stated.

"What's so special about that book?"

"It was written by a man named Myrddin Wyllt. He was a Welsh hermit who lived a long time ago. He traveled all around the land collecting forges and information from all the covens and foundries and he put them in this book."

"It's a book of magic?"

"Right."

"Couldn't you just make a copy of it like other books?"

"It has a forge on it. If you ever copy the words from it, what you have written disappears."

"What if someone could remember it and teach others by talking?"

"That is how it is done. But there are over a thousand forges in there. Very few Forgers can remember all of the words. Those that do are definitely the most powerful." She looked at Min. "Min, tell me…is it possible for Hongdeng Zhao to live to be 200?"

"There are stories of shifu up to 500 years old, but those people were wushu masters."

"So, it is possible."

"Those people were masters, with years of practice and discipline."

"By practice, you mean lots of fighting?"

"Some of it; why are you asking?"

"I talked to someone recently who told me the life I wanted to give you, Thomas, Abel, and Helga would be a short one and would not end well. I talked to another person who said danger doesn't matter when you have family looking out for you." Mary turned to Min. "I'm sorry, Min. I want you to live to be 200 year's old."

"Does that mean you'll let me help you?"

"Yes. But like I said, it will not be an easy life. It will be fraught with danger."

"My grandmother told me: 'Your enemies can only bring you danger and death. It is your duty to bring them death, and hell'."

"That's lovely," Mary said sarcastically and then laughed. She realized she sounded just like Mary White. Min laughed. "Okay, Min, go upstairs and put on the prettiest dress you hate. Me, I'll do the same."

"Where are we going?"

"To the ball, Cinderella."

"Who?…What about Helga and Abel?"

"We don't have time to track them down and make it in time for the party. Don't worry. I think Little Tiger and Doll Face can handle one Forger, correct?"

"Yes!" Min went to the stairs and started running up. She stopped and looked down at Mary. "Mary!"

"Yes Min?"

"Can you call me Butterfly?"

Mary smiled. "Of course. Butterfly, let's bring them hell!"

Part Eight
JUMP OVER THE FENCE

Abel drove the Silver Ghost down the avenue. Helga sat in the back seat to keep the police from investigating the sight of a Colored man in the front seat of a fancy car with a White female. Helga looked forlornly out the window.

"Don't fret on it too much, Helga," Abel said. "We knew this day might come one day."

"I know. Doesn't make it any easier. She let us go, just like rubbish, after all these years." She gripped her teclyn, on her lap.

"She thinks she's trying to protect us."

"And you, she fired yeh. She can't do that, yur his son as much as Leo is."

"I know. That's why I don't feel guilty for taking the car. But I think for now, it's better we just do what she wants. If we pressure her too much, it could backfire."

"I suppose." Helga looked at all of the tall buildings passing by. "What do yeh think we should do, now?"

"Find a place to live, I imagine."

Helga thought for a long moment. "You know...The Goldsmith circled an area down by the docks near the 100th block, next to the East River. And labeled it as rent is cheep 'ere."

"Strange. Why is he so interested in real estate?"

"I 'ave no idea. But I think it's worth investigating. After all, we can't pass on a cheap place to rent, can we?" she said sarcastically.

"Too right. We can't pass on a good tip on a rental."

Abel turned the car in a U-turn and they headed in the opposite direction.

"Can you get me a glass of Champagne?" a woman wearing a fox stole asked Thomas. For a second, he was going to oblige because he felt she had just asked the closest person standing next to her, but then he realized she was asking him because she thought he was a servant. He looked at his cheap tuxedo. 'It may be outdated and a little disheveled, but surely I'm dressed better than the servants.' he thought. "I'm sorry, I'm actually a guest."

"Oh, dear me. I'm sorry," she said before moving on to find a real servant. Thomas put the incident behind him and strolled around the ballroom. As advertised, the ballroom in Mrs. Astor's house could hold at least 400 people. The large room, decorated with multiple paintings, each at least five foot tall, and massive chandeliers, was at full capacity, which made it difficult for Thomas to look at each of the faces. The Vanderbilts, the Carnegies, the Rockefellers and the Morgans intermingled with the newly arrived foreign visitors, well known, in their respective countries, for their wealth. Thomas overheard one mentioning he was actually a prince. Thomas kept his ears open for anyone with a French accent. So far his search came up empty-handed. iI was hard to hear people sometimes because of an eight-piece orchestra playing Beethoven's Symphony No. #3 in E-Flat Major. Thinking of French people made him think of Madam Blanche. 'Maybe she can point out the other French speakers.' Thomas left the ballroom and entered a large hallway. Many more patrons also congested this area, intersected with a wide, two story marbled staircase with a red carpet down its center. The stairs were illuminated by a skylight and a large chandelier. Standing halfway up on a large landing, underneath the chandelier were two figures, Alva Vanderbilt, and Madam Blanche. Thomas climbed the stairs and greeted them. Madam Blanche, as usual, wore all white. The frilly dress had a very long train of fabric covered in white, cloth roses. Thomas couldn't imagine her walking downstairs without someone stepping on it.

"Ah, bon soir, Cousin Thomas." Madam Blanche said. She stuck out her hand. He kissed it. "I see you have made it. Where is your lady friend?"

"Like I said, she's not feeling well."

"So sorry to hear that," Alva said.

"Does that mean you will dance with me only?" Madam Blanche asked.

"Maybe later. I do have to ask you some questions first."

"You may ask me anything, and I do mean…anything." She smiled with her blood- red lips.

Thomas cleared his throat. "Are their any other French speakers at this affair?"

"Mais oui," She pointed down below to an older gentleman with spectacles "There is Monsieur Dumas." She pointed to a woman holding a fan."That is Madam Chanel—she always smells so nice—and somewhere is my brother-in-law, Maximilian."

"Oh, You're married?"

"Non. I am afraid my husband died in 1897."

"Sorry to hear that…Wait…'97? That means you were…"

"Quite young…And we shall leave it there, shall we? I was young, but my love for him was ancient."

"How did you two meet?"

"He saved me from a terrible train wreck."

"Train wreck? Good lord, you're lucky to be alive."

"Yes, more alive than you can imagine."

Abel finished talking to a dock worker. Nearby, Helga was engaged in her own conversation with a fisherman. She finished her talk and they came together to compare notes. "He says he's just started working down here," Abel said. "He didn't have any information."

"Well, I think I fared better than yuh. That bloke said the warehouse a few blocks down was abandoned for years until recently. There seems to be lots of activity, and get this: says they could be some kind of animal traders, because 'is friend says 'e 'eard an elephant sound."

"Elephant!"

"Indeed."

"My. Not many of those in New York."

"Quite."

"Shall we?"

"Yes, we shall." Helga put her teclyn on her shoulder. Abel took out his revolver, checked to make sure it was loaded, and put it back in his coat.

The warehouse lock was easy to open, thanks to Helga using a simple forge. Abel pulled the door open and peered inside. The vast room was full of large wooden crates. Helga steadied her teclyn and prepare for a fight. With caution they walked inside, looking around at any object which could be construed as suspicious. The building was old, but the boxes seemed new. Each one was marked with writing. Abel read one of them. "Garde Lourde."

"It means 'caution, 'eavy,'" Helga translated.

"If it's in French, at least we know we're in the right place."

"Quite right. Let's see what's in 'em." Helga took the end of her staff, inserted it between the lid and the box like a crowbar and pried the top off. The inside caused disappointment; the box was empty. "Let's try another one." They proceeded to open box after box, each one empty. After the tenth one, they concluded all of them were probably empty.

"Hmm. Perhaps we've come too early and they haven't had time to load them with things."

"Or, they've already unloaded them; either way, our timing is bad."

"I'll say!" yelled a voice from the door.

"Pardon?" Thomas asked

"Dance?" Madam Blanche asked again. She held out her hand.

"I suppose." She put her hand on top of his and he started guiding her down the stairwell. Madam Blanche stopped mid flight. Thomas looked to see what she was staring at.

Mary had entered. The crowd on the ground floor parted before her and formed a path for her to walk to the stairs. Some people murmured and others seemed confused or shocked when she walked past. She wore all black and the fabric train on the dress was equal in length to Madam Blanche's. The dress had a pattern of vines in certain places and had large, black peacock feathers on the sleeves, protruding outwards. The black dress in itself was enough to look at, but walking beside her was Min, the illegal Asian child, also dressed in a little black, frilly, Victorian dress, and on her head perched a little hat with black feathers on it.

"My word," Thomas said.

"Extraordinary," Madam Blanche said.

Mary arrived at the stairs and ascended to the midway point where Thomas and Madam Blanche were standing. Mary's black dress stretched to the bottom floor and Madam Blanche's white dress stretched upwards to the top, creating an image of light and dark. She looked at Thomas and then Madam Blanche's hand, resting on his. Min walked around Mary and glared at Thomas.

Madam Blanche took her hand off of Thomas'. Alva came down the stairs. "Mary, this is Madam Blanche, Madam Blanche this is Mary Wh…"

"Black!" Mary interrupted.

"Pardon?" Alva asked.

"Black. My last name is actually Black." Alva looked very confused.

"Charmed," Madam Blanche purred." She stuck out her hand, and Mary shook it. Madam Blanche walked down the stairs while looking at Mary's dress and singing a little tune: "Miss Mary…

Black...all dressed in...black..." She looked at Mary's back. "...With silver...buttons?...all down her...back."

Thomas and Alva looked perplexed.

"Rather catchy, don't you think?" Madam Blanche asked. "Nice to meet you, Miss Black. If you'll excuse me, Mr. Vanderbilt has promised me a dance."

"Well, not promised..." Thomas corrected.

"Monsieur Vanderbilt?" Madam Blanche said, holding out her hand. Thomas came down stairs and offered his arm. "I...She asked me before you..." he said to Mary. He looked at her back. "Mary? What is that?" He had discovered what everyone else had; her dress was exposing at least six of the buttons on her bare back, thanks to the large opening in the dress. "What is that? Jewelry?"

"It's who I am," Mary answered.

"Monsieur Thomas? Our dance?" Madam Blanche asked. Thomas continued guiding her down the stairs.

"Mary? What's going on?" Alva asked.

Standing in front of the warehouse exit was a man wearing all black, holding a pistol. "What are you doing here?" he yelled.

"Forgive us sir," Helga pleaded. "We were just passing by and noticed this door was open so we just wanted to peek and see what was inside."

The man looked over at the boxes. "That's a lie. Those empty boxes point more to you two being thieves than explorers."

"They were like that when we came in."

"Lier! Put your hands up."

Abel started to move forward.

"Steady," Helga suggested. He stopped and they both raised their hands. The man held the gun on them for a long moment. "Well?" Helga asked.

"Well what?"

"Aren't you gonna call for a policeman."

"Policeman?"

"Yes. Usually when one catches a couple of thieves, yeh call the bobbies. They come around and take them away to jail." The man didn't respond. "Unless..."

"Unless what?" he said angrily.

"Unless yur not the owner or worker in this building and yur pretending to be on the lawful side is about as fake as your accent."

"What accent?"

"Yuh American accent, it's rubbish. You're German, ain't ya?"

The man's expression went from angry to sinister. "You are very smart...Und very foolish." Another man, wearing a fedora entered the building. He was also holding a pistol. The two men began talking to each other in German.

"Now?" Abel asked."

"'Old on a tick, luv. "The more they talk, the more info we get...See, that one with the 'at on said, 'Should we wait until the Beast shows up?'"

"Beast?"

"Perhaps it's a nickname for their boss...Now the one without the 'at said, 'No we should just shoot them now and dump their bodies in the river.'"

"Now?"

"Hold on...Oh, the first one just referred to you as a schwarzer."

"What's that?"

"Not a very nice word for a Colored man."

"Hmm. Remind me to kill him first."

The two men pointed their guns at Abel and Helga. This was a sign that their time had run out. "Warten sie, schießen sie uns nicht! (Wait, don't shoot us!)" Helga yelled

Thomas danced with Madam Blanche in the ballroom. He seemed a little distracted and Madam Blanche picked up on it. "Monsieur? You are dancing with me here, yet your gaze is elsewhere."

"I'm so sorry," Thomas apologized. "I was thinking about something."

"Is it the Miss Mary all dressed in black?"

"Yes, sorry."

"Do not be sorry. I am never sorry for anything, or anybody."

"Well...you have to be empathetic for those in need, right?"

"Non. Have you ever read '*On the Origin of Species by Means of Natural Selection*' by Charles Darwin?"

"I'm afraid I haven't."

"It is wonderful. It is all about how the strong shall survive and how the weak disappear purely by the way nature is."

"You mean evolution?"

"Correct. We are the strong. And those that do not make it, is as God wants it to be."

"I respectfully disagree. Humans have evolved to have empathy and can be charitable. We're not a bunch of animals."

"Most humans are either wolves or sheep. It is up to us to be part of the pack. Which one do you want to be, Mr. Vanderbilt?"

This conversation was not sitting too well with Thomas. He changed the subject. "...So...you're from France?"

"Belgium."

"Oh, right."

On the top of the stairs, Alva closely examined the buttons embedded in Mary's back. She ran a hand over one of them. "Do they hurt?"

"On the contrary, just the opposite."

"And you have had these since you were a child?"

"Yes."

Two women on the bottom of the stairs pointed up at Mary and murmured to themselves.

"Very daring of you to wear that dress Mary, but even more so to show your disability," Alva said.

"I don't consider it a disability. It's the real me, Alva."

"I can appreciate that, but some among the elite may not. Why do this now?"

"Simple, it's bait."

"If it's for men, I can assure you it's working."

In the far dark corner at the top landing of the stairs, behind a column, a figure watched Mary. An eye-patched Lo Fang sneered a rolling smile with his razor sharp teeth. "Found you!" he hissed. Without being noticed, he got down low and crawled across the floor like a cat until he was out of sight. He walked down a long hallway decorated with sculptures and vases until he reached two large doors off to the side. He knocked twice and then once.

"Come in," said a man's voice. Fang entered. The man with the silver cane sat at a desk, smoking a cigar. One of the helpers leaned up against a bookshelf, cleaning his fingernails with a large hunting knife.

"I can't believe my luck," Fang said.

"What's that?" the Belgian asked.

"That Mary dame and Qing Min, my best fighter, are both here!"

"The ones who have caused us so much trouble?"

"Same ones."

"Let me have a look." The Belgian stood up and walked into the hallway with Fang. They arrived at a corner and were able to peek down at Mary and Alva. When the man saw Mary's back, his eyes widened. "Ahrion!" he loudly whispered.

"What?"

"Her back has ahrion on it!"

"How do you know that?" Fang asked.

"A good Forger can tell ahrion by sight. Some can even smell it."

"That means she's like you?"

"No, she's nothing like me. When you and the boys chased after her, did she ever forge?"

"Not sure. The Beast said the Colored man and the witch did. She might have, to cause a wind storm, but she was with a man."

"What man?"

Fang looked down and saw Leo coming up the steps toward Mary and Alva. He was well dressed in a tuxedo and had his hair slicked back. "THAT guy!" Fang pointed at him.

"What are you doing here?" Mary asked Leo.

"Isn't it obvious? I'm here to ask you to dance."

"Sorry, I'll have to decline. How did you know about this? And where did you find that suit?"

"A little birdie told me, and I altered my suit with a little help, if you know what I mean." He winked

"Speaking of help, Leo, I told you I didn't want your help."

"Too bad, you've got it."

"Mary, to whom are you speaking?" Alva inquired.

"Sorry Alva, this is Leopold Bianca My...my friend...from Italy."

Alva offered her hand and Leo kissed it. "Signora," he said.

The man with the silver cane looked at Leo and sighed. "And now, him. Tonight is filled with many failed attempts at murder. That man is supposed to be dead."

"Want me to kill him when I kill the Mary woman and the girl?"

"You fool. How many times has she foiled your attempts to dispose of her and managed to fool us into believing she lived in a light house?"

"But this time for sure."

"So far violent methods have yielded very little results and lots of destruction. We need to be smarter about this. That woman has some connection to Professor White and could know the real location of the book." He walked back to the office and picked up the telephone. When the operator picked up, he asked to speak to the police department in the Bowery.

"Why are you calling the cops?"

"I have a feeling someone has been withholding information from us."

The song finished and Madam Blanche and Thomas ended their dance. Leo cut in and asked Madam Blanche if she wanted to dance. She reluctantly obliged. Thomas excused himself and returned to Mary, Alva and Min. Min was missing. Thomas inquired about it.

"She said she wanted to do some exploring," Mary informed.

"Not exactly safe."

"And why wouldn't it be safe to look around this manor?" Alva asked.

"Er-ah. She might break something."

"I see. Well, if you two will excuse me, I have to go mingle."

Thomas and Mary nodded to Alva's departure.

"Am I mistaken, or did I see your gentleman caller here?" Thomas asked.

"You did, and he's not a gentleman caller."

"Brother?"

"Closer in definition. He's here for the same reason we are all here, to find the trouble-makers."

"Just be careful. We don't have Helga and Abel as back up."

"We'll be fine. You do worry too much about me."

"That's because…"

"Because of what?"

The orchestra started playing the 'Second Waltz' by Dmitri Shostakovich. "Oh, this is a nice piece, care to dance?"

Mary raised an eyebrow at him for not finishing his sentence and extended her hand to him. He guided her down the steps and into the ballroom. The eyes of the crowd followed Mary and her long black, backless dress. Thomas found the attention very unwanted. He put his hand on her back and felt the metal rivets. They were warm, which threw him off. "Are these made of that metal Forgers use?" She nodded. "Then you're like Helga? Or are you a Stryker?"

"I really don't know what or who I am anymore. I just want to find that man and…"

"And what? Kill him? Can you do that? I can tell you from experience, killing is not as easy as you think."

"I'll do whatever I can to give Min a good life."

"What about you?"

"What about me?"

"Ever since that incident with Leo, you've seem to have lost a part of yourself, and now you're calling your last name Black."

"The person you knew as Mary White is dead, Thomas."

"I don't fully understand forging or magic or any of this, but there is one thing that I know."

"What's that?"

"Black or White, I will always be your friend."

Mary looked like she was going to cry. She smiled and kissed him on the cheek. Thomas blushed and looked around embarrassed. "Mary…not here."

She giggled. "Somewhere else? Why, Mr Vanderbilt are you saying you want to be alone with me?"

"No…Yes…I mean, not now…I mean we have to find the Belgian."

Mary giggled again. "Don't worry, Min is already searching the house."

"Min? By herself? That's dangerous!"

"The more dangerous, the better for her."

"Have you lost your mind?"

"Yes…I have, and now I'm back."

The men lowered their guns a little. "You speak German?"

"Ja. Und ich habe eine Frage, bevor Sie uns erschießen. (Yes. And I have one question before you shoot us.)" She walked over to her teclyn and put her foot on it.

"What's that?" asked the one with the hat.

"Sind Sie zwei, die für einen Belgier arbeiten? (Are you two working for a Belgian?)"

They looked at each as if wondering if they should answer.

"I thought so," Helga said. "Okay Abel, we have enough info." Her teclyn shook for a second and then in an instant, flew across the room and hit both men in their chests. The force sent them reeling against the wall and pinned them.

One of them fired a gun at Helga. Instead of hitting her, it sparked off Abel's arm. In a nanosecond, he had managed to block the bullet. It ricocheted back to the man and hit his hand, forcing him to drop his gun to the ground.

Abel lowered his arm, reached into his sleeve and pulled out a large dagger the size of his forearm. *"Dückweh luhg!"* he said. The dagger turned into a small magnifying glass.

"No need to worry," Helga told Abel. "I had a coin on me."

"Good to know for the future. Shall we continue investigating?"

"Quite. Long as there aren't any further interruptions. Yeh check the other side of the warehouse, behind them big boxes, I'll check and see if these wankers have any identification."

They separated. Abel made his way to a large area around the boxes. It started to get a little darker the further in he went. *"Glo-le-oh,"* he said. The magnifying glass transformed into a large silver lantern which illuminated a large portion of the room.

On the other side of the warehouse, Helga looked through the contents of the assailants wallets while interrogating them. "Für wen arbeitest du? (Who are you working for?)" There was no answer. She read the information she had pulled from his wallet. "Long way from Düsseldorf, eh Herr Braun?" She looked at all of their money. "No American bills. Guess you don't live here or yeh just got off the boat. But not many tourists point guns at the locals and talk about waiting on the Beast—how about yeh give me a clue as to who the Beast might be?" The men didn't answer. "Quiet types, eh? That's all right. Teclyn, little tighter, please." Her teclyn pushed into them. They groaned and complained from the pain. "Now, once again. Wer ist das Biest? (Who is the Beast?)"

Madam Blanche and Leo twirled around the ballroom. They gathered as many stares as Mary and Thomas, but due more to elegance and grace than aberrant appearance. She looked at him in the eyes, waiting on him to say something. "Haven't I seen you somewhere?" she asked.

"Afraid not. I doubt we travel in the same circles."

"You would be surprised with the circles I travel in."

"That sounded almost like a challenge."

Madam Blanche smiled.

Leo looked over at Mary and Thomas, dancing. Madam Blanche took notice of this.

"Ahh, the green monster appears."

"Pardon?"

"Jealousy."

"What are you talking about?"

"You love her, non?"

"If I do or don't, it's none of your business."

"By your overreaction, I can tell your love for her is deep and unrequited." Leo didn't respond. "I can help you, you know."

"What?"

"I can help you win her heart."

"Really, how?" Leo asked unconvincingly.

"I will be in touch." With that, she put an end to the conversation.

In one of the many upstairs hallways, behind a white door with gold trim, the sound of a toilet flush was heard. A short time later, Min exited the bathroom and fixed her dress the best way she could. "Why do these people wear clothes so hard to take on and off?" She walked down the hallway and thought of an excuse for why she was wandering the hallways in case anyone asked. Being a child made it easy if this happened. She took advantage of her status and occasionally opened a door to peek inside. The manor was huge. She pondered if she could get though the entire house by the time the party was over.

From the corner of her eye, she saw something move. Down the hallway, something disappeared around the corner. She ran down the hall to catch up with it. It was gone. More movement appeared around the corner to the right. She ran down to this area. This game of hide and seek stretched on for at least three wings of the manor. It finally ended at an open door. When she entered. She could have sworn she saw a shape exit the window and go up. She ran to the window and looked up. She saw a foot disappear over one of the house's gables. She took a deep breath and within a second had crawled out on to the window sill and started climbing after the phantom shape.

On the ballroom level, Detective Douglas constantly tipped his hat to excuse his presence. He saw Mary and Thomas waltzing nearby. He narrowed his eyes at them and looked like he wanted to punch something.

10 p.m., April 18, 1912

The RMS Carpathia had been docked at pier 54 in New York for almost an hour. The weary survivors of the RMS Titanic departed the rescue ship and were greeted by the White Star Line company as well as nurses, doctors, family members and thousands of gawkers. Police officers Thomas Vanderbilt and Clarence Douglas were on assignment to serve as security for the many rich faces who had survived the harrowing experience. Looking down from the pier's upper level, Douglas expressed annoyance at having to watch after a bunch of rich people. "They got what they deserved," he complained.

"I don't know about that..." Thomas countered. "...There were rich and poor on that ship."

"Yeah, and guess which ones went down with the ship?"

Thomas didn't respond.

Douglas gazed at a scene going on near the gangplank. A young lady with red hair was having a very engaging conversation with someone who appeared to be the captain of the Carpathia. "Hey, Vanderbilt. Look at the cute little chickadee with the red hair, talking to the captain."

"Hmm. Oh, yes, ravishing."

"Hands off Vanderbilt, I saw her first."

"If you say so...Oh!" Thomas saw an older, white-haired woman coming off the ship, carrying a suitcase which seemed to be very heavy for her. "Oh, that woman looks like she needs help."

"Go ahead, Vanderbilt, that one seems more your level," Douglas laughed. He watched Thomas make his way down to the pier. He walked up to the older woman and offered to help her with her luggage. She at first refused but Thomas seemed to insist. She handed the bag over to him and it was like it weighed a ton. It dropped to the ground, almost causing Thomas to flip over it. Douglas laughed at the whole scene. The redhead walked up to them both and started talking to them.

"What the?" Douglas asked. "Is she with that old dame? Damn you Vanderbilt!" Douglas ran down to the pier and interrupted their conversation, "What's going on here?" he asked.

"Douglas? This is Mary from the House of White, and her maid, Helga," Thomas answered. Mary offered her hand. Douglas shook it like greeting a man. "I was just helping Helga with this small bag, which for some reason weighs a ton."

"Poppycock, Vanderbilt. It's because you're a milquetoast. Here, let me have it." Helga picked it up and gave it to him. The result was the same as it was with Thomas. The bag ended up on the ground. "For the love of Saint Joseph. Do you have an entire house in here?"

"No sir, just the furniture," Helga answered, with a deadpan expression. A second passed. Thomas laughed, assuming it was a joke. Helga picked up the bag.

"You're very strong," Thomas complimented. "They let you carry this on the life boat?"

"No, sir, I wouldn't 'ave dared take up space for rescuing souls. It floated after the Carpatia, like a faithful dog. I just fished it out of the water."

"Fascinating."

The captain walked over to the group. "Miss White, Your father informed me that he will meet you in the immigration office."

"Thank you, Captain Rostron. And I hope you get a picture of those sea monsters one day."

The captain excused himself.

"Sea monsters?" Douglas asked.

"Oh, yes. We talked in length about it. Captain Rostron is a firm believer in sea monsters. After I told him how unusually the iceberg moved when it hit our ship, he said perhaps instead of icebergs it could have been the spiny back of a sea monster.

"That sounds terrifying," Thomas said.

"That sounds like a bunch of rubbish," Douglas corrected. "There's no such thing as sea monsters. Did he see mermaids too?" Douglas laughed.

Mary didn't seem amused. "Well, I for one believe him."

An African man walked up to the group. He smiled at Helga and Mary.

"What are you looking at, boy?" Douglas asked aggressively.

The Black man was taken aback. "Boy?" he asked."

"Douglas!" Thomas complained.

"I'm sorry…" Mary asked. "Did he just insult my friend?"

"Your friend?" Douglas asked.

"Yes. This is my my good friend and butler, Abel."

"Oh…I thought because he was Colored he…"

"You didn't think at all!" Mary interrupted. "Now, if you'd excuse us…Officer Vanderbilt, could you please escort me to the immigration office?" She linked her arm in his. They walked away toward the exit. Douglas sneered at them.

Douglas hurried around the crowd of dancers, to the stairway, and climbed up and traversed down the hall until he arrived at the door of the nefarious group. He knocked twice and then once on the door. Fang opened the door and let him in. The Belgian was busy talking to an elderly woman. She had her back to Douglas. She was signing a piece of paper while he calmly talked to her the way one would a small child.

"…Yes, very good," he cooed. "Now you shall return to the party and you will forget all about our conversation, Mrs Rockefeller, and the second you leave this room, you will be released." The woman stood up, turned around and walked towards the door. The deadpan expression on her face combined with the red eyes only gave her even more of a macabre appearance. Douglas felt uneasy when she walked past him like an animated corpse. She left and they closed the door.

Outside, Mrs Rockefeller's eyes turned back to normal. She looked around, lost and confused, before continuing on her way.

The Belgian looked at Douglas with uncomfortable familiarity. "Bon soir, Detective Douglas. Cigar?" He offered one to Douglas, he was not amused.

"Why did you call me here? It's dangerous for me to be seen with you!" he yelled.

"Do not worry. No one knows who I am, here…No wait, there are a few who might recognize me. Did you see them?"

"Who?"

"The ones who we have had several run-ins with: Little Oriental girl, policeman I saw in front of your station who stabs Fang with ahrion pen, and the Mary woman who apparently has an entire back of ahrion!" Douglas was speechless. "Yes, nothing to say?

Isn't it interesting that Professor White has no address but you were able to tell us where his office was. We search records and find nothing, which I thought was <u>his</u> doing, but now...I am thinking: it was <u>your</u> doing, non?"

"What are you talking about?"

"Mr. Douglas, we paid you a lot of money to help us find Professor White, but I am starting to think we are not getting our money's worth."

"That's ridiculous. I found out he was on the Lusitania. Not my fault the Germans blew it up."

"That is true. But during all of this, you failed to ever tell us about that woman downstairs hanging out with that policeman, who apparently have access to ahrion and is probably a Forger or Stryker."

"I don't know anything about that."

"Of course you don't...or you've been holding back on us."

"What the hell are you talking about?"

"You've been keeping her a secret."

"Who?"

"That Mary woman."

"And why would I do that?"

"I watched you when you came in, I watched you as you saw them dancing together, that cop and that Mary woman. Holding close together like cake and icing. Even now, as I am talking about it, your jaw is tightening. You want her, non?...No answer? I am right?" He stood up and walked around Douglas. "Do you know why I haven't bended your mind to help us, Mr. Douglas?"

"Because I agreed to do it without it?"

"True, true. Your gambling debt has been very motivational in making you compliant; but non. Whenever we bend someone's mind, you can only do it once and you also have a victim that walks around with the spooky red eyes. That makes it hard to have a spy working for you. Much better to just pay someone like you <u>lots</u> of money. But, now I am afraid we are going to have to ask you to do something which I hope will not need your brain bended."

"What?"

"You must prove to me that all this time you have been feeding us clues to find the book, yet you have not been throwing us off the path and protecting your sweetie-pie, who is downstairs dancing with your rival."

"That's ridiculous, he's not my riv—"

"Kill her!"

"What?"

The Belgian took a revolver out of his coat pocket and offered it to Douglas. "Kill her. If you are on our side, you will take this gun and go down there and kill her."

"Now?"

"Oui." He started writing something on a note.

"That's stupid! In front of all these people?"

"Not to worry, once you kill her, we will do some...hocus-pocus and no one will remember your face, it will all work out." He finished writing and handed the note to Douglas. "Read this magic spell..." He lifted one finger. "...only after you have finished the job or else it won't work out." Douglas took the note and tucked it into his coat pocket.

"But that..."

"But?"

"Still, why her? How about the guy? You said he was getting in your way too?"

"You are right...Okay, kill them both. But make sure it's her first." There was a very long period of silence. Douglas reluctantly took the gun. "Tre bien. Now, off you go. And remember, do not read the note until you have finished, or else it won't work."

Douglas turned around. "Isn't there another way?"

"Non. Kill her...or we kill you—right now. How is that for another way? Bon soir."

Douglas turned around and left the room.

"If he kills her, we may never find out where the book is," Fang suggested.

"Not to worry. If she is a Forger, regular bullets can't harm her."

"Then why do this?"

"To gain her trust."

"Her trust?"

On the large roof of Astor Manor, Min surveyed every place someone could hide: behind pipes, chimneys and any object big enough. The search resulted in no success. She turned around and realized the one called Muggsy was behind her. He tried to punch her but she jumped backwards and landed on top of a chimney.

"You're fast," he complimented.

"No, you're slow," Min said before kicking one of the chimney's bricks loose and sending it flying into his face. He fell back onto the roof. He stood up, dazed and dizzy. After he spat out a tooth, he became aware Min was back on his level. Three quick punches to the face and chest sent him reeling back against a pipe, bending it. The final blow was a flying roundhouse kick to the left side of his head. This action launched him spinning off the roof. Min didn't investigate to see if he hit the ground or not. She waited for almost a minute before speaking. "I know from what I've seen, you people are not so easy to beat. I'm sure you are waiting for me to look over the edge before you show yourself and attack me. Why don't you just show yourself, now?"

"Sssuch a sssmart little girl," the man's voice hissed through the air. He slowly floated up until she could see him from the waist up. "You must know about the powers of the sssilver liquid."

She got a good look at him. His skin turned more and more green and his teeth formed into two fangs. Min readied herself.

"Too bad you won't be able to shhhhare your knowledge with the world." He rose up even more. His legs had been fused together and scales started to form. His elongated lower half had exposed his deadly new form of a snake-bodied man. He hissed at her and launched at incredible speed. She bent backwards just in time. He struck over and smashed the brick chimney behind her. Before he retracted, she kicked him twice in what used to be his stomach. He went upwards and then struck downwards. She rolled away and he imbedded his head into the roof, sending tiles everywhere. Two painful elbows to his head caused him to retreat. Min stood up and prepared for another attack.

"Fang was right!" she heard him say. "You are good. But it doesn't matter, even with your ssskills, you can't kill usss. Eventually you'll be worn down and then I will eat you like a sssnake eats a little moussse!" Min twisted her body sideways just in time to avoid a sneak attack from behind. She managed to avoid his hands and upper body but his tail acted like the end of a whip and smacked into her back, sending her flying against a stove pipe. Before she could steady herself, the tail whipped her repeatedly, each time launching her in different directions, like a lifeless doll. On the last whip, something burned his tail. He screamed and then grabbed her chest. He felt a necklace. With a quick yank, he pulled it off by the chain, revealing it was Min's copy of the special key. "What do we have here? Don't know what this isss for, but if it burnsss my ssskin, it must be important. Sssure my boss will appreciate this gift, as well as your dead body!"

"N-no," Min struggled to say. She realized the absolute tragedy which awaited Mary now that this monster had the key, and how foolish it was for her to have it on her. The snake man grabbed her throat. "Looks like Fang was wrong, you're not tough, you're just a ssscared little mouse."

Min reached into her hair bun and pulled out a silver hair pin. Her bun unraveled and her hair draped down.. She tried to stab the monster in the eye. He was too fast for her and grabbed her wrist. "What'ssss that? Sssnnneaky one, aren't you."

Two hours earlier...

Mary called for Min to come into the parlor. She shuffled in wearing the frilly black dress she hated. "Oh my, you look absolutely adorable." Mary walked over and fixed certain things on the dress. Min became angrier but didn't protest. Mary took a step back and looked at her. "Lovely. Now you do need one more accessory..." Mary walked over to a book shelf and pulled a box off the shelf. She placed it on a side table next to the Siv Myrddin, turned to a certain page and read. She then opened the box. Inside were various silver objects. She took the hair pin out and handed it to Min. "Keep this with you at all times at the party."

"Why? What is it?"

"It's a hair pin."

"That's it?"

"Of course not, silly goose. In this house?" Mary giggled. "If you need to kill a Forger or an anghenfêl, only objects made of ahrion will work."

"But a pin?"

"It's only in that shape for easier storage. It's a teclyn, you can turn it into whatever weapon of your choosing, but only if you're a Forger or a Stryker."

"How would I know?"

"Did it burn your hand when I handed it to you?"

"No?"

"Well. That proves at least, you're not an anghenfêl. This is why silver crosses are rumored to repel vampires or silver bullets for werewolves. Forgers and Strykers are one out of 100 million. Those that can't do anything are the Normalau, or the Dayfides. If they dabble in forging and especially drink ahrion, they ether die instantly or turn into beasts, like your friend, Fang. But, unfortunately, the only way to find out if you are special is to test you. Hold this pen in your hand. Think of…think of a weapon you would like to use and say the words. Eh-ha-gu avuh."

The Snake man tightened his grip on Min's neck and was about to dig his sharp fingernails into her jugular. With her last breath, Min said the words: *"Eh-ha-gu avuh."* The expression on the snake man's face went from triumphant to bewildered. He looked down at his stomach area and saw Min's hand, now holding a silver Chinese qiang, imbedded in his side. He hissed and glared at her with green slit eyes and slithered away from her to the edge of the roof. Min spun the spear and assumed a defensive stance. The snake man looked at the large, simmering wound on his side.

"You little brat!" he yelled. He rolled over the edge and started to escape.

"Nuòfū!" she yelled.

"What?" He stopped his retreat.

"Coward!"

This enraged him beyond self-control. He tried to whip her with the end of his tail. It made it within five feet of her before she cut the last three feet off of it. The tip flopped and writhed on the roof. His scream filed the air. He grabbed the severed edge of his tail and with furious rage launched himself at Min. With two quick swipes at him with the spear, the man was now cut into three cylindrical pieces. One final blow removed his head. His body parts landed in separate areas and within a second, burst into shimmering sparkles of light. There was the sound of the key hitting the roof. Min bent down, picked it up and tucked it into a pocket on her dress.

"Helga!" Abel called. She looked over in Abel's direction, and then back at the Germans. "Don't go anywhere, yeh twits." Helga walked over to Abel. She felt something underneath her feet when she got closer to him. "What am I walking on?" she asked.

"Here, let me give you a hand," Abel said. "Glo-le-oh." His lantern became even brighter and illuminated the grounds around Helga's feet. Scattered about, there lay many volumes of books.

She bent down and picked one of them up. "What's this?" She read the cover. It was a copy of the Karma Sutra by Vātsyāyana. "What's this doing here? Is this from...?"

"Yes, Abel said. The library in the lighthouse."

"Wonder what they did to the lighthouse?"

"Look to your right."

When Helga did, she saw the huge object, lying on its side, reaching almost to the ceiling. It was Mary's lighthouse, still intact.

"Cor blimey!! 'Ow did they git that down 'ere?"

"One can only guess. Two pachyderms?"

"Yuh think someone would have seen somethin'. Not the most subtlest of operations."

"Indeed. At least Mary will be happy that we've found her lighthouse."

"And as soon as I threaten to cut off their stones, they'll tell us who this Beast fella is." The second after Helga said that, there were two blood curdling screams coming from the area they had been in earlier. Helga and Abel ran back to the two Germans. They were still pinned against the wall by Helga's teclyn. They appeared lifeless. "What 'appened to them?" Helga asked.

"It appears they were attacked. Are they dead?"

"Looks like. Not many people can survive without an 'ead."

"What?" Abel asked. He rose the light up higher. It now revealed the men's headless bodies.

Mary examined the four people out on the balcony deck. None of them came close to looking like a Belgian male. Leo came outside and joined her. "Any luck?" he asked.

"I'm afraid not."

"Oh, well, guess this was a waste of time. Perhaps you and that flatfoot should go on home."

"That would please you, wouldn't it?"

"Sure would. You have no business playing gumshoe. You should just stick to socializing and tea parties."

"You obviously know nothing of the life of Mary White."

"I'm afraid not. Been away from you for 17 years. Missed the whole life of Mary White soirée."

Mary looked at the lights reflecting off of New York Harbor in the distance. "I remember being happy most of the time. Whenever I became sad, it would pass by fast, until my father... Professor White died. His death somehow stuck with me, it still sticks to me."

"Maybe it's because the man that bent your mind died."

"Perhaps..." She looked at Leo. "...I guess I should thank you, Leo."

"For what?"

"For releasing me from the coal. From now on, if I'm happy it's real and not just a forge. I'm finally me again."

Mary reached over and was about to kiss him on the cheek. She stopped one inch away.

Thomas came from the inside. He saw Mary and Leo on the deck. He turned away in anger and went back inside.

"...But, I won't," she whispered to him. And pulled away.

"Huh?"

"You've also ruined my life."

"I did it for you."

"You did not. This is between you and your constant fight against Aunt Gwenhwyvar."

"What does she have to..."

"Revenge, Leo. For all of the times she disciplined you. And Prof...I should just say my father! I was with him for 23 years, and Mary White for 17 of those. That's longer than all the years I remember with Noah Black. It might not have been a real life, Leo, but time does not lie. He played his part for 23 years! Abel and Helga played theirs for 17! They sacrificed their lives for my happiness—can you imagine? They did that for me and you, you just wanted revenge!"

"It's not like that!" he yelled. Some guest stared at him. "...I did it for you!"

"I wish I could believe you, Leo. But here we are. That horrible man killed my father and hundreds of others, chased after us and destroyed my lighthouse. And all you could think of doing was change me back to your childhood friend? Not to stop him or to warn me in any way. All you wanted, was to erase the mistake my father did to me."

"Stop calling him your FATHER! Your Name is Mary Black!"

"That was 17 years ago, Leo. She's gone."

"STOP SAYING THAT!" he yelled. They both looked around at the staring party-goers. "Fine! Do it on your own!" Leo turned around and stomped back inside.

Thomas eventually came back outside and joined Mary. She seemed to sense something was wrong with him. "Thomas? Are you okay?"

"Yes…I'm fine. Any luck?"

"No. I've looked at the faces of 300 guest to no avail."

"I as well. I even checked the kitchen staff."

"Perhaps Min found something."

"Perhaps." Thomas stared at the same lights off the harbor which Mary had gazed at.

"Thomas?"

"Yes?"

"Something is bothering you."

"I'm fine."

She put her hand on his shoulder. "Thomas? I can always tell when something is bothering you. Please tell me."

"It's…it's. Leo. What exactly is your relationship to him?"

Mary rolled her eyes. "I told you. He's like a brother to me." Thomas looked away. Mary touched his face and turned his head so that he looked at her. "I said Leo is like a brother to me, Thomas, nothing more." Mary and Thomas slowly turned and saw Leo had returned. They stared at him. He was angry. He quickly turned around and hurried away.

"Leo?" Mary called out. Before Mary could give chase, Min appeared. "Butterfly! Find anything?"

"And how!" she raved. "I killed an anghenfêl on the roof!"

"That confirms it! Did you search all of the rooms?"

"All but a few on the second and third floor."

"Okay, Thomas! Can you and Min check the third floor? I'll double check the ones on the second."

"All right," he wavered. Do you need a weapon?"

"I am a weapon." Mary departed for the second floor.

"*Headvan Tân !*" Helga said. Bright fireflies appeared out of her palm, flew to different parts of the warehouse and illuminated the inside. She held out her arm. Her teclyn left the German corpses and flew into her hand. The bodies flopped onto the ground. "See anything?" she asked Abel.

"Not yet."Abel held two pistols. And walked around kicking the sides of the wooden boxes.

"What are you doing?"

"Empty box is a perfect place for hiding."

"True, but we've already checked…"

Abel checked a box which produced a dull sound and didn't move like the others. He looked at Helga and nodded. She walked over and pointed her teclyn at the box. Abel reached into his pocket and took out a silver bullet. He loaded it into one of his pistol's chamber. He then nodded at her. She used her staff to slowly open the box. There was a moment of silence. Suddenly, someone burst out of the box holding a pistol.

"*MELLT!*" Helga yelled. A bolt of lightning traveled from her teclyn to the man, through his chest.

Abel wasted no time and shot the man twice in the chest. The man flailed back and then forwards, over the edge of the open box. Abel and Helga stepped back and waited for a follow-up attack which never happened. Helga stepped forwards and used her teclyn to push his body back so they could see his face. He was dead, also a human. "Not an anghenfēl."

"Damn it!" Abel cursed. "I wasted two of my ahrion bullets on him."

"That's too bad!" yelled a voice. "That mean you can't shoot me?"

Abel and Helga looked around for the source of the voice.

"Show yourself!" Helga yelled.

"Why? So you can shoot me with your little lightning stick?" the voice said, echoing through the warehouse.

"Why did you kill those two men?"

"No reason. I just wanted to."

"Where is it coming from?" Abel asked Helga.

" 'ard to know. Sounds like 'e's far away and yelling, could be outside, even.

Abel thought about the anghenfēls they had battled so far. "It's not the one with wing—you killed, and it doesn't sound like Fang, so…most likely it's the one I fought that…"

"That, what?" Helga asked.

Abel looked up and then at Helga. "RUN!" He started running forward and dragged her behind him. A heartbeat later, an entire tug boat crashed, stern first, through the roof of the building and landed, not far behind them, on top of the lighthouse. Like a loud explosion had taken place, wood, concrete, metal pieces and various parts of the boat and lighthouse flew in multiple directions. The back of the boat, reaching higher than the ceiling, fell downwards toward the runners like a falling tree., unzipping the entire roof onto them. Helga put her teclyn ahead of her, a propeller formed out of its front and rapidly spun. It flew forward and dragged her and Abel across the floor at an incredible speed. By the time the boat had settled onto the ground and all of the wreckage had spread as far as it was going to go, Helga and Abel had brought themselves to a stop and stood in an upright position again. They looked back and surveyed the damage.

"Is it a Forger?" Helga asked.

"No, an anghenfël."

There was a racket coming from the wreckage. A person appeared from behind it and climbed on top of the heap. It was the anghenfël Abel had battled back at the train yard.

"Watch out..." Abel warned. "...He's strong."

"Yeh don't say?"

The anghenfël jumped off the boat and ran towards them. Abel took out his pistols and repeatedly fired shot after shot at him. The bullets slowed him down and seem to cause discomfort but his trajectory was not changed and he continued towards them. Helga said the word: *"Mellt!"* Her lightning bolt missed its target because the monster had jumped up high into the air. Before he could come crashing down on them, Helga and Abel scrambled away to different parts of the warehouse. The beast, focusing his attack on Helga, jumped again and landed no less than five feet away from her. With his excessively muscled arm he swung at her. She lifted her teclyn up and he struck it, hard. It hit into Helga and she went flying back at an incredible speed and hit a back wall 30 feet away, imbedding her in it. She quickly shook off the attack and the bricks, lifted her teclyn and rose into the air. A loutish hand grabbed her ankle and yanked her down until she crashed onto the concrete floor.

"Going somewhere?" he asked raising a fist to strike a fatal blow. A shotgun's barrel appeared next to his face and fired. Abel had managed to get right beside him and fired another shot at him. The creature held up his hand to defend himself and backed away. The shots deterred him enough for Helga to make her aerial escape. The anghenfēl took a swing at Abel and missed. His fist came within six inches of Abel's face and the sheer force of it knocked Abel across the room onto a pile of ship debris. "Abel!" Helga yelled. He got up as quickly as he could. "I'm all right, I just got hit by the wind of his attack."

"Don't let him touch you. One punch from that bloke could shatter yuh 'ead!"

"You don't say?"

Unable to reach Helga, the anghenfēl started chasing after Abel. Helga fire multiple lighting bolts at him but he zig-zagged out of the way before any could make contact. Abel's running speed was more than the creature's. Out of frustration, it began to grab whatever box, or boat part he could find and threw them at Helga and Abel. Helga was unable to concentrate her attack forge because of the multiple crates flying in her direction. Abel dodged the flying objects until one in particular–the ship's anchor—came too close and the bottom curve of it pushed him forward and pinned him against the wall. The anchor prevented his escape as well as causing what he felt were multiple broken ribs. With great pain, he twisted his torso so that he faced the anghenfēl, stomping towards him. Abel pointed his pistol at him and said: "*Gwella!*" His silver pistol enlarged and transformed until it had turned into a small, hand cannon about the size of a shot gun with a very large decorative barrel. The creature marched towards Abel and the cannon. "You think that's going to hurt me?" he bragged.

"No," Abel answered. He fired the cannon. The recoil felt like it cracked another rib.

The projectile hit the monster in the face and knocked him back. He screamed in anger and pain and as quickly as he could, stood up. One of his ears was missing a piece.

"Won't kill you, but it will still hurt like hell," Abel said.

"I'm going to crush your skull like a grape!" he yelled. He took a leap in the air. Abel prepared himself for what ever horrible death awaited. The anghenfēl landed in front of him but didn't move. It looked at it's chest and saw something. A copper staff was sticking through the front. It pulled out. He turned around and looked at Helga, holding her teclyn. "You Wi..."

"Hey! Abel yelled. Causing the anghenfēl to turn back around and look at him

With a quick swipe from his ahrion dagger, Abel sliced the anghenfēl's throat. It staggered around, moved forward and put his hands on Abel's throat, and with his last breath he tried to break Abel's neck, but failed as his body burst into bright sparkles.

Helga stepped forward and tried to pull the anchor out of the wall. "Alright, Luv?"

"Not really, got several broken ribs."

"Sorry luv. Got any silver medicine?"

"There's some in the car's glove compartment."

"Brilliant. 'ave you up and running in no time...Soon as we get this anchor off of yeh." Helga laughed.

"What?"

"Sorry, luv. That's a punch line to an old off-color joke."

Thomas and Min exited different rooms and regrouped in the third floor hallway of the Astor manor.

"Anything?" Thomas asked. Min nodded no. "Well, that's all of the rooms. Let's see how Mary is doing." They ran to find Mary.

On the second floor, Mary opened an office room door and peeked inside. Satisfied there wasn't anyone inside, she closed the door and walked down the hallway to one more door. "Well, this is the last one." She nervously turned the doorknob. It clicked loudly and opened with a squeaky, long whine. With calculated steps, Mary slowly tip-toed inside. She felt something weird about the room. Taking great care not to make any noise or disturb anything, she looked at everything, from the office desk to the old cigar left in an ashtray. She stopped and listened for almost a minute. The room had a feeling of being full of something which she could not see, like thick air. After realizing the room was really empty, she walked normally out and closed the door. She was startled when she came face to face with Thomas. "Good heavens!" she yelled. "Scared me half to death."

"Sorry."

Min approached Mary from behind and scared her again.

Shaken, Mary put her hand on her bosom and caught her breath. "Did you two fare better than I?"

"Afraid not," Thomas answered. "They either left or that one Min battled could have been an assassin or a scout."

"Come to assassinate who?"

"Any of us, even Leo. Maybe he even followed Leo in here."

"He and the Belgian didn't part on good terms. It's possible they chased after us just to get to him."

"Perhaps I should have a word with him?"

"The time for talking with him is naught. He seems pretty tight-lipped about sharing info with us."

"Still worth a try. Let's go find him."

The group departed and headed down the stairs. In the room Mary had left, the old cigar sitting in an ashtray lifted up. The vision of the Belgian's body warped into view. He lit the cigar and put it into his mouth. Another visual disturbance, next to him, focused into view and became the solid form of Fang. "She was right there!" he yelled. "With one finger, I could have slashed her throat like it was paper. Why didn't you let me do it?"

"Two reasons: one, the minute you attack using Fatuus in oculis, invisibility, you appear again."

"So I would then kill her."

"Yes, I'm sure. And number two, if you kill her, who will tell us where the book is?" Fang thought for a moment. "Do not worry. The second we have the book, they all die horribly. But for now, we will play a game of chess with them. Starting in just a moment with Detective Douglas."

Near a buffet table, Leo stuffed his pockets full of hors d'oeuvres. Alva took note of this and questioned him about it. "Are you feeding a dog at home, Mr. Bianca?"

He was startled. "Oh, hi…Er, no, just saving some for later."

Alva raised an eyebrow. "So, what exactly do you do, Mr. Bianca?"

"What don't I do," he joked. She didn't laugh. He cleared his throat. "Er, well…I'm, I'm a magician."

"A magician?" Alva's eyes lit up. "Oh, how wonderful! Can you do a trick for me?"

"Er, ah…Sure." He reached into his coat pocket and pulled out a deck of cards. "Pick a card." She did so. "Now look at it, but don't let me see it. When you're done, put it back in the pile." She returned the card. "Now, I'm going to tell you what your card is, excuse me…" He touched one finger on her head. "*Oo-aid vell ur woove ur aid dwaid!*"

Alva stepped back. "Excuse me?"

"Huh?"

"What was that language you just spoke, is that part of the trick?" Leo stood in stunned silence. "Mr. Bianca?"

"Er, ah, sorry…Er."

"What card am I thinking of?"

"Oh…" Leo looked at the deck. "Uh, Queen of Hearts?"

"Afraid not."

"Eight of diamonds?"

"Hardly."

"Jack of spades?"

"No. I'm sorry."

"Oh, well. Guess I'm a little out of practice."

"Perhaps you are better at making hors d'oeuvres disappear?" She excused herself.

Leo looked at her as she talked with guest. "Maybe I didn't use the right words." He picked up an apple out of a bowl and tossed it in the air. When it came down, it landed in Mary's hand. She put it back in the bowl. "Yes?" Leo asked.

"I have some questions for you."

"Sure, go ahead and ask." He continued to stuff little snacks into his pockets.

"Do you have a dog at home?"

"These are my dinner. Don't have a fancy cook like you…or money."

"With the talents of a Forger, making a living should have been easy for you."

"Well, some people don't like swindling Dayfides out of dough."

"Are you insinuating my lifestyle is built on deception?"

"Only Professor White."

"He's been very helpful in inventing various machines to help with everything from mining to washing clothes."

"Yeah, sure. And it had nothing to do with using abracadabra. He thought of everything himself."

Mary took breath. "I need to know more about your Belgian friend."

"Subject change, eh? Guess I hit the right chords with you."

"The Belgian—information, please!"

"Don't think so, Miss White—or is it Miss Black? Which one am I talking to?"

Thomas stepped forwards to punch Leo. Mary stopped him.

"It's okay, Thomas."

"Say the word Mary, and I'll run him in," Thomas suggested. "He'll get plenty to eat in the hoosegow."

"Or I could beat it out of him," Min added

Leo laughed. "You think I've never been beaten or locked up before? You have no idea how easy it is for a Forger to escape and erase his records."

"He's right," Mary said. "There's nothing we can do to make him talk. He's always thought about himself, nothing has changed." Mary turned around and left.

"I guess she was right about you…" Thomas said. "…You are nothing more." He joined Mary.

Min stayed behind and stared at Leo.

"WHAT?" he yelled.

"Nuòfū," she insulted before walking away.

"So, what shall we do now?" Mary asked.

"We need extra help. We need to find Helga and Abel," Thomas suggested.

"I made a grave error telling them to leave."

"They've been with you for years, and didn't you grow up with Abel? He's practically family"

"I know, I know. I plan on finding them and bringing them back."

Mrs Astor walked over to Mary and Thomas. "Hello, Mary."

"Hello, Mrs. Astor. Lovely party."

"Thank you, Mary. I was wondering if you might do us the pleasure and provide us with a song?"

"A song?"

"Yes, dear. Louise Homer told me you've been learning Madama Butterfly."

"I have, but I don't know if my performance could even come close to hers. Perhaps she would be better suited for such a task."

"True, but we would love to hear you sing. You have such a lovely voice."

"Well, I…" She looked at Thomas.

"You should do it. It will gather everyone in one room and make it easier to find You-Know-Who."

"I suppose it would be okay. Min, can you check to see if there are any guests leaving? Perhaps we can catch him trying to escape my performance," she joked.

Min saluted and said: "Shì de fū rén" (Yes Ma'am) and went away towards the front door. She walked too close to an elderly dowager. The woman couldn't resist pinching the cheeks of the cute, little Chinese girl in the black dress. Min behaved herself and resisted the urge to pummel the woman.

The party guests assembled in a large, ornately decorated room with a grand piano in the corner. Once everyone had settled in, Mrs Astor took center stage and introduced Mary, who would be accompanied by her teacher, Louise Homer, on piano. Mary felt embarrassed, which was a strange feeling for her. She speculated this was related to her new self. Once ready, Mary nodded to Louise, who started playing Un Bel Di Vedremo, from Madama Butterfly. Mary started to sing. She noticed something peculiar— the song felt different for her. It was not as mechanical and methodical, as she had always performed it before. She could feel the character singing it, she could understand the heartache, the drama and the tragedy of the opera. Madam Butterfly, realizing she could never have the American, Pinkerton, choses to kill herself with a knife. A wave of emotion came over Mary. She felt unsafe and vulnerable, another new emotion. She came close to losing her voice but re-channeled her feelings into the song and used it. Members of the audience sighed, and some women teared up at her rendition. Her teacher smiled with pride—her student had finally understood the piece.

As Mary caused the guests to swoon, Thomas walked around the room looking at every face in the crowd. None came close to the one who had caused so much trouble. When Thomas had almost made a full circle around the room, he saw Detective Douglas enter. He looked different, almost worried, which was a strange look for him. "What's he up to?" Thomas asked. Douglas arrived at the bottom step and leered at Mary. His expression was more than entranced, it was obsessive. He had one hand constantly in his coat pocket. Thomas was concerned. He tried to make his way over to Mary and Louise without alarming anyone, especially Douglas. Whatever reason Douglas had attacked Thomas over, it could culminate tonight. Another figure approached from across the room: Madam Blanche. She also looked at Douglas with concern. This made Thomas even more uneasy. Douglas made his way closer to Mary and Louise. The other guests started to look at each other and point. A butler was gestured to go get Douglas a seat. Douglas stood, transfixed on Mary. He was deep in thought as he fondled something in his coat pocket. Thomas moved faster towards them. After Mary had sung the lyrics: 'I nomi che mi dava al suo venire.Tutto questo avverrà, te lo prometto. Tieni la tua paura,' (...The names he called me at his last coming. All this will happen, I promise you this, hold back your fears), Douglas pulled his revolver out of his pocket. Mary instantly stopped singing when two women screamed. Douglas looked around the room, confused, and then refocused on Mary.

"He's got a gun!" someone yelled. Some men walked to get behind Douglas.

"Stay where you are! Or else!" he yelled at them. They stopped running. Thomas made it within five feet of Mary.

"You, too!"

Thomas stopped running. "What's this about Douglas?"

"Shut up, Vanderbilt!"

"Who is he?" a man asked.

"Shad-up, ya bunch of snobs!"

"Is this a robbery?" a woman asked.

"Douglas! Put the gun down!" Thomas demanded.

"Shut up Vanderbilt, or you'll be first!"

Mary stood in front of Thomas. "Don't you dare hurt him!" she yelled.

Douglas face transformed from anger to sadness, to almost crying on furious rage. "Why not me? WHAT DO YOU SEE IN HIM! WHAT DO YOU SEE IN HIM!" He pointed the gun at her. In a half of a second, he fired his pistol. Instead of hitting Mary, it hit Thomas, who had pushed her out of the way of the bullet. He fell backwards on the ground. A scream rang out, and people scrambled in different directions. Mary reached down to Thomas. "NO! Thomas, no!"

Douglas became confused again. He pointed the gun at his head but changed his mind and pointed it at Mary. He reached into his pocket, took out the note which was given to him and read it aloud: "Mistress Mary, Quite contrary, how does...your garden grow?... What is this?" Another shot was fired but not from his gun. Douglas looked surprised. He lowered his gun and slowly turned around. There was another shot. He dropped to his knees then flopped forwards and rolled over. Standing behind him was Madam Blanche, holding a smoking derringer. She stepped over Douglas' lifeless body and hurried over to Mary and Thomas.

Thomas' head lay in Mary's lap. Min came into the room. "What happened? People are running out the door like there's a fire!"

"That man shot Thomas!"

"Oh, no! I knew I should have stayed here!"

"Oh, Thomas, I'm so sorry I got you involved in this, this is all my fault!" Mary cried "Oh my dear, sweet Thomas!" She kissed his forehead and then his cheek. Thomas coughed. "Thomas?"

He opened his eyes; "Yes?"

"You're alive?"

"Apparently?"

"Are you hurt?" Madam Blanche asked.

"I just got the wind knocked out of me?"

"But...How?" Mary asked.

He sat upright and felt around inside his shirt where the bullet had hit him. He pulled something off that was stuck to his chest. It was the coin Helga had given him earlier. It now had a scratch in it. "I guess the bullet hit this coin."

"My word!" Mary exclaimed.

"You are one very lucky man," Madam Blanche praised.

"Strange thing though..." He looked at the coin." This coin was in my pants pocket. How did it get to my chest area?"

"It's like magic," Madam Blanche answered.

"What happened to Douglas?" Thomas asked.

"She shot him." Min pointed at Madam Blanche.

"You did?" With what?"

Madam Blanche stood up and held up her derringer. She reached down, pulled up her dress and exposed one of her legs which had a garter belt holster on it. Thomas averted his eyes. "I heard in America, it is customary for everyone to carry a gun, like in the Western picture shows, so I always carry one. I never thought I would use it." She re-sheafed the derringer and lowered her dress.

"You killed Douglas?" Thomas asked.

"Yes...Oh! I suppose I did." Madam Blanche became woozy and then fainted away into Min's arms. Thomas stood up. They all bent down and did their best to revive Madam Blanche. She regained consciousness. "I'm sorry. I realize I killed a man. I feel so bad."

"Don't be," Thomas said. You saved Mary's life."

"Oh?" she asked.

"He's right," Mary agreed. "Thank you! I guess I owe you my life."

"Mai non. I was glad to do it, but why did that man try to kill you?"

Min looked around Douglas body and kicked him to make sure he was dead. She noticed a note he was holding in his hand. "Hey, what's that?"

A crowd gathered around Douglas' body. Thomas bent down and picked up the note. It had blood on it.

"What does it say?" Mary asked.

Thomas read it:

Mistress Mary, Quite contrary,
How does your garden grow?
With Silver Bells, And Cockle Shells,
And pretty maids, all in a row

Clarence E. Douglas

"Was that a love letter? A suicide note?" Madam Blanche asked.

"Well..." Thomas folded the letter and put in his notebook. "...appears he was completely insane."

Alva came up to Thomas and hugged him and then hugged Mary. "Thank God you two are all right. Who was that madman?"

"He used to be a police officer."

"A police officer? What is this world coming to, where even the police are trying to kill us?"

"Believe me, this is not the strangest thing we've seen lately," Mary said.

Mrs Astor joined them. "Oh, dear. This is tragic. This is going to ruin our name once the press gets hold of this."

"Not to worry, I'll tell the papers to put a lid on any rumors about a shooting here," Alva said. "Any violation will be seen as impeding a police investigation, right Cousin Thomas?"

"Huh? Oh, sure. Yes. You seem rather calm at this whole situation, Alva."

"I know, it's strange...it's like I've done this before. Perhaps I'm in shock."

"Possibly."

"Well, there you go." Alva gestured to some butlers. They walked over. "Now, how about we move him to a better place so that the police coroner can pick him up? Move the guests that didn't run off to the drawing room, tell them it was all a scene from a play we're working on, and treat everyone to a very large glass of brandy."

Mary, Thomas and Min followed Alva out of the room as some butlers dragged Douglas' body away.

"Do you think he was connected with the Belgian?" Mary asked Thomas.

"He seemed very adamant about me not coming to this party. It could have been crazed jealously, but we can't discount Min's encounter with the anghenfêl. That suicide note, or whatever it is, doesn't make sense, either."

"But he was mad."

"But why not say: Dear Mary, I can't live without you. Your hair is like a field of red roses that smells so sweet. Your eyes are like the morning mist on the emerald hills of an Irish mea...?" Thomas looked over at Mary. She had a happy and excited look on her face.

"Yes? Please go on!" she pleaded.

He cleared his throat. "My point is...a children's nursery rhyme may point to insanity, but the expression on his face was one of surprise, as if he'd brought the wrong note."

"Gold forging has the ability to hypnotize people to do anything. Killing me would be an easy task."

"It would, except another missing piece."

"What's that?"

"No red eyes. Apparently, when the Belgian released a bunch of prisoners from jail, he hypnotized the captain into doing it. A witness said his eyes turned red."

Mary stopped walking.

"What?"

"I just remembered something: Elephants with eyes as red as fire...They killed my parents...My first ones..."

"I'm so sorry."

She sighed. "And now elephants being used to destroy my lighthouse and my life."

"Same person?"

"The man that killed my parents was killed by Professor White."

"Revenge?"

"But, by who?"

Leo watched from the upstairs as Mary and the rest walked out of the room. Madam Blanche climbed up the stairs and joined him. "You handled that pistol pretty well for a rich dame. Hard to hit somebody from that distance," he complemented.

"I used to practice with my late husband."

"Uh, huh," he commented, skeptically.

She looked back where Mary and the rest had disappeared. "I thought for sure you would have saved her from that man, but instead, it was her dance partner."

"I was in the toilet."

"I'll say. Now it will be even harder for you to win her heart."

Leo walked up to her and got within one foot of her face. "Who are you, really?"

"Pardon?"

"Who are you? I've been around for a while and I know when someone is pretending to be someone they're not."

"Let's just say I'm an old friend."

"Friend, eh? Of who?"

"Of my cousin, Mary, of course." Leo stepped back. "My original name was Shirley Black."

"Shirley Black? But…Professor White said you were killed in a raid! You're supposed to be dead! "

"And so is Leopold Bianca, yet here we both are."

"You should… you should tell her!"

"In due time. So much has happened in her life recently. She should rest. Now, if you will excuse me…" Shirley walked away. She stopped before entering a room. "…The men that wish you dead are very near, you may want to stay away from her…If you care about her…and I know you do."

Leo turned and hurried down the stairs. She entered the room and closed the door.

In the room, Shirley walked over to a window and looked outside. "Well, that worked out well."

The Belgian and Fang reappeared behind her.

"What happened?" Fang asked.

"I saved her life and now we can become the best of friends." Shirley picked up a cigar off the desk and the Belgian lit it for her. "Thanks, Maximilian."

"My pleasure. So what's next, chief?"

She took a drag on the cigar and exhaled. "Cousin Mary will trust me enough to show me the book. I shall take it and then you can kill everyone." A long stream of smoke flowed out of her mouth like a white snake.

End of Book 1

Don't Miss Book 2…

Alexander G.J.

Mary & I

Black Blood

The Real Story Of
Miss Mary Mack

About the Author

Alexander G. J. grew up in Charlotte, North Carolina. He moved to Atlanta, Georgia to study commercial art, then to San Francisco, California, to bolster his writing and fine arts skills. He currently lives in Richmond, California.

Novels by Alexander G. J.

Mary & I: The Real Story of Miss Mary Mack
Mary & I: Black Blood. (coming soon)
Flaming Jackass: Sex, Drugs, and Pizza
Flaming Jackass: In Love
Flaming Jackass: Returns

Blog: marymackandi.blogspot.com
Facebook: facebook.com/rabbitstudiosbigpush

www.ingramcontent.com/pod-product-compliance
Lightning Source LLC
Chambersburg PA
CBHW031238120726
47905CB00002B/641